Shades of Gray

OTHER BOOKS BY
RACHEL ANN NUNES

Imprints

Saving Madeline
Eyes of a Stranger
Fields of Home
Flying Home
A Greater Love
To Love and to Promise
Tomorrow and Always
Bridge to Forever
This Very Moment
A Heartbeat Away
Where I Belong
In Your Place
The Independence Club

HUNTINGTON FAMILY SERIES
Winter Fire
No Longer Strangers
Chasing Yesterday
By Morning Light

ARIANA SERIES
Ariana: The Making of a Queen
Ariana: A Gift Most Precious
Ariana: A New Beginning
Ariana: A Glimpse of Eternity
This Time Forever
Ties That Bind
Twice in a Lifetime

ROMANTIC SUSPENSE
A Bid for Love
Framed for Love
Love on the Run

PICTURE BOOKS
Daughter of a King
The Secret of the King

Shades of Gray

A Novel by

RACHEL ANN NUNES

SHADOW
MOUNTAIN

© 2011 Nunes Entertainment, LLC

Visit us at ShadowMountain.com

Library of Congress Cataloging-in-Publication Data

Nunes, Rachel Ann, 1966– author.
  Shades of gray / Rachel Ann Nunes.
      p. cm.
  Summary: Though the police believe Dennis Briggs left voluntarily, his wife is convinced something sinister has happened and turns to Autumn Rain for help. Autumn has the extraordinary ability to receive impressions from objects that have special meaning to their owners, but what she discovers about the victim only leads to more questions.
    ISBN 978-1-60908-051-8 (paperbound)   *4859 8923*   *05/12*
  1. Clairvoyants—Fiction. 2. Psychometry (Parapsychology)—Fiction.
3. Missing persons—Fiction. I. Title.
  PS3564.U468S53 2011
  813'.54—dc22   2011001391

Printed in the United States of America
Malloy Lithographing Incorporated, Ann Arbor, MI

10   9   8   7   6   5   4   3   2   1

To my family,
who love science fiction
and fantasy as much as I do,
and who never tire of the question,
"What if there were . . . ?"

Acknowledgments

I'm grateful to Anne McCaffrey, Piers Anthony, Frank Herbert, Roger Zelazny, and other great science fiction and fantasy authors whose books showed me new worlds as a teen and who taught me to dream the impossible dream.

Thanks also go to the folks at Deseret Book, especially Jana Erickson and my editor, Suzanne Brady. From covers to marketing, thank you for all the work you did to bring this book to my readers.

And, lastly, thank you to my readers for going on this journey with me. Many of you asked for a sequel to *Imprints,* and here it is! Thank you for the many e-mails of encouragement. Don't worry. I won't quit writing.

Psychometry. The word sounds like a method for measuring a person's mind, not a scientific term for reading emotions mysteriously imprinted on random objects. I hadn't even heard the word until I'd been reading imprints for nearly a year. In no way did the term reflect the vivid scenes or the raw feelings that often left me dazed or confused.

Neither did it convey the lives I'd saved.

Or those I hadn't.

I hoped today's imprints would be the saving kind.

"Sophie should be here any minute." My sister, Tawnia Winn, sat on the tall stool behind the long counter at my antiques shop, her swollen belly stretching all the way to the counter. With four weeks left of her pregnancy, I didn't see how she could grow any larger and not be pregnant with twins, but the doctor had assured her there was only one baby. "I called her before I left work, and she was already on her way."

Traffic was often busy in the Hawthorne District of Portland,

Oregon, especially on Fridays, and I knew Tawnia was worried about the possibility of Sophie not arriving before she had to return to work. Since I was the one who had to read the imprints, I wasn't as anxious.

"What about naming the baby Lark?" I asked, leaning over to move an antique toy soldier closer to its opponent. For the safety of my younger customers, I carried only the plastic kind, not the lead figures. "Or maybe Saffron or Rose?"

Tawnia let out a long-suffering sigh. "How do you know it's even going to be a girl?" She took a last bite of the sandwich she'd bought on her way to the shop. White bread, mayo, processed turkey with preservatives—I was proud of myself for not mentioning how bad it all was for her.

"How about Sky or Cyan? Those could be for either sex, I'd think," I said. Tawnia wanted the baby's gender to be a surprise, a decision that had both me and her husband, Bret, mad with curiosity. I planned to have the child in my shop a good portion of each day, and I wanted to know if I should focus on buying more soldiers or antique dolls, though when I thought about it, they were actually the same thing.

"I think we need something a little more traditional. You know how my parents are." Tawnia's dark brown hair had grown thick and long during the past months, and she had the means to buy the latest maternity wear. Her face was a little bloated, but the added roundness and a good base made her absolutely beautiful. By contrast, when I looked in the mirror I saw a gaunt copy, a shadow twin, with numerous freckles and chopped hair dyed red on the top, who looked decidedly on the scroungy side in camouflage pants and a T-shirt.

Of course, the adventure that had landed me in the hospital three and a half weeks ago while rescuing two women from a cult masquerading as a commune hadn't helped, but my broken rib was healing, my cuts were gone, and the bruises faded, except for the narrow green half moon across my left cheekbone. My right wrist gave me problems only when I carried something heavy.

Reading imprints had definitely made my life more interesting, if not exactly safe.

"Look," Tawnia said, moving from behind the counter, one hand resting on her stomach in the agelong way of expectant women. "If it's something really terrible, go easy on telling Sophie, okay? It's hard enough with Dennis gone and having to take care of the children by herself. I don't know how she's going to handle bad news."

She meant, of course, if Sophie's husband had left of his own free will. "Either way, he's missing," I said. "It can't be good."

Tawnia frowned. "She's such a sweet person, you know. I couldn't ask for a better neighbor."

Tawnia and Bret had built their new house in a cozy settlement of houses owned by couples who were in the same stage of life—married and having children. Sophie Briggs and Tawnia had taken to each other instantly, and though I really liked Sophie, I missed having Tawnia around as much. At least for now my sister still worked in town and we could have lunch together, so I could make sure she ate decent food for my niece or nephew. Tawnia was the only person I knew who consumed as much as I did, but she tended toward junk food while I was a health nut. It wasn't really my fault—growing up with hippie parents who owned an herb shop had a tendency to do that to a child.

"How about Sunwood or Gypsy?" I asked, moving my bare feet into a patch of sunlight that came through the window. You'd think the shop would be warm in July, but I felt cold in anticipation of the imprints waiting on whatever Sophie was bringing for me to read.

Tawnia wrinkled her nose at the faint shadow of dirt on the tips of my toes, though they were as easy to wash as her hands, which touched far worse things in the course of a day. Doorknobs, for instance. "Sunwood? You're joking, right?"

I was, a little. "Okay, how about Tempest, if it's a boy?"

"With a name like that we'd have nothing but tantrums and rebellion."

Children did tend to live up to expectations. Tawnia and I had, in our separate adoptive homes. Tawnia had grown up to be an organized, forceful, wildly successful art director, while I had become an herb-loving, shoe-hating free spirit. I loved cooking and was good with a needle; Tawnia burnt everything she cooked and hated sewing. We both were directionally impaired, which was why Bret had finally bought Tawnia a GPS so she would stop getting lost while driving her car.

Strong brown arms came around me at the same instant I perceived Jake's presence. He turned me around and gave me a kiss that warmed me far better than the sunshine, but I noticed he didn't hold me too tightly, and his gaze lingered regretfully on my bruised cheek. He thought he'd failed at protecting me, though I was perfectly capable of taking care of myself. Rescuing two women, putting two bad men behind bars, and freeing that tiny community had been worth everything I suffered while undercover at the commune. That and learning Jake loved me.

Tawnia beamed at us as though she was personally responsible for our relationship. Maybe in a way she was. She'd kept throwing us together when I'd given up hope of ever being more than best friends.

"Tea anyone?" Jake asked, releasing me. "I have a new one to try before I start selling it." He held up a hand. "Don't worry, Tawnia. No caffeine or anything weird. It's completely safe for little Indigo."

"Indigo?" Tawnia guffawed. "You're as bad as Autumn." Her smile vanished as the electronic bell above my door sounded. "She's

4

here." She hurried over to meet Sophie before I could tell her not to look so devastated—she was probably thinking how awful she'd feel if Bret had gone missing. I knew how I'd react if it were Jake.

As though reading my mind, Jake, already a few steps away, looked at me over his shoulder and winked. "I'll put the water on and be right back, okay? Don't start without me."

Since the commune and a few imprints that had left me barely conscious, he'd been a bit overprotective. Something I needed to get him over. After thirty-three years of doing things my way, I wasn't about to lose my independence, new boyfriend or no. I rolled my eyes. "I'll be fine."

"Whatever." Jake threw me a grin that melted my resistance. His brown skin emphasized his muscular build, and the short dreadlocks added an air of mystery. He was entirely too handsome, my Jake. A handful of female customers often came to buy something from my shop or his, expressly for the joy of feasting their eyes on him. I didn't mind as long as he knew he was mine. Though if I were to tell the truth, my relationship with Jake was still so new that I wasn't comfortable with it yet.

He hurried to the back room that ran the width of my shop, while I turned to face Sophie Briggs. I'd come to know her fairly well in the past month. A wholesome-looking young woman several years younger than I, she was the kind you wouldn't think twice about leaving your child with—if you had a child, which I didn't. Average height, a little baby fat around her waist, nothing really to set her off from other housewives who'd recently given birth, except an adorable dimple in her left cheek and a mass of brown hair with natural curl that was carelessly swept up in a clip, the awkwardly straying pieces betraying her state of mind even more than the reddened eyes. Lizbeth, her three-month-old infant, snuggled in a carrier next to her chest, and she pushed her toddler son, Sawyer, in a stroller.

Tawnia placed a hand on her friend's arm. "How are you holding up?"

"Okay, I guess." Sophie looked between Tawnia and me as even our closer friends still had a tendency to do, taking in our similarities, especially our eyes. Those didn't change regardless of weight or hair color.

"Hi, Sophie." I smiled to put her at ease. I'd shared a half dozen dinners with Sophie and her husband during the past month, but it's surprising how things like my unusual talent didn't come up in social situations. If she'd noticed that I avoided touching certain things on the table when we were together, she'd never pointed it out. Tawnia had only told her about my ability this morning.

Sophie came around the stroller and reached for my arm, looking ready to burst into tears. "Can you really help me find Dennis?"

The fingers that touched me were cold, and I was glad she didn't shake my hand or press the ring she wore against my skin. After the past two days of her worrying, the imprints wouldn't be pleasant. "I don't know, but I'm willing to try."

"This isn't like him. He always comes home. He doesn't stay after work to play computer games, he doesn't go to bars, he loves to be with the kids. With me. We planted a garden. We're going to paint the baby's room. He wouldn't leave us." Her voice broke, and I felt her fear. Though I knew she believed what she was saying, there was always room for doubt.

"Anything missing from his closet?" I asked, more to calm her than anything. That was something Detective Martin would ask, and it was possible, depending on the imprints I picked up in the next few minutes, that I might have to talk with him about the case. I doubted he'd be pleased to see me, however, and he was definitely not high on my list.

Sophie nodded. "Some shoes, a pair of jeans, T-shirts, and one suit, but he might have been wearing that. His shaving stuff is gone, too. There was a withdrawal from our savings—two thousand dollars."

Not a good sign. Still, if he'd been planning to leave his wife and children permanently, he would have packed far more.

"Where does he work?" I asked.

"At Simeon, Gideon & Associates. It's a law firm. He's their IT guy. He does programming and keeps their network running smoothly."

"I see." I really hoped his job didn't figure into his disappearance. A law firm would be careful to cover their tracks.

"What did you bring for Autumn?" Tawnia asked.

"I wasn't sure what was best. Everything's in that bag under the stroller." She reached toward it, but I waved her back.

"I can get it. I want to say hi to Sawyer anyway." I squatted down beside the stroller to speak to the three-year-old.

"Hi, Autumn." His brown hair was curly like his mother's, though better combed, and he was dressed neatly in cargo jeans and a red T-shirt. "I wanna get out." His tanned skin told of hours playing in the backyard. Obviously, he was the outdoors type and not at all used to being confined.

"Can I play with the toys?" he added, pointing at my soldiers. "I bringed the other ones you gave me." He dug a chubby hand in his pocket and brought out a blue-clad soldier carrying a rifle. At some point in the toy's history, someone had severed one of the two places where the rifle connected to the soldier's hands, and from the moment Sawyer had seen it in a bunch I'd taken for him to play with during a barbeque at Sophie's house, he'd loved how he could move it back and forth, pretending to shoot. I'd given it to him to keep, along with another soldier mounted on a horse, which he confessed he liked a "tiny bit" more.

"No, Sawyer," Sofie said. "Just play with those you brought."

"I don't mind, if you don't," I said, thinking that if Sophie could name her son Sawyer, maybe there was hope Tawnia wouldn't settle on a boring name for my niece or nephew. "He can't hurt them." I kept the most valuable toys in a glass display box.

Sophie eyed the shelf of breakable antiques beyond the soldiers. "Okay, but it's better that he stay in the stroller."

When Tawnia's baby was born, I might have to rethink the placement of a few things.

Tawnia swept up a row of soldiers and deposited them in the boy's waiting hands. He laughed and promptly started placing them at strategic locations in the stroller.

I retrieved Sophie's bag from under the stroller. It was one of the reusable grocery bags that were popping up everywhere and heavier than I expected.

I gently tipped the contents onto the counter. Books, several tools, a letter, a recent family portrait, a tie, a stamp collection, a notebook with baseball cards, a signed baseball packed carefully in a little box, a phone charger, an electronic book reader, and an elaborate pen and pencil set.

"He doesn't like a lot of extra junk around, you know," Sophie said. "Not like me. I have a lot of knickknacks and keepsakes, but he doesn't care about that sort of thing. I got a lot of this stuff from his office, but I'm not sure how he felt about any of it. His keys are gone, and his phone. So is his car. I didn't know what else to bring."

"This is a great start." As usual, I was struck with how little was left behind, a mere hint of who Dennis had been to those who didn't know him well. "You know what it is I do, don't you?" I wanted to make sure she wasn't expecting miracles.

"Tawnia said you could sometimes see scenes or feel emotions left on objects."

"Not just any object. It has to be something frequently used or treasured by a person, articles that aren't often washed or forgotten.

Or it can be something a person touched while experiencing a great emotion—love, sadness, anger." Hate. Guilt. Terror. Jealousy. The list was long, but some were better left unsaid.

Sophie frowned. "I don't know if I brought anything useful."

"I can always go to your house later. Or to his office."

"Thank you." In her chest carrier, Lizbeth was moving restlessly in sleep, her dark, fuzzy head tilting side to side. Sophie swayed back and forth to soothe the child.

"Not at all." I removed the four antique rings from my fingers, including a tourmaline and a black-and-white hard-stone cameo. Two of the rings were silver, another a tricolor of elaborately twisted gold, and the cameo was set in rose gold. Each had once belonged to a woman who'd given them comforting imprints, now long faded into a pleasant buzz, a barrier for me against any sudden shocks when I was out and about in the world, which happened more often these days than was comfortable. In the year since my gift had appeared, I'd gone from being open and friendly to everyone, even strangers, to being careful not to touch personal items belonging to anyone. You'd be surprised at how often we do that without thinking twice.

Jake was usually my official ring-holder, but he was still in the back room making tea, and the anxiety on Sophie's face nixed any idea of waiting for him.

I needn't have worried. He was there before I set them on the counter, his warm fingers giving mine a subtle squeeze as he took them from me. I smiled at him, and he winked.

Slowly, I extended my hands over the items. Imprints were there—I could feel them already, but I didn't know what they would tell me. The moment of truth was here. I let my hands drop.

Sometimes when I did a formal reading like this, I'd flash back to the day my ability first manifested itself. On the day of my adoptive father's funeral, I'd picked up the picture of my mother that

9

he'd treasured, but instead of seeing her face as I'd always seen it, I was looking at her through Winter's eyes, experiencing his love for her as his worn finger stroked the lines of her face. Though the imprint was tender, I'd dropped the picture in my shock, shattering the glass. In that moment the photograph, always cherished, became even more treasured.

I touched Dennis's books first, but they had nothing to tell except a hint of concentration. If Dennis had loved these books, it was not for themselves but for the information he'd long ago internalized. The baseball was different. It held a distinct imprint of love and pride, yet it was an old imprint, one from a young boy. It made me smile.

"What?" Sophie asked, sounding out of breath.

"He really loved this ball—when he was a boy, I mean. He hasn't left any recent imprints on it."

The hammer gave me an image of hitting a thumb, the screwdriver a sense of satisfaction. From the letter, I felt a sense of deep love, followed by an image of Sophie's face. I ran through the rest quickly—the portrait (hint of pride and love), the stamp collection (fading youthful eagerness), and the baseball cards (vague regret). From the phone charger and the electronic book reader there was nothing except a slight annoyance that might have derived completely from my imagination. While reading vivid imprints was similar to experiencing a real event, especially of late, some of the fainter imprints often made me wonder if I was reading my own feelings instead of the owner's. The pen and pencil set and the tie had no imprint at all, real or imagined.

I shook my head and met Sophie's eyes. "I'm sorry. There's nothing here that says he was planning to leave or that he was in trouble." I motioned to the letter, whose address was facing down on the counter. "That's from you, isn't it? He loves you very much. I can feel how much he treasures that letter."

Tears filled her eyes. "What am I going to do?" She brought a hand to her mouth as though to stop from crying out loud.

I put a comforting hand on her shoulder at the same time Tawnia put an arm around her. Sophie blinked rapidly, calming herself, before patting my hand in silent thanks.

My stomach jolted. "Wait," I said, grabbing her hand. Around her slim wrist was a gold charm bracelet decorated with a variety of interesting charms, including several heart lockets for holding miniature pictures.

"What?" Sophie asked, alarmed.

"There's an imprint on your bracelet. Can I see it?" Though it had only brushed against me, the imprint had been strong, sending me the image of a suitcase.

Sophie struggled with the clasp, finally allowing Tawnia to undo it for her. Tawnia slid it into my hands.

I saw Dennis on Wednesday, two days earlier, standing before the mirror of the dresser he shared with Sophie. Also reflected in the mirror was a small suitcase with the tags still on it, sitting on the bed. Items had been haphazardly thrown inside without care for organization. The imprint was strong and vivid, pulling me inside until I was looking out of Dennis's eyes into the mirror. He/I stared down at his hands at the bracelet, the anniversary gift he'd bought for Sophie. There was a sense of disconnection, a surreal, subdued determination. He/I was leaving. I wanted to leave. Now. It was the right thing to do. I reached out to set the bracelet back in the box on the dresser. The image vanished.

There were no more imprints, and there was no use trying again. I never saw any more. Never. Even if I didn't understand what I saw the first time, or if what I saw wasn't complete, the images and emotions wouldn't change. The bracelet slipped through my fingers to the floor before I realized I'd let it go.

Sophie gasped. "What did you see?"

I looked at Tawnia, who watched me with her mismatched eyes, the right eye hazel, and the left one blue. *Heterochromia* was the medical name, and in our case the condition was hereditary, but we didn't know from which side of our birth family it had come. She started to shake her head but stopped, knowing that I wouldn't hide any information from Sophie. She deserved to know.

Jake's hand went to my waist, his warmth encouraging and comforting all at once. Since the day of Winter's death, he'd been there for me—no, even before that. First as a friend and now as something more. We'd spent hours together, working and playing. We'd faced danger together more than once, and I trusted him without question.

I found my breath. "I saw a new suitcase with tags attached and things piled inside. He was standing in front of a dresser with a mirror holding that bracelet. It was on Wednesday afternoon." Pinpointing the exact day was easy this close to the day of imprinting. "I'm sorry, Sophie, but it seems he left of his own will. He thought it was the right thing to do. You weren't home, were you? He knew that."

"Then why go out and buy me this bracelet?" She bent down awkwardly to pick it up, the baby in the carrier giving a sleepy grunt of discomfort. "Our anniversary isn't for two months. He never remembers. I found it this morning before I drove here. That has to mean he left it for me to find. Why would he do that if he wanted to leave me?"

A good-bye gift? I wouldn't say it aloud. "I'm sorry," I repeated. "I know it's not the full picture, but Dennis bought a suitcase and packed his own bag before he left. He planned it."

Sophie stared at me, tears leaking from her eyes. "There has to be an explanation. He loves me!"

"I'd be willing to try to find out more."

"I don't know. What if . . . what if . . .? What about his job? He loved that. He'd never quit."

"Have you talked to the police?"

"Yes, but I didn't get the feeling they thought anything was suspicious. They gave me odd looks. I caught one rolling his eyes and looking at the kids as if they were a disease."

"We'll do whatever we can to help," Tawnia said to her.

Sophie was shaking her head. "No. This was a mistake. I won't believe it. Any of it. Dennis loves us!" In two steps she was at the stroller, gathering the toy soldiers from her son and tossing them onto the nearest shelf.

"Wait! Those ones are mine!" Sawyer protested. Sophie gave him back one of the soldiers and then a second one he pointed at before hurrying to the door.

"Sophie, stop!" Tawnia started after her friend. "What about Dennis's things?"

But Sophie shrugged her off and fled outside.

I sighed.

"Not good, huh?" Jake placed a small poetry book in my hands, and joy arched through me as if someone had turned on the light. A man and woman stood together exchanging wedding vows. My adoptive parents, Winter and Summer Rain. My energy level soared. Sometimes Jake knew me so well it was scary.

"It wasn't a bad imprint. Just vivid. Determined. And sad because he left of his own will." Though I appreciated Jake's foresight, I tucked the little book under my arm, keeping my contact as brief as possible. I didn't want my parents' imprints to fade under my own. The imprints of that book and the other few possessions they had left meant everything to me.

"You ready for tea?" Jake put an arm around me.

"I am." Tawnia moved down the aisle like a woman with a purpose. "But first I have to show you both something. Autumn, I

13

know you've never been wrong about an imprint before, but maybe there's a first time."

If she'd experienced imprints herself, she wouldn't suggest such a thing, but I'd hear her out. She was my twin, and I knew she didn't take my ability lightly.

She reached for her oversized bag on the counter next to the items Sophie had left. "I was so sure you'd find someone had taken him or something. Because what you said doesn't explain this." She slapped a sketchbook down on top of Dennis's books. "If Dennis wanted to leave Sophie, why did I draw this?"

I stared at the paper. My sister also had an unusual ability that we'd only become aware of within the past month. During the problems at the commune, she had used her talent to help solve the mystery, but since then it had disappeared.

Apparently not for good.

The sketch showed a man in a sedan, fear distorting his handsome features. Behind him were two men in another car, one with his hand out the window firing a gun.

"That's Dennis," I said, recognizing the man in the front sedan.

"And his car." Tawnia chewed on her lip. "I don't know who the other men are, but I was trying to come up with a new billboard for Mr. Lantis today, and this is what came out instead. It's why I urged Sophie to come here."

"Did you tell her about this?"

"No." Reluctance laced Tawnia's voice. She still didn't admit to having an ability, but I'd already seen proof that she could draw things happening miles away, involving people she'd never met.

"So, it's okay if you have a weird sister, but not if you're weird yourself."

"It's not like that, Autumn. I just—this comes from the pregnancy. I know it. Or something connected to you. It's not me."

I sighed. It wasn't like my sister to hide from the truth. The woman had moved to five different states in ten years searching for something—for me, it turned out—and she still didn't believe she was special.

"Whatever it is," Jake interrupted, "this guy needs help now."

I turned back to study the page, thinking that if Tawnia had drawn the reality of Dennis's situation, we might already be too late.

CHAPTER
2

No one said anything for several seconds, and then Jake was pouring tea and pushing cups into our cold hands. Tawnia moved heavily around the counter to sit on the stool, while I stood staring at the drawing.

"We have to do something," I said. The imprints on Sophie's bracelet hadn't hinted of danger, but regardless of why Dennis had left, he was in trouble, about to be in trouble, or had already been in trouble. We didn't know how time factored into Tawnia's drawings, though I suspected her drawings came from past events, like my imprints.

"What about that detective?" Tawnia smiled as Jake poured a bit of raw agave nectar in her tea. She would have preferred sugar, but I never had the stuff around.

I knew Tawnia was talking about Detective Shannon Martin. We'd worked together before, and he'd even saved my life when Tawnia's pictures had urged him to the commune.

Jake snorted. "Him?" He and Shannon didn't get along, and

lately he had tolerated the man even less. Whether because Shannon had saved me when Jake hadn't, or because Jake viewed Shannon as a threat, I really didn't know. Whatever the emotion, this reaction wasn't like the normally easygoing Jake.

"Tawnia's right," I said. "I'd better go see him."

"Sophie said she went to the police already, and the imprints didn't show anything new for us to tell them, right?"

I met Jake's gaze without flinching. It wasn't my fault, this rivalry between him and Shannon; I'd done nothing to encourage it. "If I show Shannon the drawing, he'll understand the importance of finding Dennis right away. I know he will. He believes in us that much." Reluctantly, of course. Most days I had the feeling Shannon would rather see me behind bars than reading imprints. "He can get information that I can't."

Jake's frown deepened, but he didn't object. He cared about Tawnia's friend every bit as much as I did. He was a lot like my adoptive father that way. Winter had cared about everyone.

"Maybe you should try to read more imprints first," Tawnia said. "For proof."

I tapped her drawing. "This is all the proof I need."

"What if Shannon wants to interview me? He makes me nervous."

Her and me both.

Tawnia glanced at her cell phone. "Great. I'm going to be late getting back to work. I'll return this cup later, okay?" Grabbing her bag and blowing a kiss, she ran toward my door where she hesitated, raising the tea. "What is this anyway? It's really good."

Jake laughed. "A ginger blend. I told you I'd find one you'd like."

"Amazing. Save me a few packages." She ducked out the door.

I drank a couple of hot swallows before setting down my cup, the ginger plainly obvious to me. I wasn't normally a fan of ginger, but this wasn't bad. "I'm going to talk to Shannon."

Jake sighed. "I'll watch the shops." The recent change in our relationship hadn't affected the way we ran our businesses. He owned the Herb Shoppe, which had once been my father's, and the double connecting doors between our stores and our networked computers allowed us to help each other during the busy times. We also shared two part-time employees, one of whom was Jake's sister, Randa, who was still in high school.

"Thera and Randa will be here soon." Not that it'd matter. Friday afternoons were always slow for Autumn's Antiques. I did most of my treasure hunting on Fridays.

"Don't forget your rings." Jake pulled them from his pocket.

"Thanks." I slipped them on one by one, enjoying the pleasant buzz of a life well-lived. Of laughter. I made sure that everything in my shop had either a good feeling around it or no imprints at all. I hadn't yet discovered if there was a way to remove negative imprints, and until I did, I wanted nothing that had them in my shop.

Jake caught me in his arms and gave me a kiss that made me wish I could stay. We'd come a long way, the two of us, and though neither of us seemed to know exactly where to go from this point, I was confident we'd figure it out.

The real jingle bells at the door to his shop broke us apart. Jake rubbed my hands, his fingers dark against my white skin. "If Shannon acts up, tell him he'll have to answer to me."

"He'll just threaten to put you in jail. Don't worry. I can handle Shannon."

Jake nodded and swaggered to the double doors connecting our stores, muttering something under his breath about Shannon and jail.

Grinning, I made sure the outside door to my store was locked, turning over the sign that told customers to use the Herb Shoppe entrance instead. Most of my regulars knew the routine by now. This way if anyone tried to swipe something, they'd have to sneak past Jake.

The warmth on the sidewalk traveled through the tough skin of my feet and warmed me. The last time I'd worn shoes was all those years ago in college when the dean threatened to expel me. I hadn't missed them since, and not wearing them was now a part of who I was. I liked being as close to the earth as possible. Lifting my face to the sun, I took a deep breath. I adored July, the heat, the glare of the sun. It made me feel happy. Lots of vitamin D.

My rusty red Toyota hatchback, a sad-looking vehicle that had cost me more in repairs the last nine months I'd owned it than I'd paid for it in the first place, awaited me by the curb. I knew the way to the police station by heart, but I wasn't looking forward to the visit. If Detective Shannon Martin was there, he'd drop everything, and it would only be that much more awkward because despite my assurances to Tawnia, I didn't have much proof to give him. Okay, any proof. But Sophie needed someone, and I thought he'd help her because of me. For the most part, he never gave any hint about his feelings for me—his reluctant feelings—but I knew he was attracted to me despite his mistrust in my strange ability. I suspected he also felt somewhat responsible for me since I'd begun working as a consultant with the police department, a responsibility that had only increased since the commune affair and his saving my life.

As for me, well, I'd loved Jake for a year now, and my feet hadn't touched the ground since we'd finally admitted our feelings for each other about three weeks ago. Yet if there had been no Jake and if Shannon hadn't hated and mistrusted my ability so much, well, things might have taken a different turn.

At the police station, I was quickly ushered into a room sparsely furnished with two chairs and a small table. It wasn't the cubby he normally worked from, but since the room didn't seem to be an office, I figured this change didn't mean he'd been promoted. More likely, he was trying to keep me and my big mouth from disrupting the precinct. I'd become a bit famous around here of late. Or infamous, rather.

Shannon appeared the same as he always did, sturdily built and compact, only a few inches taller than I was. His features were rugged, and he spent a lot of time outdoors, the sun prematurely crinkling the skin around his eyes and giving him a healthy, wholesome glow. His hair was somewhere between brown and blond, though the blond seemed to be winning now that summer was in full swing. He was wearing it longer these days, and a bit of unruly curl had appeared at the ends.

"So," he said, indicating a chair, each movement undeniably graceful. "What's up? Not thinking of joining another cult, I hope."

I met his eyes and experienced a jolt of shock as I always did. His eyes are not like other men's, or anyone's, really—both compelling and beautiful. The green-blue color, framed by heavy, light-brown lashes, studied me not with impatience but with an intensity that made me want to trust him.

Big mistake.

"Oh, I haven't ruled it out," I replied a little too casually. "What about you? Need some help finding your bad guys?"

He scowled, hating the reminder that he had come to me for help first, though it wasn't a case either of us wanted to remember. It still haunted me. "I think I got it covered."

"Good. Where's Tracy?"

"Getting a late lunch."

"Oh." I liked his partner better than I liked him. She'd come by nearly every day when I'd been in the hospital, always dressed in one dark pantsuit or another. Occasionally she'd brought objects from cases they'd been working for me to read, and at first I'd been reluctant, but when none of the imprints were overly traumatic,

I'd begun to look forward to her visits. Neither of us had ever told Shannon. When Shannon had come to visit, it was to urge me to take self-defense courses or to warn me not to track down any more bad guys. He'd given me orders and several vases of flowers, but she'd given me something to do. I'd never heard if the imprints I'd read had led to any arrests. A part of me didn't want to know.

I sank into the chair, bringing my bare foot up under me as I made myself comfortable. Shannon sat across from me, still waiting. I bet he could wait all day. His prisoners probably confessed in order to get out from under those intense eyes. His fingers didn't even tap impatiently on the tabletop.

I had the strange urge to ask him if he was growing any herbs on the acre of land he owned on the outskirts of Portland. I knew he planted things, or at least worked around the house on the property, but that's all I knew. Not that it was any of my business.

"Tawnia has a friend whose husband left home on Wednesday afternoon and hasn't been seen since."

"Has she contacted the police?"

"She says they didn't seem very interested."

"They don't think foul play is involved?"

"Oh, he left on his own. I know that much."

"Because of an imprint?"

There was a challenge in the words, but I ignored it. "I saw a packed suitcase. He left because he wanted to."

"I'm not sure what you want, then." Shannon tilted his head and leaned back in his chair to study me. "It's a free country. A man can leave his home whenever he wants. We certainly can't go after every errant husband who disappears for a few days. He'll probably come home soon. Or file for divorce."

"Maybe. The real worry is this." I pulled Tawnia's picture from my bag and set it between us on the table.

Shannon stiffened, and I knew he recognized the significance because of the earlier drawing of me when I'd been in trouble. "Your sister drew this?"

I nodded. "Dennis has two little kids, and I know he loves his wife. Something's not right. This has nothing to do with imprints but with my gut feeling. I was hoping you could do some checking, track down some leads. Maybe the law firm he works for knows something. Or his friends. You could put out a search for the car."

He studied the picture without replying. "This isn't proof. I'm not sure how I can put things into motion because of a feeling."

"You mean because of *my* feeling. If it was your feeling, it would be completely different, wouldn't it?" We glared at each other, and I felt no little satisfaction when he dropped his gaze first.

"Look, I'm asking a favor." I hated to put it that way. I didn't want to owe him anything, especially since I already owed him my life. "It's for Tawnia and for those children. If he's a creep, then his wife deserves to know so she can get on with her life. And if he needs help, the faster we find him, the better."

"Okay, I'll do some checking, but I want you to stay out of this. If something is going on, I don't need you getting in the way."

The perfect retort came to the tip of my tongue, but I swallowed it. He was doing me a favor, and I could at least pretend to go along with his heavy-handedness. "Don't worry," I said, flashing him a fake smile. "I'm only going to Sophie's to see if I can find more imprints."

"Give me the man's name. And his wife's number. I want to chat with the officer she contacted." When I'd obliged, he stood and swept up Tawnia's drawing. "I think I'll get some copies of this. I'll be back in a bit." He glided out the door. Too bad he was so annoying or I might actually like looking at the man. I mean, if I didn't already have a boyfriend.

I leaned back in my chair and put my feet on the table, rubbing my bare arms against the chill. They must be hot in their uniforms to keep it so cold in here. There wasn't even a window I could open to let in some heat.

I was shivering by the time Shannon returned. "The officer Sophie talked to found nothing out of the ordinary," he said, "but I asked to have the case transferred to me."

Hopefully, that meant he'd go a little beyond ordinary protocol. He'd done it in the commune situation, which had been so successful that his partner told me everyone had begun to think he had some kind of intuition about cases. Shannon would be upset if he ever heard the gossip, but for now it worked in my favor.

"Thank you," I said, rising to my feet. "Show me out of here. It's freezing. How do you stand to work in here anyway?"

He flashed me a flat little grin. "I don't sit around much."

He walked me out but didn't leave me at the door as I'd expected. "Are you following me?" I asked after taking a few paces down the sidewalk, reveling in the sudden heat.

"I'm going with you."

"What?"

"I'll drive. I've seen your car." Again the flat grin that was as fake as anything I'd given him.

I shook my head. "I need to get back to work."

"I thought you were going to Tawnia's friend's house."

"Later."

"Really?"

I'd halfway decided to go now, but I didn't want his company.

Shannon shrugged, his expression bland. "If she lets me look around, I might find some clues. I am a detective, after all. She might feel better knowing someone's taking her husband's disappearance seriously."

He had a point. A huge point. I hadn't been able to forget Sophie's face or her uncertainty. She was living a wife's worst nightmare, and if the irritating Shannon could give her any hope, I would welcome that.

"She doesn't know I'm coming," I said. "I'll have to call Tawnia to set it up for us."

"Okay."

"Is Tracy back yet?" I liked the idea of having her as a buffer between us.

"Any minute now."

We both pulled out our phones, him to check on his partner, and me to text Tawnia so she could let Sophie know to expect us. Given Sophie's distress when she left my shop, I preferred not to be the one to call. She might not want to see me again so soon.

Tawnia texted me back before Tracy appeared. Sophie would see us.

"I'll meet you there," I told Shannon, forwarding Tawnia's address to his cell phone. It probably said something that I had his number in my contact list, but we'd worked together enough that I'd felt it necessary. He might be abrasive and annoying most days, but he did help catch criminals. "You can follow me when Tracy gets here. The address I sent you is my sister's, but Sophie lives right next door. On the left."

He didn't protest, which showed he was learning a thing or two about me. Humming to myself, I opened the door to my Toyota and started the engine. The radio didn't work, but at least the new battery and alternator were fairly dependable—and I didn't have to feel Shannon's eyes on me.

Putting in my earphone, I called Jake to let him know I wouldn't be in for a while longer. No use in having him wonder what I was doing so long with Shannon or tempting him to come rescue me.

"It's me," I said when he answered. "I decided to go to Sophie's to see if I can find something else. I didn't like the way she left."

"What about the detective?"

"He promised to look into it. He and his partner are going to search her house."

"That's good."

The honk of a car came through the phone. "Where are you?" I asked. "You don't sound like you're in the shop. Everything okay?"

"I'm just walking out the door on my way to my grandmother's. She called and asked me to come over. Randa and Thera are at the store, and they'll be okay until one of us gets back. I had a bit of a rush on herbs, but it was steady when I left."

"She's not sick, is she?" I knew Jake well enough to feel there was more he wasn't saying. His grandmother had raised him and Randa after their mother died, and she meant a lot to him. He'd do anything for her.

"No. I'd rather not explain over the phone, but an old friend showed up on her doorstep and asked for me. She's in a bit of trouble, I guess. Not sure exactly what happened."

Was the friend the one in trouble or was it his grandmother, because of the sudden appearance? I wasn't sure I wanted to know, but I had no reason not to trust Jake. I knew how he felt about me. "Okay, then. We'll talk later. Let me know if you need me."

"I always need you."

A shiver rippled down my spine. He'd been worth waiting for.

"Be careful," he added.

"I will. You, too."

We hung up, and I had twenty more minutes on my drive to wonder about the friend and what the visit might mean. Jake sounded apprehensive, not at all looking forward to the visit, and yet, there was also a sliver of curiosity in his manner, an anticipation. What did that mean?

I pulled my mind from Jake's mysterious visitor when I arrived at Sophie's, a two-story tract home similar to Tawnia's, though both

Sophie and Tawnia had chosen extras that made their houses different from each other. Attractive, up-and-coming, comfortable suburbia. I liked the green lawns, the new trees, the feel of the neighborhood. Maybe if things went well between us, Jake and I would move here someday. Having grown up in an apartment building practically in the middle of the city, I thought the area felt wonderfully open and uncrowded.

Certainly not the type of neighborhood where a man went missing.

My hand paused on the car door release as doubts assailed me. What if I discovered nothing new for Sophie? Worse, what if I discovered Dennis Briggs was seeing someone else? Everyone said I was confident about my decisions and my direction in life, and many days I felt decisive, but today I was as confused as my sister was each time she entered a kitchen.

Only my trust in Tawnia's drawing started me up the walk. My sister would have laughed at that, but she felt the same about my ability. Maybe both of us were crazy. Detective Shannon Martin certainly thought so.

Sophie answered the door, her eyes less red now and her hair wet and loose as though she'd washed it. "Thanks for coming," she said, surprising me with her graciousness. To give her even more credit, I noticed she didn't look twice at my bare feet as she usually did when I'd come to her house before.

"You're welcome. I hope I find something more helpful."

"I've been thinking. Maybe Dennis was in trouble, and he thought leaving would keep us safe. Couldn't that explain what you saw?"

"Yes." I looked away from the eagerness in her eyes. Though her explanation could be right on, especially in view of Tawnia's drawing, I didn't want to get her hopes up that Dennis would come home soon or in one piece.

Little Sawyer was sitting on the far side of the living room floor where it met the hallway and opened into the kitchen. Next to him was a small toy box, and he was busily taking out miniature cars and making revving sounds as he set each down on the carpet. The baby was nowhere to be seen.

I explained to Sophie about my talk with Shannon and how he'd be arriving shortly to look around. Sophie brightened at the news of his interest. "Except that I can't imagine what he hopes to find here," she said. "Nothing's out of place. Nothing's unusual."

"What about your husband's debit or credit cards? Are they missing?"

"Yes. But he hasn't taken out any money except the two thousand I told you about. Do you think they could trace the cards if he tried to get more?"

"Maybe. You'll have to ask the detective."

"Did Dennis take any medications?" I'd found some of the most telling imprints on prescription bottles; people almost always felt strongly about their medications.

"Yes, something to help him sleep. He took it with him."

I wondered what had made it difficult for Dennis to sleep.

Sophie looked at me, a wariness growing in her eyes. "What would you like to see first?"

"Would it be okay if I just wandered around and touched things?"

She relaxed. "Yeah. Go ahead and open closets and stuff, too. I don't mind. I'll be in the kitchen if you need me."

"Okay."

She smiled vacantly, her thin face lost and forlorn. I was so filled with pity that for a moment I was frozen in place watching her leave. In the kaleidoscope of her life, I hoped these next few days would be one of those gray areas that soon changed to brightness, instead of a black stain that bled into and saturated every other color for years to come.

Sawyer pulled out a realistic-looking cell phone from his toy box, opened it, and clapped it to his ear. "Daddy, come home now. I wanna play cars with you. Hurry, 'kay?" Without closing the phone, he tossed it to the floor by my feet where it landed with a heavy thump.

"Careful," I said, giving his head a pat as I stepped past him down the hallway.

I was looking for a bedroom, particularly the master, and found it at the end of the hallway, unlike Tawnia's, which was on the top floor. The room was exactly how it had appeared in the imprint—the sleigh bed and matching dresser with the mirror, the picture of a sailboat above the bed. I hadn't seen the rocking chair or the baby cradle, but neither would have been reflected in the mirror from where Dennis had stood with the bracelet in his hands. I tiptoed over to the cradle, but it was empty. Good. No worries about waking up Lizbeth.

I slipped my antique rings into my pocket and spread out my hands, running them quickly over the knickknacks, candles, and magazines that lay artfully here and there. I didn't know how long it would take Shannon to arrive, but I wanted to finish before he came to look at the room. None of the items gave off imprints of any consequence, so I opened the drawers of the nightstands. One was filled with books, the other contained a few baby toys, a pacifier, and a journal. Sophie's, by the imprint, but it was faded and didn't tell me anything. I wasn't interested in the words it might contain—that was Shannon's jurisdiction.

I put my hands inside the dresser drawers and ran my hands along the clothes. Nothing there or in the closet, but I hadn't expected clothes to hold lasting imprints. The blanket on the bed, obviously not often washed, did retain something, but as the most recent image always came first with multiple imprints, I released it after catching a tiny glimpse. Too old to be related to Dennis's disappearance and too private for me to pry.

Moving on.

I wondered what Jake was doing and if his friend was good-looking.

Upstairs I found a bedroom that must be Sawyer's and another bedroom scattered with painting and wallpapering supplies. Probably intended for Lizbeth. At the end of the hall was a smaller room with a set of weights. Running my fingers over these, I received a vague impression of sweat and effort. Not vivid. At least two years old.

Stifling a sigh, I went back down the stairs and through the hallway, where Sawyer was now running a car up the wall. The doorbell rang. My private time was up.

Sophie hurried from the kitchen, her eyes asking a question.

"Nothing," I said. "At least so far." Without waiting for her to answer the door, I headed into the kitchen myself. Lizbeth was there, sleeping in a little swing. So small and fragile. It'd be some time before she'd be doing anything with dolls or soldiers besides putting them in her mouth.

I began touching objects, but everything was too new or too generally disregarded to have vivid imprints. Occasionally, I caught a glimpse of Sophie's emotions, but there seemed to be little Dennis had felt strongly about here except his wife and children. Not surprising if he worked long hours outside the home. But Sophie had said he'd done yard work, so maybe I'd have more success in the garage, which was supposed to be a man's domain.

"She's right in here, I think," Sophie was saying as she appeared in the kitchen doorway.

"Well?" Tracy Reed asked eagerly. As usual, Shannon's partner wore a dark suit, this time navy, and her long blonde hair was

29

iron-straight. She was in her mid-twenties, ten years younger than Shannon, but she had risen fast through the ranks, due more to hard work and eagerness than to the fact that her grandfather, father, and brother had also worked as police detectives.

"Nothing. Maybe I'll have better luck in the garage or at his office."

Tracy nodded. "I hope so."

"Can you show me around the house?" Shannon asked Sophie.

Tracy didn't follow them from the room. "That expensive pen you read?" she said to me in a low voice. "Well, you were correct. It did write the threatening letter. We tracked it to the seller, who remembered the purchase, and we were able to trace the payment and get our man."

"I'm glad." Pens often carried good imprints. "What did Shannon say?"

"Oh, I didn't tell him where I got the information." Tracy winked. "Or about the identification you made of the camera owners who witnessed that bank robbery. They did have another memory card, exactly as you saw in the imprint, with all the photographs they'd taken of the area just before the robbery. Got some great accidental photos of our culprits staking out the place. Good thing the perps didn't guess about the full memory card they'd just replaced, or they might have done more than trash the camera."

All that with a few simple imprints. At least I had helped someone.

I was itching to get out to the garage, but I was also curious about what Shannon might find. Better to chat a bit more with Tracy, who squatted down near the swing to look at Lizbeth. Fortunately, Shannon didn't spend even as much time as I had in the other rooms.

"So you didn't notice if he was preoccupied," I heard him say from the living room.

Motioning for Tracy to follow, I moved into the hallway to hear the answer, stepping over Sawyer's toys on the carpet.

"No more than normal. He—he got depressed sometimes, you know, and he'd withdraw a bit. Usually when the kids were being more of a handful, or when he had to work a lot of evenings. But this week was good. He wasn't any different."

"Do you know anyone who'd want to hurt your husband?"

"No."

The questions went on, from money issues and any fights they might have had to extended family and past relationships. Some of the questions were too personal, and I was beginning to feel a little defensive on Sophie's behalf.

"Leave her alone," I said finally. "She doesn't know where he is or why he left. Can't you track his car? Or what about Tawnia's drawing? Wasn't there a building in the background? Couldn't you identify that and look for the car nearby?"

Shannon arched a brow. "I'll get to it." I couldn't tell if he was being serious or patronizing.

"What drawing?" Sophie asked.

I was saved from answering when Sawyer threw his phone at my leg. I gasped but not from the impact. A scene flashed in my mind, disappearing before I could tell what it was.

"Sawyer, no!" Sophie said, closing the space between them and bending down to talk to her son. "We don't throw things. You're not going to be able to play with your phone today. Daddy's—" She broke off suddenly and then said in rush, "Daddy will be very sad you used his old phone that way." Sophie was reaching for it as she spoke.

"Wait," I said.

Her hand froze in midair. No one spoke as I hesitated over the cell phone. It was an old one, large and unwieldy but comfortable to hold to your ear. The perfect toy, I supposed, for a rough little boy, though I wasn't sure it was safe to have kept the battery in. The imprints on the phone practically sparked toward my fingers.

I lifted my gaze to see everyone staring at me, Shannon's beautiful eyes the most intent. He gave me a slight nod, which freed me from my sudden paralysis. My hand tightened over the plastic.

I saw Dennis's face, felt Sawyer's delight as his daddy handed him the phone. "This is yours now, okay? You can stop trying to take mine." A giggle as Sawyer took the phone and hugged his daddy.

How easy it was to give a child joy.

This recent imprint was immediately replaced by something older and much darker, an imprint which sucked me in and held me tight. Dennis's shock and terror as he/I dialed a number. A man sprawled on blacktop, unnaturally still, a well of crimson covering his chest. Another man standing over the corpse, his features obscured by the darkness, an ominous black shape in his hand. His eyes lifted in Dennis's/my direction. Chills crawling up my back. Hide. Run! Footsteps following.

"What happened?" A tinny voice demanded from the phone.

"I need you to pick me up."

"What about Bart?"

"He killed him. He's following me!"

"Who killed who?"

Running faster. Had to get away or he would shoot me, too. Run. Terror.

"Autumn?" a voice said from far away. I didn't know whose.

"Tell me where you are," the tinny voice said from the phone.

Dennis/I rambled off street directions that made no sense. Stumbling. Falling. The sidewalk smacked him/me in the face. Footsteps moving closer. Turning. A man lifting his gun. A face of shadows. Terror filling every part of me. Looking into the face of death. Heart fluttering like a moth pinned to a board.

I was going to die.

CHAPTER

3

I was falling. Falling. Fear pounded in my ears. I couldn't breathe. Arms came around me, and I touched something. A watch. I saw it in a man's hand as he turned it over to view the inscription on the back, *To my grandson, Shannon. You have been my greatest joy.* The face of an older man as I reached to give him a hug. Love seeping into all the deep cracks the terror from the other imprint had cut into my soul, infusing me with rationality and comfort in exactly the way my parents' book of poetry or my mother's picture had soothed other terrifying imprints.

I remembered that I was Autumn Rain and I was safe in Sophie's house, not lying in a street somewhere facing a killer. In fact, I was encircled by Shannon's arms, my back against his chest as he crouched on the carpet. I clung to his wrist with a strength that surprised me, my fingers greedily soaking up the imprints associated with the watch his grandfather had given him.

"Are you okay?" Shannon asked after too many minutes had passed and it had begun to be awkward, his holding me while I clung to his arm. He bent his head around to look at my face, and the concern in his eyes was apparent, the way he held me tender, his attraction leaking through the mistrust. Usually, I felt the slightest bit of pure human satisfaction that Shannon liked me, however hard he battled against it, but I was so shaken by the imprint that I didn't feel a hint of gloating.

"Give me your watch," I managed, my tongue feeling thick and gummy.

He blinked once but unfastened it. I didn't lose contact with the metal as he did this but curled my fingers around it possessively, probably gouging his skin with my fingernails as I kept hold.

Once the watch was in my hand, I curled forward, away from Shannon's chest. He let me go. I breathed in steadily, shutting my eyes. Shannon had loved his grandfather so much, but there was a sadness in the imprints too, because one of them took place at the old man's funeral. Even that had a sort of beauty about it, a comforting inevitability, of belief in an afterlife.

Better than Dennis and the gun.

I had to tell them. They were still waiting, all of them sitting or kneeling on the carpet where the hallway intersected the living room and the kitchen, wanting to ask questions but giving me time. Even Sawyer waited, his eyes going between me and the phone on the carpet.

"Sawyer, take your toys and go up to your room." Underneath the calmness of Sophie's voice, I heard her fear. When the boy seemed ready to protest, she added, "If you're good, I'll take you to the park later and buy you an ice cream."

"With chocolate on the outside?"

"If that's what you want."

Sawyer picked up his toy box and gave his phone one last longing look before tromping upstairs to his room.

I took another steadying breath. "Dennis saw a man murdered,

34

a man named Bart. He was calling someone, but the murderer came after him. He was going to kill Dennis, too, but that's where the imprint ended. I don't know what else happened. It was . . . disturbing."

Sophie gasped. "Do you think the man is after Dennis?"

I shook my head. "I don't see how. The imprint is very vivid, but it happened over five years ago. Around April or May, I believe, though I can't be sure." I didn't see dates when I read imprints but rather imagined a calendar in my mind with a highlighted area around the event. Unless the imprint was less than a few months old, it was hard to pin it to an exact date.

"Well, the one thing we do know is that Dennis didn't die five years ago." Shannon moved away from me so gradually that at first it was hard to tell he was moving at all. He picked up the phone and stared at it thoughtfully. His voice didn't hold as much disbelief as it normally did by this point, but that was probably because I'd been right often enough before.

I wondered if I could remember the address Dennis had given without touching the phone again. I really, really, really didn't want to do that.

"I need paper," I said.

Tracy produced a pad and pen from somewhere, and I jotted down what I could remember of the address. "I think this is what Dennis told whoever he called. Maybe you can find out if something happened there. I have no idea what state or even what country it was in."

Shannon took the paper and rose to his feet. Everyone else did the same, even me, though my legs were shaky. "They were speaking English?" he asked.

Oh, right. "Yes. Definitely American."

"Has Dennis always lived in Oregon?" Tracy asked Sophie.

"No. He's from Kansas. We met when he moved here." Sophie

paused, her brow furrowing. "That was five years ago. We got married in three months. It just seemed right, you know?"

Tracy and I nodded agreement while Shannon asked, "Have you ever met his family?"

"An aunt once, a couple years ago. His mom and dad were older when they had him. They died before we met."

"He have any siblings?"

Sophie shook her head. "Look, if Dennis did see someone killed, then do you think it might have something to do with why he's missing now? What if that guy has been searching for him all this time and finally found him?"

"It's a possibility," Shannon said. "Or it might be unrelated. Have you contacted his work?"

"They called me. Apparently, Dennis was supposed to do some computer systems update on Wednesday night and he never did it. I told them he hadn't come home, either." Sophie glanced at me. "I learned later he did come home while I was out and packed a few things. I told his boss that I'd called the police."

"I think I'll pay them a visit," Shannon said.

"Maybe they did it!" The words burst from Sophie as if they'd been held in a long time. "I get a bad feeling about them sometimes, you know?"

Shannon's eyes narrowed. "What about Dennis? Did he ever say anything negative about his work?"

"No." Sophie's voice was soft. "I mean, he didn't always get along perfectly with everyone, but he loves that job." She put her hands to her cheeks and began to sob. "I'm so scared!"

Shannon put a hand on her shoulder, a comforting hand. I'd seen him to do the same thing to a woman at the commune after her husband had been shot and killed while trying to protect her. It gave me the same unsettled feeling now as it had then, though I couldn't pinpoint why. "We'll get to the bottom of this," he said. "I promise."

I felt a short-lived surge of triumph. Shannon was convinced something was wrong with Dennis's disappearance and that meant he would give the case his full attention. He might be an irritating cynic most of the time, but he was also a dedicated cop who didn't give up easily once he'd grabbed onto something.

Meeting Tracy's gaze, Shannon glanced quickly toward Sophie.

"If I could just ask you a few more questions," Tracy said, retrieving her notebook from Shannon.

"Okay, but I need to check on my baby." Sophie rubbed her hands over her face several times, wiping the tears. The two disappeared into the kitchen, and I could hear them talking, Tracy's voice slow, deliberate, matter-of-fact, Sophie's high-pitched and anxious.

"Are you planning to rub the metal right off?" Shannon asked with an amused smile.

I looked down at the watch still in my hands, my thumbs working over the metal on the back as if I were trying to mold it into something else. "Oh, yeah. Thanks." I extended the watch, and he took it from me. I could feel the roughness on the tips of his fingers that told me he didn't sit at a desk all day. I wondered if he'd been working on his acre. I'd never seen his place before, and some part of me really wanted to.

"My grandfather gave me this watch," he said as he fastened it on his wrist.

"I'm sorry about his passing. You were named for a man who saved his life, weren't you?"

He gave me a measured stare. "How did you know?"

I'd known for months, since almost the beginning of our acquaintance, but now for the life of me I didn't remember how I knew. "Didn't you tell me?"

"No."

That meant I'd probably picked it up from an imprint on something at the precinct when we'd worked together on that first case with the missing child. "Oh, well. It's a sissy name, you know."

"So you've told me. You and just about every cop I know."

I smiled. "Well, I'm going to take a peek in the garage and then get out of here. I need to go meet Jake." Because underneath all the excitement, I hadn't forgotten his visitor. A need to see Jake was building inside me, the primordial urge to stake my claim.

"You sure you're okay to drive?"

There, his concern was peeking out again. "Don't tell me you're finally starting to believe." I'd seen all degrees of belief and skepticism, but I'd thought no one could use my information without at least some kernel of belief, as Shannon seemed to.

"Oh, I believe you," he said. "Tracy hasn't suddenly become the most intuitive detective on the force on her own. Don't think I didn't notice the evidence in our cases disappearing from time to time."

Okay, so he believed—and now had actually admitted it to me. Not that his believing would make a difference in how he felt about me and my ability. I was weird, odd, unusual, strange. Something to be examined and used at arm's length. No matter what his inner emotions urged, he wouldn't allow himself to feel anything more. I felt no regret at that, as I had when we'd first met. Such a waste, I'd thought then, to share an attraction with someone who would never let you close enough to really know him.

Now I had Jake, and Jake loved me for everything that I was—and wasn't.

"You know where to find me if you need me." I forced a smile.

Shannon watched me go. "Autumn."

I stopped. "Yes?"

"Be careful."

Why did everyone think I needed that warning? Almost as though I had the words *Looking for Danger* stamped on my forehead. "With what?"

"Leave this investigation to me."

I shrugged. "Without me, this investigation wouldn't even *be* an investigation. If Sophie needs my help again, I will help her." Giving him a smile full of confidence I was far from feeling, I turned and left. I didn't look back.

•   •   •

Jake's grandmother lived in an older section of town, but though the buildings were old, they weren't neglected. Most of the neighbors had lived there a long time and knew each other by name and helped out when needed. I loved being there. The people had started to recognize me, in part because of the publicity surrounding Winter's death in the bridge bombing and in part because Jake and I were friends. Their smiles in my direction were genuine.

The place felt a lot like the area where my apartment was, though I lived closer to the Hawthorne District. I had thought there was a large concentration of African-Americans living there, but Jake told me that was purely in my imagination. According to him, his people were still in the minority by far. His people. That separation was silly. Jake's father, though he'd never known him, had been white, which meant Jake was as much white as he was black. Not like his younger sister, Randa, who'd come from his mother's second marriage.

I'd called Randa at the Herb Shoppe to make sure she and Thera didn't need help. My store was usually as dead as an ancient tomb on Fridays, and I often took the opportunity to visit yard and estate sales or second-hand stores to search for antiques to add to my inventory. Friday, however, was one of Jake's busy days, and it surprised me that he had stayed away so long. That he had was probably why I decided to make this little visit. His visitor must be someone special—or big trouble.

I took the elevator to the third floor, where Jake's grandmother opened the door. She was slender and strong and stately like a black walnut tree, her shoulders only slightly beginning to hunch with age. Thick lines of gray ran through her dark hair, which was combed and wrapped into her customary knot at the base of her head. She had raised six children and a dozen or more of her grandchildren after their parents' deaths or when their trials in life left them incapable. Stalwart and opinionated, she'd been the heart and soul of the family. Since the only family I'd known growing up consisted of Winter and Summer, the adoptive parents I'd always addressed by their first names, I practically worshiped this woman and the many ties she'd created.

"Autumn! So good to see you, child." The edges of her brown eyes crinkled as she drew me into the middle of a narrow hallway that ran the length of the house.

"You, too, Marme." The name meant grandmother, but even Marme, who was an educated woman, didn't know where the word originated. "Is Jake still here?"

"He's in the parlor."

That was what she called her formal sitting room, a name left over from her childhood in the south. "He tells me you're on another case. Are you sure that's wise?"

I gave her a half smile. "Not in the least, but doing something with my ability helps me control it a bit." What I meant was that purposefully reading imprints helped me develop an instinct about where stray imprints might lurk before I touched them. That made accidental readings easier to avoid, though the accidental ones weren't necessarily worse than planned ones, as Dennis's phone imprint had proven today.

"That's understandable." We had reached the door to the parlor, but Marme stopped me before going in. "Look, you should know, he has a visitor," she said quietly.

"He told me."

"He went to high school with Kolonda. They were very close."

Her inflection told me their involvement had been more than a simple friendship. I met her gaze without voicing the questions in my heart. Jake loved me, and I loved him. That's all I had to know.

Marme dipped her regal head and led me into the room. Jake was seated on the sofa, studying papers spread on the coffee table. Next to him was an attractive woman with black hair that fell around her face in gentle waves. Her skin was the color of rich, dark caramel, her large eyes a brown several shades lighter than Jake's. She wore a happy, spring dress with a designer cut that advertised she had money to spare—not to mention a figure most women only dreamed of having.

I wanted to hate her immediately, but when Jake jumped up and gave me a kiss, she smiled. "You must be Autumn. I'm happy to meet you."

Jake led me to the sofa. "Autumn, this is Kolonda Lewis. We went to high school together."

Kolonda stood, and I shook her hand. "So Marme was telling me. Nice to meet you."

"How'd it go?" Jake asked, a hand on my back. "With the detective, I mean. Was he as irritating as always?"

I thought of how Shannon had held me after I'd read the imprint on the phone. "Not quite, but then Tracy was there most of the time to ward him off."

"Did you find anything?"

"I think so." My eyes slid to Kolonda. No way did I want to discuss this with her here. "I'll tell you later."

His strong hand caressed mine. "Bad, huh?"

I nodded.

"I'm sorry. I wish I'd been there."

"Me, too." Then I wouldn't have had to depend on Shannon.

During our exchange, Kolonda seated herself again and picked up a paper from the coffee table. Unless I wanted to sit between her and Jake on the sofa, I'd have to take the chair. I chose the chair.

Jake hesitated before returning to his seat on the sofa next to Kolonda, his dark eyes troubled.

"So what do you think?" Kolonda asked into the silence, apparently polite enough not to pry.

He turned his gaze back to her. "After reading this contract and hearing your story, I'm coming to the same conclusion as you did. The work had to have been shoddy, and this offer to buy the place instead of fixing it is definitely an attempt to get the property."

"The question is why," Kolonda said. "It's a convenient location, but the area's a little rundown. It won't make anyone rich. Anyway, I can't sell my buildings. I need the rental income."

Jake gave her a grin. "I guess a college teacher's wage doesn't do it these days."

Kolonda wasn't offended. "Daddy left me the apartments so I'd be taken care of, and I do admit the income allows me to pursue my love of teaching."

"Uh, so what exactly is the problem?" I asked, not quite following the conversation. Why did I feel so strange? Kolonda seemed a perfectly nice person—not a woman out to reclaim her first love, if that indeed was what Jake was to her.

"Kolonda had some work done in the two apartment buildings we're talking about," Jake explained. "Less than a year later the ceilings collapsed in several of the units. There is considerable structural damage. Since the work Kolonda had done was to avoid this kind of thing, she suspects negligence on the part of the contractor."

"But he won't take responsibility," Kolonda added, "and any other professional I've had look at the place refuses to back my suspicion. Officially, that is." She snorted delicately. "It's like they're all afraid to say anything. Then I remembered that Jake spent a lot of years in construction and hoped he might be able to tell me what's really going on. I don't have money to repair the place again, and every day I'm losing money from the tenants I could have there."

"And now the contractor is offering to buy the place?"

"Yes—at a very reduced price, of course, because of the damage." Kolonda tucked a strand of hair behind her ear and pushed the papers across the coffee table toward me. "This is the contract, if you want to read it."

I wanted to read it, but not the way she was talking about. Taking a breath, I set my fingers on the papers. Jake's eyes narrowed expectantly, but I shook my head. Whoever had prepared these papers either hadn't cared about them or hadn't handled them long enough for any imprints to remain. After the phone, the nothingness was almost a comfort.

Jake frowned. "Look, I'd be glad to take a look at the buildings. I haven't worked construction for a long time, but I bet I could tell if there was negligence, and I still know a few people in the business. If I can't give you an answer, I'll find someone who can."

"Thank you so much." Kolonda reached out and set a small hand on Jake's arm. "I really appreciate it. I know I have no right to come to you for help after the way Daddy treated you."

Jake shrugged, giving me a decidedly uncomfortable glance. "It's okay. I don't mind."

So Daddy hadn't liked their relationship. Well, that made two of us.

"You don't happen to have anything belonging to this contractor, do you?" I asked. "You know, a business card, something he left behind when you talked?" It was a long shot, but you never knew.

Kolonda started to shake her head but then nodded. "A pen. He gave me a pen to sign the contract. I told him of course that I wasn't going to sign anything right then, but he didn't listen." She was rummaging in her small black purse now. "It was a fat one, engraved. I purposely didn't give it back because I was mad." She gave a wry giggle. "He came to see me at my office, and I envisioned throwing it out the window at him as he left. Of course I couldn't do it, not with all those impressionable freshman out there waiting to walk with me to class."

I could imagine half her male students were in love with her and would jump at the opportunity to walk her to class. Well, that was good for us because it meant she hadn't thrown the pen. As I'd already proven with the evidence Tracy had shown me, writing instruments often held great imprints.

"Great. I don't see it. Maybe I took it out." Kolonda began emptying the contents of her purse onto the contract. A jeweled compact, not the disposable kind and obviously unusual, drew my attention. Of anything she had in her purse, that was most likely to contain imprints. I reached for it.

"Autumn?" Jake caught my eyes. He knew I didn't touch things lightly, especially when I hadn't remembered to put back on my antique rings.

I drew back my hand. He was right. I didn't want to read any of her imprints or invade her privacy. "It's a very pretty compact."

Kolonda picked up the compact and pushed it into my hand. "My father gave it to me when I was sixteen. The jewels are real."

She loved it. I felt it the minute my hand closed over the piece. And that wasn't all she loved. I saw her determination to contact Jake, felt the fluttering of her heart as she checked her makeup in the compact before she saw him again after all these years.

Kolonda still cared for Jake.

An earlier imprint showed Kolonda clutching the compact and

weeping as her father told her Jake would never amount to any-thing. My heart wanted to break with hers. Older scenes followed, fading but still clear enough, especially when she'd used the com-pact in Jake's presence. They had spent a lot of time together, and Kolonda had cared deeply for Jake. I could tell by his expression in the imprints that he'd felt the same way.

He'd looked at her the way he looked at me now.

Slowly and deliberately, I set the compact down. Jake leaned forward and caught my hand. "You okay?"

Did he notice the slight trembling? Probably. He was that care-ful of me.

"Your rings. Where are they?"

I fished them from the pocket of my camouflage pants, relieved when the comforting buzz blurred Kolonda's imprints in my mind.

It's not like I thought Jake had lived in a box before he met me. I'd known him a year before we began dating last month, and he'd been one of my anchors when Winter died. Though the seed of attraction had always been there, I hadn't loved him then as I did now. I'd dated other guys, and he'd dated as well. We'd often teased each other about our choice of dates—and how the rela-tionships always ended in disaster. But despite all the women he'd dated, I hadn't figured there was someone who'd once meant as much to him, possibly, as I did now.

"I guess I left it at my office," Kolonda was saying. "Or maybe he took it after all. But why? Is it important?"

"I'll let Jake explain," I said, rising to my feet. "I'd better get back to my shop."

Kolonda looked at Jake uncertainly. "You probably need to get back, too. I'm sorry about interrupting your day. I can arrange for you to look at the buildings another day, if it's better." Her gaze shifted to me, her reddened lips curving in a smile. "Jake's changed so much. I never imagined he'd own an herb store or go back to college."

"Oh, he told you about the classes."

"I'm glad he's gone back. Some things you really must learn in a classroom."

I couldn't think of one thing that wouldn't be better learned by actually doing it, but I wasn't about to argue with Kolonda, a woman whose life was teaching. Besides, finding hands-on opportunities wasn't easy for working adults these days, much less for college kids, so in that respect even dull classes were better than no education at all. I had to agree with that. Besides, where Jake was concerned, I'd prefer Kolonda to be as far removed from hands-on experience as possible.

"It's only a few botany courses," Jake grumbled, moving closer to me. "Helps me with the herbs."

I took Jake's hand and squeezed it. "You coming?" I was considering leaving my car and riding back with him on his motor bike.

"Actually, I think I'll zip on over to Kolonda's building right now. She has the time, and we might as well get things rolling. Can you lock up for me if I'm not back in time?"

"Sure." I gave him a quick kiss and made myself walk to the door. I had nothing to worry about. Jake was as reliable as a mountain.

"Oh," Kolonda said, noticing my bare feet for the first time. "Were we supposed to take our shoes off at the door? I do that at my house." Her eyes landed on Jake's shoes with relief.

"No, I just don't wear shoes." I tossed the words over my shoulder, leaving Jake to explain that as well as the possible imprints on the pen. "It was nice to meet you, Kolonda."

"You, too." Her smile was genuine. If she was still in love with Jake, she must not know it yet or hadn't dared to admit it to herself.

"I'll come by tonight," Jake called as I moved down the hallway.

Marme heard me and came from the kitchen, reaching the door before I did. "Take care of yourself," she said, opening it for me.

"I will." Mentally, I gave her an invitation to join Shannon and Jake's Autumn Should Be Careful Club.

As I drove back to my store, I thought about Kolonda and what I'd learned. Whether she admitted it or not, she was still in love with Jake, and he still cared a great deal for her or he wouldn't have dropped everything on a Friday to check out her buildings.

No. I was overreacting. That was the kind of guy Jake was, always eager to help people, just as I liked to do by reading imprints. I refused to be jealous.

Well, maybe just a little.

CHAPTER

4

When I returned to Autumn's Antiques, Thera Brinker had things well in hand. "It's been really slow, I'm afraid," she said, wiping her hands on her pants, the same sky blue color she normally wore. The color was calming, she'd explained, and she yearned for calm after all the excitement she'd endured with her deceased husband. On her ample chest she wore her favorite bulky, blue bead necklace. "But I did get a chance to reorganize the music boxes so the new ones will fit in."

"Wonderful." They were my biggest seller these days.

"Is something wrong?" Thera had been my friend before she became my employee and a regular customer as well. She knew me better than anyone except Jake and Tawnia.

I explained about Sophie and Dennis and the imprints, and soon Thera was clucking over me, reminding me never to feel sorry for myself out loud again.

"Really, I'm fine."

Thera nodded. "If you want, I can stay late and lock up for you."

"No, you go ahead. I have a little restoration to do in the back."

"Okay, then. I am looking forward to a hot bath and a nice evening in bed watching TV."

Which sounded exactly like what I'd been doing the past few weeks as I healed from my adventures at the commune. The inactivity drove me insane, but I didn't think my ribs were up to dancing quite yet.

I was stretching a delicate piece of fabric over an antique chair in my back room when my cell phone rang. Sighing, I let the material go. I wasn't exactly doing a great job on the reupholstering, anyway. I'd refinished my Victorian couches at home and read three books on the subject, but the chair's oddly curved shape presented a challenge. Perhaps taking a class to learn how to do it would be a good idea. Score one for Kolonda and her formal education crusade.

"Hello?" I said, stifling disappointment that it wasn't Jake.

"I've got news," Tracy said. "A murder did take place at that address you gave us but not in Oregon or in Kansas. Try Michigan. And it might be related to organized crime—namely, the Franco family. The police have been suspicious about them for years. Bartolomeo Franco was the man killed that night. What's more, a man named Alex Trogan witnessed the murder and called 911. The police showed up in time to place him in protective custody, but after a few months in hiding he went missing and never testified. They assumed he'd been found and murdered."

"Oh, wow."

Tracy laughed. "My thoughts exactly. Shannon's ordered an entire background check on Dennis. He's wondering if maybe Alex and Dennis are one and the same and that he went underground with a fake identity instead of being caught by those wanting to stop him from testifying."

"Do they have a picture of this Alex?"

"Yeah, but it's old and not very good. Could be Dennis. Maybe the call you saw him make in the imprint was to 911."

"I guess it could have been, but it didn't seem like it to me. I think he knew the man he called."

"Well, you've said yourself that imprints don't record exact happenings, just the person's emotions and impressions of the event, so there might be several interpretations."

"I suppose." I didn't like my words thrown back at me. Sometimes Tracy had too good a memory.

"If Dennis did witness that murder, it could be a huge break for Michigan police."

"Funny, I never thought of Michigan as a center for organized crime." I tucked my phone between my ear and shoulder and picked up the fabric again.

"Organized crime is everywhere."

"I'm glad you're looking into it. Sophie doesn't deserve this, and those kids need a dad."

"Hopefully we'll find something in Dennis's office that will lead us to him. We're going over there now."

"Good." But what if the clue was an imprint they couldn't see? "I don't suppose Shannon wants me along." I twisted a section of material to see if that might be the look I was aiming for.

"No."

"Big surprise there."

"He's really not so bad once you get to know him."

"Really?"

She laughed. "Well, it beats working with a lot of these guys. He doesn't make comments about what I wear or brag about his conquests. He's respectful of my ideas, and he's about given up trying to force me to like pasta. Deep down he's a nice guy. For what it's worth, Autumn, when you were hurt last month, he had a hard time with it. He blamed himself."

He could get in line behind Jake. And Tawnia, too. She'd never let me forget how I'd almost gotten myself buried alive and shot. If Sophie hadn't been her friend, she would never have wanted me to read Dennis's imprints. "I make my own choices. Shannon had nothing to do with that commune."

"I know. Look, I gotta go. Shannon's giving me the evil eye. I'll stay in touch."

"Thanks." I hung up and stared into space for a long while until I felt the invisible connection I always experienced with my sister grow thick and close. Throwing down my fabric, I stood up as she waltzed into my back room, beaming and happy.

She hugged me. "Thank you so much for everything you've done for Sophie. She was a lot more positive when I talked to her a little while ago."

Her words brought back the memory of the imprint on Dennis's old phone. Death. Fear. I smiled wearily. "I'm glad."

"That bad, huh?"

"Yeah. But Shannon had a watch, and it helped."

She rolled her eyes and sank into the ratty easy chair, whose comfort was more important than its indeterminable color. "Oh, I bet he liked that. You spying on his personal life."

"He didn't seem to mind." Yet I knew Shannon would hate that violation once he thought about it—once the urgency of the moment was forgotten.

Tawnia frowned. "We'll have to find something you can carry around with you. Something you're not worried about the imprints fading or being replaced by your own."

"Let me know when you figure that out." The best comforting imprints came from objects most treasured by people—wedding rings, photographs, keys, or other jewelry. I couldn't exactly ask to borrow irreplaceable treasures.

"I will. Hey, what's up with Jake? Randa seems to be all alone in the Herb Shoppe, and she's got a bit of a line." She held up a hand to stop me from moving. "No, not enough for you to need to rush in there to help. She can handle it. But where's Jake?"

I didn't feel like talking about Kolonda Lewis.

"Have you tried to draw another picture?" I asked, sitting on the edge of my long worktable, my legs stretched out to the floor. "Of Dennis, I mean."

"Every chance I get." She shook her head. "Nothing. But I was able to finish all my work early today." She eyed the door to my bathroom at the end of the room somewhat regretfully. I knew how she felt. Once you settled in that chair, you wished you never had to get up, even for something as urgent as pregnancy bladder. I slept there some nights when I was working late.

I extended my arm to help her up. "We need to go see Dennis's office."

"Won't the law firm be closed by now?"

"Well, the police are there, so probably not yet."

"Then let the police take care of it."

"I have to go. Something doesn't feel right. I'm all jumpy." Of course that might be because Jake was somewhere with a beautiful, accomplished woman who loved him, but at least going to Dennis's office might help me get my mind off their relationship.

"Okay, but I need something to eat. We'll have to stop some-place on the way."

"No way. I'll throw something together while you're in the bathroom." I opened my mini refrigerator next to the bathroom door. "You've been eating nothing but white flour and preservatives all day."

Tawnia laughed. "So does most of the world, and we do just

fine. But if you insist, at least make it something edible, okay? None of that rye bread junk you tried to give me last week. Talk about a meal that haunts you."

"Don't worry. I have meat rolls, freshly baked last night." I'd meant them for our lunch today, but she'd had that awful sandwich instead, and I hadn't begun to make headway on them, despite my large appetite. "Wait," I said before she could close the bathroom door. "I just thought of something. What about naming the baby Unity? That might inspire some good."

"Unity? For a baby's name? Oh, come on." She shut the door in my face.

Randa had finished with her customers by the time Tawnia emerged from the bathroom, and I let her go a few minutes early as I closed and locked up both shops. Then Tawnia drove us to the law firm where Dennis worked because if she didn't do the driving, she tended to become nauseated. We ate as we drove to the address I'd looked up on the Internet and programmed into her GPS. I didn't know if I was in a hurry to get there before the police left so I might be let in, or if I'd hoped the police were gone and the office still open so I could talk my way in. Either way didn't bode well for my success. My only advantage was Tawnia, the queen of getting her own way. We'd have to play it by ear.

The offices of Simeon, Gideon & Associates were even more prestigious than their name. The ultimate of cutting edge architecture, though the rather abstract statue in the spacious lobby, obviously designed to impress, looked lumpy and lopsided to my antiques-trained eyes.

Tawnia eyed the statue appreciatively. "Is that a man fighting a bear or a woman giving birth?"

I laughed. "Take your pick."

"So how do we get permission to search the place?"

"I don't know. If Tracy's still here, she might find a way to get us in, at least to Dennis's office." Belatedly, I thought about calling to let her know I was here. Then again, she hadn't invited me along in the first place—not that I blamed her. She was the one who had to work with Shannon.

"May I help you?" asked the blonde at the tall reception desk.

I put my hands on the desk and leaned forward. "We're working with the police on Dennis Briggs's disappearance. I'd like to see his office, please."

She eyed us doubtfully. Tawnia was dressed the part in her office wear, a stretchy maroon maternity suit to be exact, but in my comfortable camouflage pants, baggy after my hospital stint, and my fitted T-shirt, I probably looked more like a teenager on her way to high school. "The police just left."

"It will only take a few minutes," Tawnia said. "We couldn't get here sooner."

"Let me call someone."

I had visions of Tawnia talking to the guy in charge while I sneaked around and searched for Dennis's office. Not going to happen from the secure look of this place. Besides, with my luck, I'd end up tackled and earn myself another broken rib.

Removing my rings and shoving them in the pocket of my pants, I trailed my hands over the objects on the reception desk. A sign-in chart, a bronze plaque, a pen, a potted flower. Nothing. I flexed my toes and slowly paced the length of the reception desk, but there were no imprints on the floor, either. No surprise since not much was felt strongly at foot level. If it were, I might be forced to wear shoes, despite the back pain most of them caused me. I headed over to the waiting area of leather couches and stacks of magazines. More potted plants.

"What is she doing?"

"It's called psychometry." Tawnia spoke as if it were the most obvious thing in the world. She didn't elaborate, and I was glad the receptionist seemed too cowed by her cool response to ask any questions.

I sensed nothing. If someone here had it out for Dennis, they hadn't left their feelings lying around this public area. A part of me was relieved. Strong imprints left in a public place were usually terrible because people simply didn't have many loving emotions about things that didn't belong to them. Rather, they felt greed, anger, hatred, desire, and revenge. The library was the exception. I'd found a lot of comforting imprints on books, though some sections I'd learned to stay away from altogether, like those dealing with grieving, weapon-making, and intimacy. No reason to destroy my life with imprints that were insidious and addictive. I did not want to become a junkie of any kind.

A man emerged from the elevator situated on the wall to the left of the desk. "I'm Ben Fuller, one of the associates here," he said to Tawnia. "May I help you?"

I hurried over to them. The man was about our age and handsome in an I-know-I'm-good sort of way. His brown hair was a little too short for seriousness, and his face slightly soft-looking for my tastes, but his immaculate suit and highly buffed shoes screamed upscale professionalism.

Tawnia began explaining our purpose, making it sound as though the police had invited us. I let her do it because fabrication has never been my strong suit. I couldn't mislead people or act if my life depended on it. Plus, she was the older twin, having been born before midnight on February twenty-third, twenty-seven minutes before me, which made me younger by an entire day. Since I was the one taking care of her in practically every other way, she needed to earn that older sibling status. Not that she would agree with me.

Ben stared at my feet, but I hadn't seen any signs saying people had to wear shoes. Contrary to popular belief, governmental health regulations did not require people to wear shoes in buildings, public or otherwise. If such notices were posted in private businesses, it wasn't because of the health department. Last I'd checked, it was also legal to drive in all fifty states without shoes, though some officers themselves didn't know the law. In my teens, I'd received a ticket for failing to wear shoes while driving. I fought it in court—and won.

I met Ben's stare evenly. For some reason I wondered if his mother called him Benny. He seemed like a Benny to me.

"The police just left," Ben said. "They took Dennis's hard drive and some other records—we are cooperating fully, of course. They didn't say anything about anyone else coming, and now the office is actually closed for the day." He said it with a finality that might have had me pleading for an exception or walking to the door.

Tawnia took it all in stride. Taking out her phone, she dialed quickly. "You know Dennis's wife, Sophie, don't you?"

"Well, uh, I've met her. I guess."

"Hi, Sophie? This is Tawnia. I'm at Dennis's office with Autumn, but I need you to please talk to Ben Fuller here. Let him know that Autumn's working with the police like she was doing at your house today. We need to get in to see Dennis's office." She handed over the phone to a surprised Ben.

"Hello?" He was quiet a long time as Sophie's voice ebbed and flowed, loud enough for us to hear but not loud enough to make out the words. "Really? That's interesting. So you think I should let them in? Well, all right." He shut the phone, obviously not inclined to make small talk with people he didn't know well. Or maybe he had a guilty conscience where Dennis was concerned. In my opinion, everyone here was suspect.

"Okay," Ben said. "His office only, but you need to hurry. As I said, we're closed." He took two steps away from us and leaned over the reception desk, whispering something to the receptionist. She nodded and glanced nervously at us over his shoulder.

Ben straightened. "Come this way." His gaze ran over me again, not altogether sneering but different now that he'd talked to Sophie. She must have told him about my ability, and I had risen in his estimation from scum to freak. Well, no matter. It was why I was here after all.

He didn't take us to the elevator but to a door near it, which opened onto a long corridor. It was the kind of law firm where everyone had his own office, even the lowly IT guy, though his was probably far smaller than those of the partners and associates. From what Ben told us, Dennis's job consisted of everything—writing programs, installing software, keeping the network working, and doing odd bits of research. Tawnia latched onto this last bit of information.

"So, he might have learned something in his research that put him in danger."

Ben stared at her. "We handle a lot of sensitive items, but I don't think anyone would want to, uh, knock him off because he stumbled across some information. It's not as if we do anything illegal here."

No one spoke, but Tawnia and I exchanged a significant stare when Ben wasn't looking. "Of course not," I muttered when the silence grew too noticeable, but my mind was working overtime. What if Dennis's disappearance had nothing to do with the murder he'd witnessed? I wasn't a big believer in coincidences, but they did happen, and after all, five years had gone by since the murder. Why would he be discovered now? The chance of uncovering something possibly damaging about his own employers or their clients was a lot more likely.

I mentally reined in my thoughts. Not only was this speculation unhelpful at the moment with Ben staring suspiciously at me but I didn't want my thoughts to influence any imprints I might find.

Dennis's office was about as large as the back room at my shop, though arranged in a square instead of a rectangle, which made it feel more roomy. Plus it had a nice-sized window that opened into a small courtyard with several large flowerbeds. Not bad at all. A wide oak desk held a neat stack of papers, an iPod dock, and two large monitors. Two extra chairs stood against the wall under a dry erase board. A tall bookshelf held numerous books and several pictures of Sophie and the kids. Much like his areas of the bedroom and master bath, the office was uncluttered to the point of sparseness. Except for the pictures, it could have belonged to anyone.

I began with the bookshelf first, running my fingers over the spines of the books. Many people were attached to their favorite books and left imprints on them. These, however, seemed new, or nearly so. I wasn't surprised that they held nothing. Not even the pictures of his family had more than vaguely pleasant imprints attached. He hadn't handled them since he'd placed them on the shelves.

My jumpy feeling was still present, though, as it had been since I'd left Sophie's. I reached the desk, pulled open the drawer with an ergonomic keyboard inside. A thin, silver pen lay at the top of the keyboard, far from the other writing utensils that filled another compartment in the drawer.

I leaned over and touched the keyboard. Flashes of concentration, contentment, frustration. Too many imprints to separate, not one standing out from the rest. The daily grind.

Okay, the pen. As my hand approached, I noticed a smear marred the shiny surface. Probably Dennis's fingerprint—nothing I needed to worry about preserving since he hadn't disappeared from here, and Shannon had probably already lifted Dennis's fingerprints in connection with his full background check.

The smoothness of the pen against my skin was immediately blotted out by an imprint. Dennis entering a room where two men sat at a large conference table. Bright daylight shone through two oversized windows on the far wall. "Ian, I have the information you wanted," Dennis said.

The men turned and Dennis/I felt the smile freeze on my face.

"Thanks, Dennis." The man with the blond hair came to his feet and reached for the papers.

I stared at the dark-haired man across from him, my eyes falling to the hands on the table and then back to his face. Fear coursed through my chest. *Maybe he doesn't know me.* The man rose slowly to his feet, dipping his head in polite acknowledgment. His eyes were intent, and my fear cranked up a notch.

"Uh, Dennis, can I have the papers?"

"Oh, yeah." My grip loosened enough so Ian could take the papers, but I clutched the silver pen desperately. Sweat made my hands slick. *Turn. Leave.* Taking a breath, I managed to do just that.

Finally, I was in the hallway, breathing heavily. One thought was uppermost in my mind, even above the fear: *I have to get out of here.* It was the only way my family would be safe. First I had to make myself walk. One foot in front of the other. Hurry!

The imprint disappeared, and I waited only a second to make sure there were no others before dropping the pen.

"Autumn? What did you see?" Tawnia gripped my shoulder tightly, as though doing so would call me back to the present.

I wished when I saw imprints that I could see them with a disconnected outsider's view. Unfortunately, that was not how it worked—at least not with the most vivid ones. These memories would become my own, and like at Sophie's today, try as I might to tell myself I wasn't in danger, my emotions refused to believe me. I was fortunate this imprint had been so brief.

"Well?" Tawnia asked. She and Ben were staring at me, Tawnia with concern, Ben with skepticism.

"I know why Dennis left," I said. "But I don't know how it's connected to the murder."

CHAPTER

5

urder?" Ben's brown eyes opened wide. "The police didn't say anything about a murder."

"That's because it's on a need-to-know basis." Shannon strode through the doorway, Tracy close behind.

I caught a glimpse of the receptionist in the hall beyond them. Now I knew what Ben had been whispering to her before he'd brought us back here. He must have wanted to throw us out but was playing it safe in case we were legit. If we weren't, he'd expect Shannon to do his dirty work.

Shannon crossed to the desk and glared down at me. "I thought I told you to stay out of this."

I lifted my chin. "I thought you knew you weren't my boss."

"This is serious."

"Which is why I'm here. Look, do you want to continue to pretend you're protecting me, or do you want to know what I found?"

Shannon's jaw worked silently for a moment, as though struggling to control what was trying to burst forth. To give him credit,

he didn't immediately slap me in cuffs and charge me with interfer-
ing in a police investigation.

"I'd like to know." Tracy was smiling, but the worried look in
her eyes and the line on her brow told me she didn't know how
Shannon was going to react to her support.

"Was Dennis murdered?" Ben interrupted, his face looking a
little pasty. "Is that what this is all about?"

To my relief, Shannon fixed his stare on Ben. "No. At least not
that we know of." When Shannon turned back to me, I found myself wishing I could ask for his watch because I still felt unsettled by
Dennis's fear. I couldn't ask, though, because that would be prov-
ing Shannon's point, if only in a small way.

"Okay," Shannon said. "What did you see?"

"She didn't see anything," Ben said. "She was sitting there the
whole time. And if you are trying to imply that something is amiss
here, I'll remind you that Simeon, Gideon & Associates is a law
firm and completely capable of protecting itself."

Shannon's face darkened, and I would have felt glad that Ben
had diverted his attention again if my hands hadn't started shaking.
I tucked them into the pockets of my pants so no one would notice.

"No one is implying anything, Mr. Fuller. Now if you would be
so good as to leave us alone a minute—"

Ben scowled, but he started toward the door.

"Wait," I said. "We'll need to talk with someone here named
Ian."

Ben hesitated, looking questioningly at Shannon and Tracy.

Without so much as glancing my way, Shannon said, "Please
bring him here, if he's available. If not, I'll need his contact information." When Ben still hesitated, Shannon added, "Both Mrs. Gideon
and Mr. Simeon promised us full cooperation, Mr. Fuller. If there's
a problem, you need to take it up with them."

"I'll be right back." Ben turned on his heel and left the office.

All eyes turned to me expectantly. I sank down into Dennis's chair, my knees growing wobbly. My rib was throbbing, too, though I hadn't damaged it again. Not yet.

I hadn't touched everything on the desk, and I wanted to. Really, I did. But I needed to find the courage first. I wish I'd brought my parents' poetry book because even if I had the energy to put them on, my antique rings were not enough to dampen that dreadful imprint.

"Okay," I began, "so Dennis was delivering some papers—research, I think—to that Ian guy. Looked like a lawyer, a few years older than Ben. But Dennis freaked out when he saw the guy Ian was with. He recognized him."

"What'd the other man look like?" Shannon asked.

"Italian, big nose, dark hair—no, I'm kidding. He did have dark hair, but he didn't look like Mafia, if that's what you're asking. He was just a guy." I remembered Dennis looking at the table, at the man's hands. "Wait, he was missing half a finger on his left hand. The middle finger."

"It wasn't the guy Dennis saw shoot that man in the street?"

"No." It should have been the same man because the fear he'd experienced had been similar, but it wasn't. That meant Dennis was terribly afraid of at least two people. What had he gotten himself into?

"What else can you tell us?"

"Nothing." I repeated everything I'd seen, describing in detail both the men in the imprint. "Dennis was scared. Every bit as scared as he'd been that night on the street. Or close."

Shannon's eyes softened, though it might have been my imagination. Standing beside my chair, Tawnia shoved her left hand into mine, pressing her wedding ring against my fingers.

Love. I felt love as my skin touched the metal. Looking out of her eyes, I saw Bret staring at her as they exchanged vows. The love in her heart was so all-encompassing that my fear seeped away, taking with it the jumpy feeling. I took a deep breath and relaxed, my muscles feeling relief as though resting after overuse.

Thanks, I mouthed. Usually, it was Jake who thought of giving me a good imprint to replace the old, but Tawnia was learning. She winked.

While everyone waited, I scooted to the edge of Dennis's chair and reached for the iPod dock on the desk. Clean. I touched the monitors, shuffled through the papers, and even skimmed my hands over the surface of the desk. Nothing. Thankfully. I didn't know how much more I could take in one day.

"You should check the last Internet sites he visited," I said. "Might give us some clues."

Shannon smirked. "Yes, ma'am."

I rolled my eyes at him.

"You feeling okay?" Tracy asked me.

"Yeah."

Tawnia glanced toward the door. "Did you see a bathroom around here?"

"Down the hall," Tracy told her. "Want me to show you?"

"And leave these two alone to kill each other?" Tawnia grinned. "I can find it." She waddled out the door, though I'd never tell her as much.

"Maybe you'd better go home," Shannon said into the silence.

I clenched my fists at my sides and urged myself to calmness. "And miss you talking to this Ian character? No way."

"It's a private interrogation."

"He won't care unless you make a big deal out of it."

Shannon did his best to give me a flat stare, which was difficult given that his eyes are too alive for such mundane expressions. "Do you know who this Ian is? Because from the description you just gave us, I'm fairly certain the man's name is Gideon—as in Simeon and Gideon."

"You mean one of the law firm's partners?"

"Not exactly. He's the nephew of Mrs. Gideon, who is a partner, but from the brief chat we had with him today, he's been here long enough to have become another partner by now. I think he's taken over a lot of his aunt's business."

Tracy nodded without checking any notes. "His first name is Ian."

"Well, this just gets more and more interesting." I sat back in Dennis's chair. Nothing could induce me to leave now. If Shannon wanted me out, he'd have to arrest me. Or at least threaten to, because I wouldn't risk experiencing the imprints former inmates might have left in any jail cell.

"Oh, let her stay, Shannon. If not for her, we wouldn't even know about Dennis's run-in with Mr. Gideon." Tracy met his gaze for a full five seconds before he stalked over to the window and peered out.

I smiled. She was learning to hold her own, which of course I silently cheered because she was on my side.

Shannon sighed. "Okay, you can stay, but don't say anything. The last thing I need is for the department to be sued by a law firm."

I pretended to lock my mouth and throw away the key, but the look in his eyes told me he didn't believe me. He was right not to. If my mouth decided to say something, there wasn't a blessed thing he or I could do about it. I strived for honesty, or so I told myself, but in truth I chattered when I became nervous. Bad habit I needed to break.

Ben appeared in the doorway. "Mr. Gideon will see you. Please, come with me."

Apparently, Ian Gideon didn't descend to the nethermost

regions of the law firm where Dennis's office was located—except, presumably to leave the building.

Ben looked us over. "Where'd the, uh, other woman go?"

"My sister's in the bathroom."

"I'll have the receptionist watch for her."

"We can't wait a minute?"

"Mr. Gideon is anxious to call it a night." Without waiting for a reply, he led the way back to the lobby and the elevator.

I exchanged an amused glance with Shannon before I realized what I was doing. I looked away quickly.

In the elevator, I was hit with an odd wave of weariness. Reading imprints may seem like a simple thing, but it took a lot out of me. I wondered if one day I might feel too much and the imprints would disappear as mysteriously as they had appeared. Emotion. That was the key to how I could read imprints, though I believe I'd felt them on at least some level since the beginning of my life, which was probably why I'd ended up opening my antiques shop. Even walking into the shop gave me comfort. Of course, there were objects I'd never sell there, no matter the deal I might get on them. I kept a safe imprint environment for myself. Profit wasn't everything.

The elevator opened onto a lobby like the one below, with lots of glass, another receptionist, a plusher set of couches. Eight-by-ten portraits of the employees covered part of one wall, the two partners at the very top, Ben and other associates under them. Dennis's portrait was one row up from the receptionists and secretaries.

Ben took us past all this to a door in a hallway I recognized from Dennis's imprint. My heart slammed into movement, causing me to catch my breath. As Ben started to open the door, I almost expected to see the dark-haired man who was missing half a finger.

So what if I did? I had nothing to fear from him.

The door opened and inside, a blond man rose to his feet. I

recognized him from the imprint, but Dennis hadn't dwelled on how tall and thin Ian was. He towered over all of us, even Ben, who was nearly a head taller than Shannon.

"Here they are," Ben said. "Would you like me to stay?"

Ian waved him away. "No, it's okay. You can go home now if you want."

"I have a few things to finish up." Ben looked pointedly at us as though to imply that we were responsible for his not already having finished. "I'll be in my office if you need me."

"Thanks." Ian turned a warm smile on us. "Nice to see you again so soon, detectives. Come on in and sit down. I hear you have new information about Dennis?"

I put Ian at thirty-eight or forty, but a young forty. He moved with a jaunty air, as though life were something exciting to experience. His suit fit his lean figure well, giving him needed bulk in the shoulders, and I knew they were tailored. The only thing I owned that was tailored was a dress I'd made myself—if you could call something you made with sale material on a hand-me-down sewing machine tailored. I wondered what it would be like never to think about money or how you were going to pay the mortgage.

I made for the closer chair that the dark-haired man had used. I slid my hands surreptitiously across the top and down the back of the seat as I sat. Nothing. Nor on the table where his hands had been. Next to me, Tracy lifted an inquiring brow, and I gave a slight shake of my head. It had been a long shot.

"We're sorry to keep you." Shannon settled into a chair across from me.

"Not a problem. I hope I can help." Ian sat at the head of the table, tenting his hands on the wood and leaning over them, projecting confidence and interest the way an attorney should. He wasn't wearing a wedding ring.

"We believe that Dennis saw you with a man shortly before his disappearance," Shannon said. "A man he knew. In fact, we think it happened in this very room." Ah, so Shannon hadn't missed my checking out the place.

"Do you have a description of this man?" Ian asked, a careful note in his voice.

"Dark hair. Missing half a finger on his left hand."

"Big guy," I added. "Not as tall as you. A little too much Italian pasta, probably." Especially if he was connected to the organized crime murder in Michigan.

Shannon scowled at me, but I pointedly ignored him.

"I believe I know who you're talking about," Ian said, tapping his fingers together idly. "His name is Nicholas Russo."

"What was the nature of his visit?" Shannon asked.

"That I can't tell you. He's a client, and I can't share his business until he gives consent."

"Can you at least tell us what business Mr. Russo is in and what research Dennis brought you?" Tracy asked. "Was it connected to Mr. Russo?"

"Sorry." Ian smiled a little too broadly at Tracy. "But I can go as far as to suggest that you look in the history of Dennis's hard drive. Everything should be there. Well, assuming he did the research from his office."

The hardness that had begun in Shannon's face relaxed. "We'll do that."

Shannon might accept that olive branch, but Ian's reticence made me angry. "Do you have any reason to believe that Dennis knew Mr. Russo?" I asked. "Or suspect that Dennis might be the reason Mr. Russo chose your firm for representation?"

Ian shook his head. "Absolutely not. Mr. Russo was referred to us by colleagues in New Jersey. He didn't ask about Dennis or react in any way when he came into the room."

"And Dennis?" I could feel Shannon's eyes burning into me,

ordering me to silence, but I didn't care. He might be bound by rules, but I wasn't.

Ian frowned. "Now that you mention it, Dennis did seem upset, but I think that was because he was late getting me the information I needed for the meeting."

"Don't you have assistants for things like that?" I asked. "Researching, I mean."

"Actually, yes. But there are times when Dennis is more resourceful. He has programs he uses to filter information, and sometimes he can cut down on the research time." Ian gave me his wide smile, which seemed to contain a hint of regret. "Look, I really like Dennis, and I'm going to do everything I can to urge my client to cooperate with you, but I really don't see how Mr. Russo can be involved with his disappearance. This was our first meeting. Before today, we've only done business on the phone."

"Did he make any comments about Dennis?" Shannon asked. "After he left the room?"

"No—wait. He did comment on the depth of the information Dennis brought me, and I told him we employed only the best."

Tracy arched a brow. "After your meeting, did Mr. Russo leave on his own?" It was a good question because for all we know, our mysterious Mr. Russo could have tracked down Dennis after the meeting.

"I went with him down the elevator and to the front door."

"No stops or detours?"

"None except to show him the portraits of our employees. The partners were not here to meet him, and Mr. Russo is a rather wealthy client, so I showed him the photographs."

"And Dennis's?" I didn't know why, but it bothered me that the man, whoever he was, knew Dennis's last name.

Ian glanced at me and then back toward Shannon. "I really

think the two have no connection. Mr. Russo didn't seem interested in Dennis in any way."

"You may be right. But we'll still need to talk with Mr. Russo."

"If you give me thirty minutes to talk with him first," Ian said, "I'll have my secretary send you his contact information. I'd like to give him a heads-up."

"Is your secretary still here?" I said, not sure why I wanted to be so contrary. Something didn't feel right.

Ian smiled, making his thin face more appealing. "If she's not, I know how to e-mail."

"Great." Shannon came to his feet and proffered a card. "Send it to this address. If there's nothing more you can tell us, we'll be leaving—again."

"I assure you I told you everything I knew earlier." Ian glanced at the card before slipping it into the pocket of his suit.

"Please let us know immediately if you hear from Dennis." Tracy also shook Ian's hand, and it wasn't in my imagination that he held on a bit too long. Tracy also noticed, and if her slight secretive smile was a good indicator, she was pleased at the attention.

I hadn't planned on shaking Ian's hand because I avoided touching strangers who wore rings on their right hands, but Tracy's interest made me shoot out my hand awkwardly as I stood. "Thank you for seeing us, Mr. Gideon."

"Please, call me Ian. And who are you, if I may ask?"

His ring held faint memories of college graduation, contentment, and concentration. Nothing more. That didn't say everything about him, of course, but I was relieved. "My name is Autumn Rain. I'm a consultant on the case." I didn't look at Shannon as I spoke, worried that he'd object.

"Nice to meet you." Ian released my hand and opened the door. "I'll walk you out."

"We can find our way," Shannon said.

"I don't mind."

We met Tawnia emerging from the elevator and stopped for introductions. Ian gave both of us a double look as he realized our similarity. He didn't notice our eyes, though, probably because his attention was mostly on Tracy. They made a striking couple. Though her navy suit was conservative and far more economically priced than his, her classic features and her ironed blonde hair would rival that of any society girl. She didn't look like a woman comfortable with guns and stakeouts.

"I can't believe he wouldn't tell us more," I whispered to Shannon as we followed Ian and Tracy from the elevator and past the lower lobby reception desk. "Doesn't he realize a man's life is at stake?"

Shannon shrugged. "He gave us a lot more than he had to."

"You really aren't going to give him a half hour to talk to his client, are you? Isn't surprise the whole point?" I wanted Shannon to be as irritated as I felt, not striding along like he hadn't a care in the world.

"Well, he definitely wasn't going to give us the information without a warrant, and we probably wouldn't find the right numbers to get us directly to Russo before half an hour anyway. So even if I refused Gideon's offer, either way there wouldn't be a surprise factor. It's not perfect, but it's how the game is played, Autumn. Plus, I need to find out a little more about this Russo before I talk to him."

"You mean to check if he's involved in organized crime."

Shannon's mouth quirked in amusement. "Or if he has priors, or why he might need an attorney in Portland. That sort of thing."

"I see."

For all his calm talk, Shannon was giving Ian Gideon a hard stare. Ahead of us Tracy giggled.

Now it was my turn to smirk. "Don't worry," I told Shannon. "I'm sure she's faking interest to pump him for information."

"I couldn't care less about her personal feelings," he growled. "I just don't want to train another partner."

Next to us, Tawnia laughed. "I don't think you'll need to. Even if his interest is serious, I bet Mr. Gideon would love to have a contact on the police force."

Shannon's scowled deepened, which strangely made him even more attractive, like a brooding hero in one of those literary films no one I knew ever went to see but that all the critics raved about. I grinned at Tawnia, and she winked. I felt a rush of that certain sort of love I'd never felt for anyone besides my adoptive parents. My twin was a part of me in a way no one else ever could be.

Not even Jake?

I swallowed hard at the lump in my throat. Where was he now? Still with the beautiful Kolonda? Too bad my ability didn't extend to reading people. Unfortunately, I had to rely on regular intuition for my personal relationships. Or go around secretly touching their personal belongings, a level to which I refused to stoop.

We'd reached the double front doors, where Ian and Tracy had paused. "Ben and I are the only ones who aren't family men," he was saying.

"Oh?" My heartbeat quickened. "I bet that makes you a better attorney, not having to worry about a wife and kids."

Ian's forehead wrinkled. "Believe me, it's not by choice. I happen to think a family is a good thing for a man."

Since I'd read that married men tended to live longer than unmarried men, he'd probably be wise to seek a wife. I smiled at Ian. "I meant for your clients, of course. Like Mr. Russo. I bet he's glad you're single so you can focus so completely on his case."

"He didn't comment either way." Was that a tint of annoyance in Ian's voice?

"Tell me," I continued. "Did that come up in your conversation?

That you and Ben are the only men in your company who aren't married?"

Tracy's gaze sharpened, and I saw she knew where I was going.

"Yes, when we were looking at the portraits."

"Is that when you told him about Dennis's family?"

Ian didn't speak for several seconds, and everyone else was also silent and unnaturally still. Tawnia's eyes were wide, Tracy's dismayed, and Shannon's intent. I felt as if I'd dropped a stink bomb in the middle of a nice dinner party. Or walked into a fancy restaurant without my shoes, which had actually happened more than once.

"Not Dennis specifically. All of my employees." Ian spoke in his usual confident manner, but there was a line between his eyes. Of concern? Guilt? I didn't know him well enough to say.

"Thank you for your time," I said. "It was nice to meet you." I offered my hand again before going past him to the door.

"An unusual woman," I heard him say in a low voice as the door began to shut behind me.

"You can say that again." Shannon, of course, spoke loud enough so I'd be sure to hear.

The heat emanating from the sidewalk felt good on my feet after the cold tile in the air-conditioned lobby. I lifted my face to the sun and absorbed the blissful rays until the others joined me.

I thought Shannon and Tracy would be annoyed at my interference, but Shannon's next words surprised me. "We'd better put someone watching the wife and kids," he said in an undertone.

"I'll do it." Tracy flicked her eyes toward me and in them I saw disappointment.

As we walked to the cars, I fell into step with her. "I hope I didn't mess things up for you and Ian Gideon."

Tracy flashed me white teeth, perfectly straight except for the slight sideways tilt of one of her canines, which gave her smile character and a bit of flare. Easily fixed, but obviously she knew it worked for her. "You didn't mess things up. He'll call. No misreading those signs."

I wished I had her confidence when it came to men. "You don't think he's too old?"

"Ian?" Tracy laughed. "Ten years is nothing these days. I find him attractive."

"Must be the suit." Though I knew what she meant. Ian Gideon had confidence, presence, and a nice smile. Being rich only helped. "I'm betting he told that Russo character far too much about Dennis without even meaning to."

Tracy's smile faded. "It's a common mistake people make. Criminals know the right questions to ask. I'm just unhappy I didn't get this information sooner. I'm worried about Sophie and the kids."

I liked her better for calling Dennis's wife by her first name—unlike Shannon. Which goes to show that sometimes first impressions weren't all they were touted to be. I hadn't taken to Tracy the first time I met her and not because I cared that Shannon's new partner was so young and beautiful. I'd crossed him off my possibility list long before she showed up.

"You really think Sophie might be in danger?" I asked as I reached my sister's car. Shannon and Tawnia were closing in behind us.

Tracy shrugged. "I don't know. It all depends on why Dennis ran, who he really is, who's looking for him, and how far they're willing to go."

"I'd say they were willing to go as far as murder," Shannon said. "Which means his entire family and anyone who snoops too deeply is in danger."

"You mean like me." I lifted my chin in silent challenge.

His eyes pinned mine. "Like you."

Unfortunately, I had to agree.

CHAPTER

6

I was in a lousy mood when Tawnia dropped me off at my shop, where I retrieved my car and drove to my apartment. My limbs felt heavy, and a dull throb had begun in my temples. I wanted nothing more than to fall into bed. If I could get my brain to turn off.

Jake hadn't called, and my mind was working overtime. I imagined him and Kolonda catching up on old times and perhaps discovering there was still a connection. The problem was that Jake and I as a couple were too new, though we'd spent considerable time as friends. That, and my luck with men had never been very good. If Jake hadn't been my best friend before, I'm not sure I would have trusted him enough to let myself proceed even this far into a relationship in only a few weeks.

Inside the apartment where I'd lived all my life, I staggered across the room and tumbled over the back of the couch, pulling my mother's crocheted afghan over me as I settled on the cushion. Faded imprints of her misted through my body like a warm breeze on a cool day. I'd never washed the afghan and wouldn't, not as long as it held a trace of the mother I still missed after twenty-two years. The ache for Summer was not as strong as it was for Winter, my father, but it was younger and more needy, rooted in the eleven-year-old child I was when she died of breast cancer.

The couch was comfortable, despite its Victorian origin, because I'd added a plush mattress-like cushion and numerous matching pillows when I'd reupholstered it years ago. The carvings on the wood were incredible, captivating me the minute I'd seen it, but the previous padding had left a lot to be desired. Now it cradled my tired body in comfort.

The next thing I knew, Jake was there, his warm hand gliding down my cheek, his lips touching mine. "Hey, beautiful. Wake up."

I loved when he called me that, especially on the days when I felt I'd been dragged out of the Willamette River all over again after surviving the bridge collapse.

"Hey, you're back. Find any interesting clues for your friend?" I tried to sit up, but the world wavered. I closed my eyes and shook my head to clear it. Big mistake. Pain knifed through my skull. "Ow," I said without meaning to, bringing up my hand to the place above my ear where the pain had originated.

"You okay?"

"I'm not sure." The pain was gradually fading, though. "I think I'm tired. It was a long day."

Jake eased onto the couch under me, pulling me close. "It was the imprints, wasn't it?"

"Dennis witnessed a murder."

Jake's arms tightened, and I relaxed my back against his chest, letting his presence soothe me. "Tell me about it," he said.

I did because I needed to tell him every bit as much as I wanted to hear about him and Kolonda. "I'm not sure what to make of it, but I wonder if Sophie's ever going to see her husband again. Even if he can avoid those people in the car Tawnia drew, what if he disappears permanently to get away from them?"

"He wouldn't leave his wife and children. Not forever." Jake put his feet up on my coffee table, careful to avoid my antique bowl and figurines. "He'll have to go to the police eventually."

Once I would have believed him, but now I wasn't so sure. Another questionable legacy from my ability to read imprints. I'd seen so many bad things lately that thinking the best of someone was no longer my first impulse. I mourned that loss of innocence. Of course now I could help people. I had to remember that.

"The key has to be Russo." I wondered if Shannon was talking to him now, or if he'd been put off until Saturday morning. I was all too aware of the time clicking by. I reached for my bag to see if Tracy or Shannon had left a message on my phone, but a wave of dizziness had me falling back on Jake.

"When was the last time you ate?" Jake asked.

"I don't remember. Lunch, I guess."

"That was nine hours ago. You need to eat something."

Nine hours? I was surprised so much time had passed but more surprised at the lateness of his arrival. "I'm not hungry."

"Maybe not, but I think those imprints are taking their toll. Do you think you should pull back a bit?"

"You were the one who always urged me to use my ability."

"That was before I knew it'd do this."

"I just need to pace myself. Rest in between. It's like using any muscle, I think."

From the corner of my eye, I could see Jake's smile. "So you've got a sore imprint-reading muscle?"

"Or something. Tell me about the apartment buildings." My eyes drifted to the miniature grandfather clock on the mantel above my fireplace. "You were there a long time, so you must have some idea if Kolonda has a good case."

He leaned back on the couch, his arms still around me. "I think so, but I'm going to have to call a few friends to verify it. I don't know if my testimony will hold up in court or anything since I'm not really an expert." He hesitated, but I didn't make it easier for him. "I didn't mean to stay so long. We got talking about old times."

I almost wished he hadn't been so forthright. "She was your girlfriend."

"How did you know?"

"The compact."

"Oh, right." There was an uncomfortable silence before he added, "Do you want to hear about it?"

"To be honest, I don't know. I mean, we've both dated a lot, but it's weird having someone you cared about come back into your life."

"If you think it's weird, imagine how I feel." He sighed. "It was high school. You know how everything was back then. All drama and no sense. Kolonda and I had it all planned. I was already work-ing a bit of construction and twelve bucks an hour seemed like an awful lot to me. She was going to teach, and I'd stay in construc-tion, and that's exactly what we started doing. She went to college to get her teaching degree, and I got a full-time job. Her father, who made twenty times what I did, didn't approve. So it ended."

"She listened to her father."

"Kolonda was his only child. His wife had died, and he and Kolonda were close. Education was his mantra, one she believed in. I didn't stand a chance." He gave a self-deprecating laugh that disturbed me more than if he'd expressed anger.

I twisted my head to get a better look at him. Brown skin with the stubble that was always present by this time of night, liquid eyes the color of dark chocolate that radiated seriousness instead of his usual humor, the prominent cheekbones giving his face charac-ter and toughness that never showed in his actions. He was a strong man with a soft heart, who cared about stray kittens and customers and, unfortunately, needy old girlfriends. And me. I knew he cared about me.

"Maybe it's good this happened," I said in what I thought was a surprisingly calm voice given the situation. "I think what happened back then really bothers you. This is your chance to resolve that." Something Winter would have said. He'd believed that if you weren't right with your past, you couldn't live properly in the present or plan for a future.

He tilted his head, leaning it against my cheek. "Doesn't make sense to feel anything about that time. It was so long ago."

"But you do." My stomach rebelled at the idea—I wasn't quite as complacent as Winter would have been.

"Yeah." Jake's cheek rubbed up and down mine, his growing stubble tickling me. "But it's not the same."

"Of course not."

"I love you."

It was what I wanted to hear. I turned enough to give him a kiss and then settled with my back cuddled against his chest. Darkness grew from the edges of my vision until it filled the room.

The next thing I knew, Jake was gently slapping my face. "Autumn, wake up. Autumn, are you okay?"

I looked at him, confused. "Here, drink this." He lifted my head and held a cup to my lips.

Green drink from my fridge, made of spinach, raspberry leaf, wheat grass, a few strawberries, fresh apple juice, and whatever else I'd had in my kitchen when I'd made it this morning. I felt energy seeping into me as the liquid reached my stomach. I also felt a craving for protein—a lot of it.

"What happened?" I asked after a few swallows.

"I don't know. I think you passed out for a few minutes. You were breathing and looked peaceful, but it didn't seem like natural sleep. I want to get some food in you to see if that's the problem. I knew you'd kill me if I called an ambulance."

He had that right. "I feel a little tired, that's all." The dizziness I'd felt upon awaking was passing.

"You stay here. I'll make something. I saw you have a couple of steaks."

"Those were for our dinner." Or would have been if he'd shown up on time.

"You rest here, and I'll make them. Yell if you need me."

Another great thing about Jake is that being an herb guru, he's almost as good a cook as I am. I was content to let him take care of me, especially because it soothed away my worries about Kolonda and Dennis and Sophie. What Jake and I had didn't depend on other people.

I'd eaten the tender grass-fed steak, organic potatoes flavored with real butter and sea salt, and lightly steamed squash and vegetables when Tawnia telephoned. It was after ten, well past her usual time to call.

"What is it?" I sat up and was glad not to feel any dizziness. I could hear the clank in the background as Jake washed the dishes.

"It's Sophie. I went over to check on her a while ago because I saw a strange car in her driveway, a real expensive one."

Exactly the type of car Ian Gideon's client Mr. Russo might drive. I felt a chill as I asked, "Who was there?"

"No one. That's just it. When I asked about the car, all she would say is that it was a gift and she didn't know who gave it to her. But it was brand spanking new. I'm sure of it."

"Wasn't she freaked out?"

"I think she thinks Dennis is responsible and that this is a message to her not to worry."

"Couldn't be from him—not unless he's been embezzling."

Although that could explain a lot. Maybe Mr. Ian Gideon was hiding more than a new client.

"Dennis doesn't seem the type," Tawnia said. "I mean, he's rather ordinary, if you know what I mean. I just don't see him living an alternate life."

"He obviously has some secrets. I told you that Tracy and Shannon think he's Alex Trogan, that witness who disappeared from police custody, didn't I? That's a double life if I ever heard of one."

"Did they show the picture of Alex to Sophie?"

"I don't know, but Tracy says it would be hard for anyone to make an identification."

"Like those pictures we have of our birth mom."

I was silent for a long moment. Our mother had lived with my adoptive parents during her pregnancy, and they had treated her like a beloved younger sister. The few pictures they'd taken during her short stay hadn't been well-preserved, though Tawnia had since made several copies of the photos and moved them to an acid-free book. Our birth mother had been only sixteen when she'd died giving birth to not one but two babies. The doctor had fulfilled her wish to give Winter and Summer a child but had also felt it necessary to honor the contract with Tawnia's adoptive parents in Texas. We'd grown up separately, but the connection between us had been strong, even then, and Tawnia had eventually found me. I'd lost Winter that same time, but I didn't compare the exchange. It just was.

"Autumn? Are you all right?"

"I'm fine." It was true. The food had restored me almost completely. I'd have to remember the protein thing if I read any more imprints.

As if I could stop.

I frowned at my thoughts until Tawnia said, "I'd better get to bed."

"Wait. Do you see a police car out in front of Sophie's?"

"There's a car I don't recognize parked down the street, but it's not a police car."

"Probably Shannon's guys. I'm glad they're not using a marked car. That's way too obvious."

Tawnia laughed. "You really have to turn off that TV and get out more. I mean, now that you're mostly recovered. I doubt anyone is after Sophie. It's Dennis who has a past."

We didn't know that for sure—Sophie could be anyone—but I didn't want to bother my sister with those dark thoughts. "Hey, what about Moonflower?"

"Autumn."

"Windsong, then."

"With a last name like Winn? Windsong Winn?"

"Why not? It could be Win Winn for short."

"You must have been all day coming up with that one."

"I don't want something boring for my niece or nephew."

"I promise it won't be. Love you." With that, my sister hung up.

Jake was still busy cleaning in the kitchen, and I debated for a full thirty seconds before dialing Shannon's cell phone.

"Hello?" His voice was gruff, though from sleep or disuse, I couldn't tell.

"Sorry for disturbing you at this hour," I said, though I wasn't in the least sorry.

"You're not disturbing me. What is it?" The impatience in his voice definitely implied that I was disturbing him. I would have to begin making all my calls to him at this hour.

"I have some news, though you might have already heard from your guys—if they're the ones sitting in the car down the street from my sister's."

"Have you been annoying my men?"

"I most certainly have not. But Sophie has a new car parked in her driveway that she claims is a gift. Tawnia thinks that she believes it's from Dennis, but if it is . . ."

"There've been no charges on his cards, but that doesn't mean it's not him. I know you don't want to hear this, Autumn, but he may be the bad guy in all this."

"Whatever. He's still in danger."

"Is there something more you haven't told me?"

"No."

"And are you okay?" A diffident note had crept into his voice.

I dismissed thoughts of my earlier faintness. "I'm perfect."

"Then let me get some sleep so I can do my job tomorrow. Good night."

I sighed, staring at the phone. Strange how if I needed him, I knew he'd come running, but he wasn't willing to trust me one more iota than he had to.

Well, that was okay because I didn't care what he thought of me.

I had to be missing something. Some little clue that Dennis had left behind. Had it been in the imprints? I felt anxious enough that if I had the phone and the pen I might try them again, despite the fear. With Jake here, it would be easier.

Except imprints never revealed anything more, so my mind already contained every bit of information. I wasn't hiding anything.

"How are you feeling?" Jake came around the couch and settled beside me, holding me close. His lips met mine.

"Wonderful. Thanks."

"Anytime." He kissed me again and for a while I forgot what I'd been thinking about.

Not until I'd said good night to Jake and was lying in my own warm bed half asleep did I finally realize what I'd missed.

Shannon's intuition was better than good because I *had* learned something I hadn't shared from Dennis's imprint on the pen. The drawback was that to learn the meaning of it, I'd have to see Mr. Russo myself.

Worse, I'd have to touch his stuff.

I blocked Edward Hodges's blow and countered it with a round-house to his shoulder that I pretended didn't strain my sore ribs. He spun out of the way but not fast enough to completely avoid my kick.

"Nice," Steve said as Edward rubbed his shoulder, only partially covered by his sparring chest guard.

I inclined my head at my instructor's praise. Edward was half a foot taller than I was and outweighed me by sixty pounds, but Steve was never effusive with his praise. One word from him went a long way toward buoying my confidence.

Edward's hand dropped as he noticed my gaze. "Lucky shot. Let's do it again."

I didn't want to because not only was Edward mean and vindictive but his dark blond hair was greasy, and I was beginning to think he showered only once a week—on Sundays. Since our semi-private tae kwon do lessons were on Saturday mornings, that was saying quite a bit about his odor.

"She got you fair and square, and you know it," said Andrea Mathews, the third student in our class. "Besides, she has to get to work. But I'll take you on."

I knew Edward regretted his rash challenge now because none of us were as fast as Andrea. She made even Steve appear slow at times. Given her strength and ability to crush her opponents, her face, framed by thick golden hair, was deceptively beautiful and feminine. Edward and I were fortunate that Steve stressed defense far more than attacking or she'd have pulverized both of us today. Even these intense, three-hour lessons that were designed to move us along at a fast pace hadn't yet caught us up to her level. I was feeling more confident each week, however. I'd taken lessons as a teen, and the moves were coming back to me.

I bowed to Andrea. She gave me a smile and winked, after making sure Edward wasn't looking.

"Fine. I'll take you on, but I need a drink first." Edward stalked off like a lion searching for weaker prey. Part of his problem was that he had a lot of natural talent and strength, unlike some who had to work for it. Namely me. And work I did. Hard. After the commune incident, I wanted to be able to protect myself.

"See you Thursday," I said to Steve and Andrea as I left the studio. That was the night we attended regular lessons with the other adult students. I also went on Tuesdays, though it was teen night, because I wanted the extra practice, and it reminded me of my previous foray into the martial arts. Besides, teens were more unpredictable than adults, which added to my sparring repertoire. This time around I'd begun lessons the week I left the hospital. I'd chosen this studio partly because Shannon had recommended Steve and partly because the adult class was on Thursday nights, the same night Jake was in school, and I was the tiniest bit worried he wouldn't approve. I hadn't actually told him about my new hobby until last week, and he'd been all for it. I guess seeing me used as a punching bag at the commune had convinced him more than anything I could say that self-defense classes were necessary.

Or maybe he liked dating a woman who wore a dobok.

Smiling to myself, I headed for the locker room, another reason I'd chosen this studio. After my three-hour power lesson, I could shower and head right for work on Saturday mornings.

Except that today I didn't plan to go to work. As long as Jake and our two employees had shown up, I'd take a little detour before going in.

I called Tracy first because my search for Nic Russo with the missing half finger hadn't gone as well as I'd hoped. On the Internet that morning I'd found Nicholas Russo's name in connection with an import company, a string of restaurants, and a construction company that was building a slew of new office buildings, but I had no idea where Russo himself might be at that moment or if any of the listed addresses were valid. Tracy might give me the information I was searching for and save me the legwork.

"Hi, Autumn," she said.

I'd put on my earphones backward so the wires wouldn't interfere with applying my makeup. Tawnia teased me about updating to wireless, but I wasn't sure all those unseen waves were healthy. I dabbed on a bit of base over the green bruise still covering my cheek, happy to see that it was almost invisible.

"So," I said to Tracy, "did you guys talk to Russo yet?"

"Shannon's over there now."

"Not you?"

"It's my mother's birthday, and I'm driving to her place."

I pulled out the addresses I'd scribbled down at my house that morning since the only printer I owned was at my antiques shop. "I noticed Russo's into quite a bit—restaurants, importing, land development, construction."

"You left out exporting, retail, and politics—though the

candidate he's backing does seems to be on the level. Simeon, Gideon & Associates was permitted to tell us that they are representing him on some real estate deals. No specifics, just general real estate for developing."

"Is Shannon interviewing him at a construction site? I mean, if it ends up that he has any connection to organized crime, isn't that rather stupid?"

Tracy laughed. "He'd be touched at your concern."

"I'm sure he'd return the observation if I was the one chasing Mr. Russo to some deep hole in the ground."

"We don't have any proof Russo's connected with anything illegal, much less the murder Dennis witnessed, but Shannon's meeting him at one of Russo's restaurants, if you must know."

I snorted. "Italian, I bet."

"Actually, Chinese. But why all the questions?" Her voice showed amusement. "Either you're developing a thing for Shannon, or you want to do some investigating on your own."

"It was my case first. Shannon should have asked me to go along with him to see the guy." Russo had been linked to two Chinese restaurants, so I still didn't have a solid destination.

"He'll call you in if he needs you to read something."

"Maybe, but probably too late to help Dennis. Shannon doesn't like what I do. You know that as well as I do." I didn't much like it myself most days, but that didn't stop me from holding his attitude against him.

We were both quiet for a moment. "Okay, look, go do your sleuthing, but promise me you won't do anything rash and that you'll call me or Shannon if you find anything interesting."

"I promise. Don't I always?" As far as she knew, that was true, though I had held back a few things, like the key to a cellar at the commune. If I hadn't, I might never have found the woman hidden there. "So if I were to feel like Chinese for breakfast," I added, "would I head to downtown Portland or up the Pacific Highway to Vancouver?"

"The Pacific Highway is nice this time of morning."

"Thanks. I owe you."

"The way I figure it, I owe you. You should have seen my last review. My closed cases are up 10 percent."

Up 10 percent? I considered this as I finished getting ready. Even on good days I had ambivalent feelings about my strange gift, but with Tracy's help, I had done some good no one could argue with, not even me.

Next I called my shop to make sure Thera and Randa had everything under control. They were accustomed to my coming in later some Saturdays when there was a particularly promising estate sale, so they didn't think anything of my absence. I tried to be there for the afternoons, though, because Saturdays were usually busy.

"Should I get Jake for you?" Thera asked.

"No need. But tell him I'll be in later."

"Will do."

My hair was still damp as I left the studio and headed north on Pacific Highway. It was only twenty minutes to Vancouver, Washington, but I allotted an hour to find the place with my great sense of direction. I should have borrowed Tawnia's GPS. Hopefully, Shannon would be gone when I arrived because he'd be angry at my interference. Not that I would let that bother me. I didn't answer to him—especially when I knew his objection was mostly because I'd been hurt before under his watch. Must be tough being a man who felt he had to protect everyone.

I ended up getting off the freeway at East Mill Plain Boulevard and backtracking down Washington to Eighth Street. I drove around searching for the right location and finally stopped to ask a passerby, who pointed to the other side of the street. I thanked him somewhat sheepishly.

The commercial area around the restaurant teemed with life, though the place itself was not yet open. In the parking lot behind the restaurant, two black sedans sat in the otherwise empty lot— one an expensive new Lexus, the other older and with a few dings but still a BMW. There was no sign of Shannon's white Mustang. That meant either I'd taken a long time finding the restaurant, or Russo had nothing to add to the investigation. The third option was that Shannon was losing his touch.

I voted for the third option because I'd felt Dennis's imprint on the pen. Fear, yes, even terror, but what I'd remembered last night was even more important. There had been also the tiniest rush of warmth in his heart, and a touch of relief that I couldn't decipher or reconcile with his overwhelming fear. I could only come to the conclusion that not only did Dennis know the man but seeing him had evoked something pleasant in his past, though whether it was the man himself or what he represented, I couldn't say because Dennis didn't know how to feel about it. Not black and white as I'd first thought but laced with a tiny swirl of gray.

I thought of Sophie and the new car that had shown up in her driveway. Where would Dennis get that kind of money? How did it tie into that long-ago murder? I'd have to get over there and talk to her sometime today. There might even be imprints on the car, though not if it was as new as Tawnia described. I wondered if someone had checked the trunk for bodies. Or made sure the car wasn't rigged to blow.

Ridiculous. Maybe I should throw out my TV altogether. Besides, Shannon knew how to do his job.

All these thoughts were not bringing me any closer to the truth, so I slipped from my Toyota and strode toward the back door of the restaurant. I hoped the door was open after Shannon's visit and that Nicholas Russo was still there, or I'd have to catch up with him someplace else, which I wasn't anxious to do. The restaurant had no customers at the moment, but at least it didn't have any open holes in the parking lot or regular cement deliveries that were perfect for hiding bodies.

I hoped.

Not that I suspected I was in any real danger. Tracy knew where I was, and she wouldn't have given me the information if she thought I'd get into trouble. Aside from that, Mr. Russo was connected with a respected Portland law firm, and he had a reputation to uphold. I simply wanted to ask him a few questions. He could always refuse.

As I suspected, the shiny doorknob on the newly painted door turned under my fingers. I'd contemplated knocking but figured Mr. Russo wasn't the type to answer doors. Then again, who knew how many thugs he had with him. Surely they did far more for him than open doors.

Don't think about it, I told myself.

I eased the door open and slid inside a small room. On the right wall were a dozen or more wooden cupboards with locks, probably their version of employee cubbies. Two couches and a table filled up most of the available space, but the room didn't look dingy or crowded like the break rooms at the few restaurants where I'd worked in my youth.

The break room opened up into a spacious kitchen with gleaming pans and utensils hanging from the ceiling. Stainless steel shelves, refrigerators, and sinks lined the walls. In the middle was a massive stove top and several ovens. Everything was perfectly organized, including the huge mounds of freshly washed vegetables that two Asian men, a young one and an older one, were deftly chopping with gleaming knives.

I stopped moving forward and began sliding toward a door on my right. Too late, the men saw me. The older man spoke in what

I assumed was Chinese, and the younger man addressed me. "May we help you?"

"I'm here to see Mr. Russo," I said.

The young man said something to which the older man replied. Back and forth they went, seemingly too many words crammed into those few seconds. Finally, the young man said. "You have an appointment?"

"Of course. And a friend of mine was just here. A police officer?"

Again the torrent of words and the exchange of significant looks before the young one motioned to another door on the other side of the room. "Mr. Russo's office is there." He nodded to me and resumed chopping. The older man didn't follow suit, and I could feel his eyes digging into my back as my bare feet crossed the clean floor.

The door opened into a narrow hall with several doors, but I knew which one was Russo's office because it was open and I could hear voices. American voices with no trace of accents. I slipped my antique rings from my fingers and shoved them into my jeans before I tapped on the open door. The well-oiled door swung wide with the movement, and the voices ceased.

"Uh, hi," I said, faking a brightness I didn't feel. One man, wearing a navy blazer, sat behind the oak desk, and another one sprawled on a chair in front of it, obviously comfortable in his worn jeans and T-shirt. Another man with a shaved head stood casually near the window but snapped to attention at my appearance, his hand going for what I supposed was a weapon in a waist holster under his jacket.

I hated guns, but for the first time I seriously considered the advantage of carrying one—not that I would ever be able to touch it again if I even used it once in a crisis. The imprints remaining would be impossible, and I'd be out a lot of money unless I could find something besides time that removed imprints. From searching for antiques, I'd learned there weren't enough lifetimes to get rid of some imprints.

I lifted both hands about chest high to show I wasn't a danger. "Sorry to interrupt, but when I tried to knock, the door opened. I need to speak with Nicholas Russo. I can wait out in the hall until you finish, if that would be okay." I clamped my mouth shut, stemming my nervous impulse to babble.

"I'm Nic Russo." The man behind the desk waved at the guy near the window, who relaxed and didn't bring out his gun after all, though I sensed he was more than willing to do so if I provoked him. Not that I'd be much of a challenge to his boss. Russo wasn't fat, but he had serious bulk that was much larger than portrayed in Dennis's imprint. The imprint hadn't shown his elegance and charisma, either, which surprised me since I'd begun thinking of Russo as an ugly thug from a mafia film. Not exactly an attractive man, yet his air of power and confidence made him compelling. He invited trust, but I wasn't falling for it. Not until I read his imprints.

I lowered my hands. "I'm Autumn Rain. I need to talk to you about something very important. It won't take long."

The man in front of the desk had turned and was looking at me with interest, grinning like a man with a secret. His blond hair and tanned face seemed familiar, but I couldn't place him. He hadn't been in any of Dennis's imprints, that much I was sure. He was as scrawny as I was, and I thought I could take him in a fair fight, if I had to. Good sign my training was working, if that's the way I was thinking.

"Alone, if possible," I added. I didn't want an audience, and the scrawny man's grin made me more nervous than the other man's hidden weapon.

Nic Russo arched a well-shaped brow. "What about?" He was

younger than I'd expected—probably in his early thirties, only a few years older than Dennis himself.

"My friend's missing husband. I need to ask you a few questions." I dared to move forward a few feet. The room seemed to have been made from two smaller ones, and another matching door leading into the hallway was partially covered by an oak filing cabinet.

"The police were already here," Russo said. "I answered all their questions."

"I'm not with the police. I have different questions."

A smile tugged at the corner of his mouth. "I'm afraid I'm really busy. Some other time maybe?"

"No." The firmness in my tone surprised both of us. The guy in front of the desk grinned wider, while the man at the window made a display of pulling back his jacket to reveal his gun.

"I don't know anything about the man or his disappearance," Russo said.

"Dennis recognized you," I countered, "and it scared him to death, but he was also just a tiny bit relieved that you'd found him. I want to know why."

Russo's eyes narrowed, and he stared at me for a full ten seconds before speaking. "You can go, Ace. We'll talk later." Russo's eyes didn't leave my face as he spoke.

"Righto." The man in front of the desk stood and started for the door. He winked at me as he passed, but I pretended not to notice. Where did I know him from, anyway?

"Charlie, wait in the hall," Russo added.

Without a sound the man by the window obeyed, shutting the door behind him. I didn't know whether to be glad or afraid now that I was alone with the man who had evoked so much terror in Dennis's heart.

And the rush of warmth, I reminded myself. Which I needed at the moment. This room was as cold as the precinct had been yesterday.

"Have a seat," Russo invited. His eyes were blue, I saw as I approached the desk, dark enough to appear brown from a distance. I tried to remember what color Dennis had given them.

If I sat in the chair, I would have no opportunity to touch anything on his desk, though looking around at the office, all the furnishings seemed relatively new, so it was possible that he hadn't yet left any imprints. It was typical upscale office gear—filing cabinet, bookcase, mini bar, nice paintings, even a plant. No personal touches that I could see. But Russo hadn't sprung up from nowhere, so he might have brought things with him from New Jersey or wherever he had originated. Something on the desk, maybe.

"Well?" Russo asked when I didn't sit, impatience in his voice.

I smiled and met his gaze, continuing up to the desk.

Surprise lit his face, though whether at my refusal to sit or the fact that he'd noticed the different color of my eyes, I couldn't say.

"I'm a friend of Sophie and Dennis Briggs. Sophie asked me to look into her husband's disappearance."

"I still don't see why people think this has anything to do with me."

"Because after he saw you, he bought a suitcase, went home, packed it, and left. No one knows where he is."

"So the police said. But you still haven't told me what that has to do with me."

I let my fingers trail over a dolphin-shaped paperweight. No imprints. I leaned forward as though to share a confidence, but really it was to touch the book a short distance away, the title hidden by an invoice of some type. "Dennis told me he recognized you," I said. A stretch, but true all the same. "I know he was afraid for his life and family after he saw you. I also know that he cared about you or something you represent." The book held imprints of personal enjoyment, nothing more. I wished I could see the title. Maybe it would tell me more about Russo than the fact that he'd enjoyed reading a book.

"When did you last talk to him?" The words burst from him, too full of intensity to be a casual comment.

"Then you *do* know him."

Russo's eyes narrowed. "When did you last talk to him?" he repeated, emphasizing each word.

Something clicked. "You don't know where Dennis is, do you? But you care an awful lot about finding him. How do you know him?"

"What do you care?"

"I told you. I'm a friend. His wife asked me to help find him."

"You don't have to worry about his wife anymore."

I stopped reaching for his stapler, though it was automatic and I doubted he'd touched it since it was placed there. "Of course I do. Sophie's my friend. She's worried about him. She's worried about what will happen to her and the children if he doesn't come home."

"She'll be fine."

"Wait. One minute you don't know them, and the next you say she'll be fine?" My thoughts were racing. "Does this have anything to do with the new car in Sophie's driveway? She thinks Dennis gave it to her, but he doesn't have that kind of money. You know what? I'm betting you gave it to her."

He didn't reply, and I continued, "Is that payment for his death? Taking care of the woman you made a widow?" I hadn't meant to sound so accusatory, but my nervousness had taken over.

"No," he barked. "I don't know where the man is. I haven't seen him since that meeting with my attorney. I think you should leave now."

I reached for the set of car keys I'd spied beyond the book, but his fingers closed around my wrist. It was his left hand, and I could clearly see where half the middle finger was missing.

"Is there some reason you keep touching my things?" he asked.

"Personality quirk." I tried to pull my hand from his, but his fingers tightened, and the wedding ring he wore touched my skin. I gasped with the vivid image of his/my hand coming down on a dark-haired woman's narrow face. She cried out. I stopped pulling my hand away and the image vanished, but the anger that accompanied it had become my own.

Russo's face was hard. "I heard about you. You're the one who claims to be psychic."

"I don't claim any such thing." In another situation, I might explain that my ability was a fluke of genetics, that a part of my mind had simply developed that didn't in most people, but I couldn't trust Russo.

"Garbage." He let me go, and I stumbled backward, nearly falling. "Charlie will show you out."

"Please don't hurt Dennis. He has a wife, children—a life."

He stiffened at my words, which I was already regretting. Me and my big mouth. "Take my advice and keep out of it," he said.

Turning, I yanked open the door and made my way out. Without being asked, Charlie accompanied me back to the kitchen, where the men were piling the chopped vegetables into large plastic containers, and through the employee break room to the warm, bright parking lot.

Behind me, Charlie cleared his throat, and I looked to find him standing in front of the doorway, smirking. Bald men should never smirk, I decided, since he looked more like a cartoon ogre than a tough bodyguard.

I grinned at the thought, but his only answer was to fold his hands across his chest and stare at me without blinking.

I started across the parking lot to my car, but the asphalt had become hot enough that even my tough feet felt uncomfortable. I dug for the keys in my pocket so I wouldn't have to spend a moment more than necessary on the hot surface.

Glancing over my shoulder as I slid inside, I saw that Charlie was now talking on the phone.

So what had I learned? Russo definitely wanted to find Dennis, but I didn't know if he'd come to Portland for that sole purpose or if it had been a happy coincidence for him. All his businesses seemed to indicate the latter, yet I didn't believe in coincidence. There had to be a connection.

As I left the parking lot, the steering wheel pulled hard to the right side. I came to a stop and jumped out to investigate. A flat tire. There was no obvious damage, so I must have run over a nail, but the timing was too coincidental. I glared toward the restaurant where Charlie had disappeared. No one else was in the parking lot, and I didn't feel anyone watching me—not that I had any special ability that way.

Nothing for it but to fill the tire before the trip back. I'd seen a station half a block down where I could get gas as well. I didn't have a working spare, but I had an aerosol bottle of goo that would plug the hole and inflate the tire enough to get to the station and maybe even last a few days.

The air hose was around the back of the station, so I headed there first. Feeling jumpy, I scanned the area to make sure no one suspicious was around. Nothing. A man finished filling his tire and drove off, leaving me alone.

I'd filled the tire and had turned to replace the air hose when a rush of footsteps warned me that someone was coming—fast. Whirling, I glimpsed a white man with close-cropped hair, the glint of a knife in his hands. He was of average build for a man, which meant he had fifty pounds and the advantage of few inches on me. I didn't have time to worry about that since I was busy forcing my brain to remember my moves. I'd had nine hours of intense private training since coming out of the hospital and six hours of group training. Add that to the hours of practice at home and my teen-age lessons, and it still wasn't nearly as much as I'd wish for in this situation. My reflexes had kicked in this morning during my bout with Edward, but real life was something completely different.

Sidestepping, I followed through with a blow to his back. He recovered almost immediately and sprang toward me again, but my clumsy success told me he wasn't formally trained. I kicked out at the hand holding the knife and felt a surge of triumph when it clattered to the blacktop. I expected him to run away, but he didn't. Nor did anyone come around to use the air, though I could hear plenty of cars driving in the street out front.

He came at me again, but I ducked in plenty of time. I beat him in agility hands down. He wasn't even as good as Edward.

I kicked again at his knee and felt the blow connect, but I was too busy dodging the fist he sent toward my face to make the kick really count. I countered with a strong left hook to his jaw that I hoped hurt him more than it hurt me. The keys still in my hand added power to my blow, but he didn't back down. He scored on my hip, which sent a shock of pain through my leg. At this rate we would wear each other down equally. My quickness was an advantage, but one slam to my healing ribs and it might all be over. I had to end this fast.

We exchanged several more blows before I connected a round-house to his stomach and followed it up with a straight slice at his groin. He grunted in pain, but he didn't collapse to the ground as I'd hoped. *Follow it up again! Keep at it!* I heard Steve's voice urging me as he always did. Letting the tips of the keys slip outside my fist, I sent a punch to his right eye. This time my blow left him writhing on the ground, grabbing his eye and moaning. I rubbed my right hand, hoping I hadn't damaged my wrist again.

As my heart rate gradually slowed, I studied my attacker. He wore jeans and a T-shirt, and his wispy goatee was accentuated by a lip ring. He looked more like a street thug than someone in the hierarchy of organized crime, but I got the message loud and clear. Someone wanted me to stop asking questions.

I was betting on Russo, though I wasn't sure how he would have put the attack into place so fast. Or could this be a simple mugging? Despite the knife, he wasn't well-trained.

Running my tongue over the new split in my lip, I took out my cell phone to call the police, but the man leapt to his feet and hobbled away. I wasn't about to go after him. Calling the police was still a good idea, though. The gas station might have cameras out here, and possibly the man could be identified from footage of the attack.

Something gleaming on the ground caught my attention. The knife. It would be taken away by the police in a plastic bag the minute they arrived. Now might be my only chance to see if it held imprints that could lead to who had hired my attacker.

I approached the knife, dread forming a knot in my stomach. There was no telling how this knife had been used, and I knew I was opening myself for a nasty imprint that might give me a worse hurt than the information was worth. Yet what choice did I have? Sophie and her children needed Dennis. I'd been attacked in daylight in the parking lot of a gas station. If I didn't use my ability to make things right, what was the use of having it?

My hand shook as I reached out, but I made it stop. Not wanting to leave a fingerprint, I bent my forefinger and touched my knuckle to the shiny blade. Rapid images flitted through my mind, scenes of death and destruction that horrified me. I tried to push them away, tried to lift my hand, but I couldn't move. My heart thundered in my ears. My energy leaked away.

Only twice before had I experienced malicious imprints jammed so tightly together that one horrific image could not be separated from the next, and both times I'd fainted.

The last thing I felt was the hard ground smacking into my head.

CHAPTER

8

I turned the watch over and read the inscription. The old man was smiling, and I could feel his love as we hugged. No, not me. Shannon. An imprint.

My eyes blinked open, and there Shannon was, leaning over me, his watch digging into the bare flesh of my arm. I was tired—oh, so tired—but I couldn't seem to move. *Just let me sleep for a while,* I wanted to say. My mouth refused to obey, which put it into the same class as the rest of my body.

"Autumn, are you okay?"

I shut my eyes and let myself float. As stuffy as Shannon was, if he was here, there was no way the street thug could get me now. I didn't seem to have any new wounds since the attack except a pounding headache, so I would be okay with a little sleep.

I could still feel the imprints of Shannon's watch—probably because I'd somehow hooked a finger in it. I was too tired to be embarrassed by my involuntary action. I had no control at the moment.

The next thing I knew, I was being lifted from a car onto a gurney. "What's going on?" I mumbled.

"You were attacked," Shannon said. "You're all bruised. We want to make sure there's no internal bleeding."

I moved my head and saw that I was heading into an ambulance. "Stop." No way I could afford this. "I'm fine. Perfectly fine." I struggled to sit up.

"Then what's this?" Shannon's finger brushed across the split in my bottom lip.

"I beat him," I said. "He ran away."

"I saw that part. But then you collapsed. Could be serious."

"It was the imprint on the knife."

Shannon looked at the uniformed officer with him. "You bag a knife?" The man nodded.

"I just need to rest." In fact, I was feeling better by the minute.

Shannon signaled the ambulance workers to give us space. "Who attacked you?"

"I don't know." I gave him a description, and by the time I was finished, I wanted to curl up in my bed and sleep for a week.

"You went to see Russo."

"How did you know?" I didn't think Tracy would rat me out.

"Never mind how I knew. That was a dangerous thing to do."

"So I found out."

"You think he sent that guy?"

"I don't think I'm on anyone else's hit list. Yet."

Shannon sighed. "Autumn, I suspect Russo is as dirty as they come, but I can't find any connection between him and Dennis."

"He was looking for Dennis, and Dennis was scared to death to see him, but he also felt something else—relief, maybe even a little liking for Russo." How else could I explain that tiny rush of warmth? "Russo gave Sophie that new car sitting in her driveway— I'm sure of it—so there is a connection." I thought of Russo's hand coming down on the dark-haired woman. "Dennis might already be dead."

"It's a possibility."

I grabbed Shannon's arm and pulled myself to a seated position. "I am not going in that ambulance. I can barely afford the mortgage on my shop as it is."

"Then I'll drive you home."

"That's not necessary."

"You were unconscious."

I didn't bother to tell him that he'd be unconscious, too, if he had experienced the imprints on the knife. "It's been a long day. You didn't have to come after me. I would have been fine after a little nap."

"On the pavement?"

"So?"

"Fine. You didn't need me, but I'm still going to drive you home." He looked anxious now, and I knew I'd have to give in.

I sighed. "If you drive me, how will I get my car back?"

"I'll drive you home in your car." The way he said "car" let me know he was being kind in calling it that. "One of the officers can take mine. You know, I would have let you come with me if you'd asked."

"Would you really?"

He shook his head. "No. But I should have."

That was close enough to an apology that I almost forgave him for trying to cart me away to the hospital.

"Knowing how you are and everything," he added, which nixed my forgiveness.

"I'm going to do whatever I can to find out what happened to Dennis," I said. For Sophie and her children but also for my pregnant sister who lived next door to them and could be in danger of getting caught in any cross fire.

"Well, we've identified the place in Tawnia's picture, and we have officers canvassing the nearby hotels and gas stations. There was a report of shots fired in the area Thursday evening, but the police concluded it was a car backfiring."

"It had to be a gun, and whoever had it was after Dennis." My money was on Russo. I pushed myself gingerly off the gurney, feeling as if I'd gained three hundred pounds. My hair was plastered to my head with the heat and humidity.

"Was there anything on the knife?" Shannon asked.

I shook my head. "Nothing I would be capable of pinpointing. No way I'm touching it again."

Shannon put me firmly in the passenger seat of my car. I would have protested more if I'd thought I was capable of driving myself home, but I was beginning to think that reading too many imprints wasn't like getting a sore muscle. It could be worse. How much worse, I didn't know.

He was back within moments, slipping into the driver's seat. The sun glinted off the blonder streaks in his hair that was starting to curl on the ends. "So," he said, "where'd you learn those moves?"

"What moves?"

"I pulled up just as you took out that guy."

"Wait a minute. How'd you find me, anyway? This isn't your jurisdiction."

His eyes narrowed. "A tip from an informant I have watching Russo's place. I came back when he told me about your flat tire. A little too late to help you with that thug, but you did okay."

I contemplated shrugging but decided it would take too much energy. "You're the one who told me I should take lessons from Steve."

He blinked at me.

"Whaaaat?" I said.

"You never listen to what I tell you."

"I do when I happen to agree with you."

He laughed. "That's a first."

We settled into a comfortable silence, and after a while I tilted my seat as far back as it would go. My brain still felt sluggish, and secretly I was a little concerned. What if one day a negative imprint was so strong I couldn't come back from it? But I wasn't going to share that thought with Shannon. Besides, it was kind of nice not picking at each other for once.

"Autumn, wake up."

I jerked awake and found myself staring into Jake's face. "Jake, I—" Looking around, I saw that Shannon had parked outside my shop. I smiled and stretched. "Hi." After the morning I'd had, Jake looked really good leaning over me.

"I thought you were going to take it easy for a while with the imprints."

"It was sort of an accident. I promise no more touching strange knives."

"Knives?" Jake got that worried look that made me wish I'd kept my mouth shut.

"Don't worry." Shannon appeared behind him on the sidewalk. "The guy is paying for his rash behavior." He winked at me with one of his beautiful eyes before turning back to Jake. "Looks like my ride has caught up to me. Keep an eye on her, would you?"

"Jake doesn't make choices for me," I shot back.

Shannon only smiled. "Good to hear."

Jake frowned as Shannon took his leave. "So," he said, "what happened really?"

"Didn't Shannon tell you?"

"I want your version."

He let me finish recounting the morning's adventures before he spoke. "Sounds to me like Russo doesn't know where Dennis is."

"Why would he give Sophie a new car?"

"Maybe Russo is someone from Dennis's past, but he doesn't actually want to hurt him."

"That doesn't explain why Dennis was so afraid after seeing him. Why would he run away?"

"The real question is, Who were those guys shooting at Dennis in Tawnia's drawing?"

I shook my head. "I don't know. Maybe we should call her and see if she's heard anything else. Maybe Dennis has tried to contact Sophie."

"We'll give her a call—after we clean you up." Jake gingerly touched my bottom lip. I could feel it swelling, but it didn't hurt nearly as much as my hip, where the thug had kicked me, or my arms, which I had used to block his blows. I'd have to wear long sleeves to hide the bruises.

Jake held my hand as we went into Autumn's Antiques, waving Thera away so she wouldn't cluck over me. "We'll explain in a minute," he said as we headed to my back room.

I cleaned up in my bathroom, while Jake put on some herbal tea. That was exactly what I needed. I also felt the need to touch something with positive imprints, but I was too exhausted to find anything, and after my fight with the thug, my fingers felt too sore for my antique rings. I left them on the sink in the bathroom and settled for two packages of string cheese in the hopes the protein would help as much as it had last night.

I settled into my easy chair, pulling my feet up under me, and called Tawnia between bites. "Hey, Autumn," she said. "I've been worried about you."

"I'm fine."

She hesitated slightly before saying, "Good."

"Have you been drawing again?" I hoped she hadn't drawn me being attacked.

"No. But Sophie called to tell me that someone has put money into her account. She's afraid Dennis is into something illegal. She was crying, and I felt so bad for her."

"I might know who's responsible, but it isn't Dennis."

"Who?"

"Someone from his past. A Nicholas Russo. I don't have a picture of him, but maybe Sophie's heard of him."

"I'll ask. But, Autumn, when I said I hadn't been drawing, I meant today. Last night after we had talked, I did a drawing of a hotel or motel room. Now, that's not odd, seeing as one of my clients runs a hotel chain and we've been brainstorming advertising ideas, but this room looked, well, not like something you'd put in a magazine."

"Maybe it's where Dennis went. Is there anything to identify the place?" I saw Jake staring at me thoughtfully without touching his tea, a frown on his face.

"It's really generic. A bed, a slice of a window, and half a table. It's more what's on the table that disturbs me."

"What?"

"Something that looked like a stained strip of cloth."

"Stained with what?"

"No clue. It was a pencil sketch. But it could be a makeshift bandage."

"Well, there's nothing we can do about that, I guess." At my words I felt more than saw Jake relax.

"I guess not. I'll be so glad when this is all over. I'm really sorry for dragging you into it."

She'd be a lot sorrier if she knew about my street thug. "What are sisters for? You know I thrive on this sort of thing."

"I know. And that worries me, too."

"Stop worrying. It's bad for little Ashberry."

Tawnia laughed. "Ashberry? Oh, that'll go over well with Bret. He was thinking more along the lines of Christian."

"Wasn't that his brother's name?"

"Yeah."

"Tell him it's already taken. Bret had enough trouble getting over your dating his brother before him, and I don't think you need that between you again." Christian had died in a fall from a tree in the mountains, and Tawnia had been with him at the time. Not a good memory for either of them.

"Right. Look, Bret and I are taking Sophie out to lunch, so I'd better help him with Saturday chores or we'll never get out of here."

"Have fun." I didn't need to tell her to be careful. Tawnia always was.

Jake was leaning against the sink watching me as I hung up. His muscled arms folded over his stomach, reminding me strangely of Russo's bodyguard. "Well?"

I repeated what Tawnia had told me as we sipped our tea. There was a tension that hadn't been between us before, but I couldn't pinpoint the reason until Jake spoke.

"Look," he said. "About tonight. I promised Kolonda that I'd show a guy her apartments. He's coming from out of town to look into her construction problems. Want to come along?"

Not my idea of a Saturday evening, especially when my limbs felt lined with lead. "Actually, I was thinking about going out to Tawnia's. I want to talk to Sophie again. She might have an idea about which hotel Dennis might choose. People tend to be creatures of habit." If he were smart, he'd be far from Portland, but I suspected his connection with his wife and children was too strong. Good for his marriage but bad for his life expectancy.

Jake was frowning again. "Maybe it's time to let the police handle this. If Russo is as connected as he seems to be, it's too dangerous."

Rising from my chair, I set my cup on the sink and put my arms around Jake. "I won't be in danger tonight. Besides, I can take care of myself. That's what all those extra tae kwon do lessons are for. You don't have to worry about me." As much as I cared about Jake, I couldn't back away from trying to solve this mystery.

His arms tightened around me as he bent and gently kissed my swollen bottom lip. "I don't want to lose you."

"You won't." I kissed him back, not regretting it even when my lip hurt.

Bells jingling at both our shop doors broke us apart, and we spent the next few hours helping customers. Among my antiques, I felt stronger. Though many of the imprints were long faded, the vibes were positive and strengthening.

I almost changed my mind about going with Jake to Kolonda's apartment building when she appeared in the herb shop. She looked amazing in white shorts and a red top, her long black hair fanning over her back and shoulders. Jake left the customer he was talking to and went to meet her, and I watched them from the register where I had come to help Randa with a short line of people. It went that way on Saturdays—a rush in my store and then in his.

I rang up my customer, deciding I didn't like the jealous streak appearing in me. I'd never had a romantic relationship worth fighting for, and the emotion was new. I couldn't help but notice that Jake and Kolonda looked like a couple who'd stepped from a magazine, their sculpted bronze faces alive and eager.

"They were going to get married once," Randa whispered as her customer left. "Doesn't it bother you to have her hanging around?"

I had to wait to finish with my customer before I could say, "I trust Jake."

"Well, I don't trust her," she said, turning to help the last customer.

I watched Jake and Kolonda as Randa finished. A few people

were in my store now, and I really should have gone to help Thera, but I wanted to hear more from Randa. "I take it you don't like Kolonda?"

"She dumped my brother because he wasn't good enough for her. I may have been really young when she did it, but I remember how hurt he was. It was months before he was himself again. Now he's doing well with this store, and she comes back? Seems too contrived. If you ask me, she just wants him for his money."

I didn't feel like destroying Randa's view of her brother's success. The truth was Jake was still making payments to me on the Herb Shoppe, and, like me, he barely made it each month. His clientele was growing, and someday things might change, but if Kolonda wanted money, she was looking in the wrong place.

"Jake's a big boy," I said.

"I know, but I still don't like her."

Leaving a simmering Randa, I went around the desk to go over to Jake and Kolonda, but Kolonda waved at me and left the shop. Her eyes were reddened, and I wondered what had happened.

"The guy I know from out of town who was going to look at her apartments called her and canceled," Jake said when I asked, his brow furrowed. "She thinks they got to him. I'll call him myself to see what's what, but it's really strange. Her two buildings aren't all that large. I'm not sure why the contractor would go to such extremes."

"Maybe it's not those buildings they want. Maybe it's the space."

He blinked. "I never thought of that. I should probably check out any future plans for the area."

"The city offices are closed today."

"That's okay. I know a few people to ask, friends of my grandmother's. And I still need to find a second opinion on the work she had done."

111

I laughed. "Now who's the detective?"

Jake didn't respond with his normal smile. "There's a difference, Autumn. This isn't going to get me attacked with a knife."

I was saved from answering by the entrance of several customers and the ringing of my phone. To my surprise, it was Shannon.

"We found Alex Trogan, the missing witness in Michigan," he said when I answered. "Unfortunately, he's dead."

9

"Oh, no. Is he—" I couldn't finish the question. If Dennis and Alex were one and the same, Sophie was a widow and her children fatherless.

"I should have said we found his bones. He's been dead at least five years. He was actually found a year ago in Lake Michigan, on the Wisconsin side, close to Milwaukee. We had to work to find Alex's dental records and when they didn't match Dennis's, the lab automatically compared them with other unsolved cases. Not sure why they didn't do that before."

"Alex isn't Dennis then." I let out a long breath. "He wasn't the witness the police had in protective custody."

"It's looking that way."

"That means there were two witnesses to that murder—Alex and Dennis."

"And Alex was killed for it."

"So what are you going to do? We have to find Dennis before

Russo does. Or whoever else is looking for him. You're having Russo followed, aren't you?"

"I can't tell you the particulars, but it's covered."

I tried not to be irritated at that. "Thanks for calling me."

"I thought you'd want to know." A pause and then, "You feeling any better?" There was a careful note in his voice, and it dawned on me that this was the real reason he was calling. I would have laughed if the idea hadn't called to life a warmth I didn't think I was capable of feeling for Shannon. Maybe we were finally learning how to work together.

"I haven't dropped over yet, so I guess I'm fine."

"Good. Later." He hung up, and I stared at the phone until Thera poked her head through the connecting double door and said a customer needed me.

I usually closed the shop at four or five, whenever the traffic eased. Jake usually had to stay open later, as people always seemed to have urgent last-minute herbal needs. Sometimes I would stay to help him, but he had things well under control in the Herb Shoppe and traffic in my shop had wound down enough for Thera to take care of it. I decided to head to Tawnia's at barely three o'clock. She and Bret should be back from lunch by now, and I could talk to Sophie.

Only when I was outside did I remember my tire. Shannon hadn't filled it on the way home, so hopefully it was still holding. Otherwise, I'd need to find someplace to fix it permanently before making the trek to Tawnia's. If Jake had brought his car instead of his bike, I could borrow that, but the bike was impossible to drive without shoes. I went around to the driver's side and squatted down to check out the tire, keeping one eye on traffic.

The tire was still perfectly inflated.

I should have been happy, but thinking about it made me uneasy. Since I'd been attacked at the gas station, I assumed the thug was responsible for the flat. That he hadn't used the knife told me he'd been trying to avoid raising too much suspicion so I wouldn't call the police. But letting the air from my tire without being seen and even arranging for the thug at all would have taken time, and my first suspect, Russo, hadn't known I was coming. Plus, the thug had been nowhere near professional, and Russo didn't seem the type to hire an inexperienced street hood.

But it had to be Russo, I thought. Maybe I had run over a nail and Russo's bodyguard, bald Charlie, had called in a favor from the thug when he'd seen the tire, wanting to teach me a lesson without it being connected to them. I'd seen him on the phone. Wait. Maybe he was the informant who tipped off Shannon.

No, Charlie wouldn't have survived this long betraying a powerful man like Russo. Shaking my head, I climbed into the car and started the engine, checking to make sure no other car parked along the block pulled out after me. Now I was paranoid.

"I wondered if you'd be coming," Tawnia said when she opened her door twenty minutes later, looking as if the humidity wasn't affecting her hair the way it seemed to affect mine. "Hey, Bret helped me hang the curtains in the nursery this morning. Do you want to see?"

"Sure, but first I'd like you to try to draw a picture of Russo to see if Sophie recognizes him. I can describe him to you pretty well. About our age, dark hair, blue eyes, high cheek bones, square jaw, face a little too wide. Not really good-looking but compelling, confident, a bit arrogant. Oh, and big eyebrows. Not the ugly unibrow, but dominating."

Tawnia laughed. "Sounds like you liked the guy."

"He hits his wife." My initial instinct before imprints came into my life might have been to give Russo the benefit of the doubt, which would have changed my attitude and my conversation with him. I would have been wrong, so this time it worked in my favor, but mistrusting my own instincts caused havoc in my personal relationships. It made me second-guess what I knew to be true. Like with Jake.

"I suppose I can try to draw him from your description."

I was hoping her other ability would kick in and do a better job than I could with my description, but I knew she wouldn't like the idea if I voiced it.

I took a step inside the house. "Thanks, I really—"

A shrill scream pierced the air, coming from the direction of Sophie's house. Tawnia's eyes went wide as she stared at me, and for an odd moment, it seemed as if I were looking into a mirror. As one we turned and ran down the steps.

The seconds it took us to cross the lawn seemed the longest I'd known in a long time. The front door was locked, and no one answered our ringing.

"Around the back," Tawnia said.

There was more screaming that quickly turned into sobbing as we ran through the gate. We found Sophie crumpled in a heap near her back fence. "Sophie!" Tawnia and I shouted together.

When we reached her, I could see a swelling red spot on her cheek the size of a man's fist. Tears wet her face as she clung to me. "They took him. They took Sawyer!"

"Who took Sawyer?" I asked, my eyes searching the yard for any clue to what she was talking about.

"I don't know. A man. I looked outside and saw him come over the fence. I ran outside because Sawyer was there, and he shoved me away and hit me when I wouldn't back off. Then he grabbed Sawyer from the sandbox and tossed him over the fence to somebody. I heard a car squeal away."

"We have to call the police!" Tawnia started toward the house.

"No need." I motioned to the gate where two uniformed police officers were entering, presumably the pair assigned to watch Sophie's house.

"Is something wrong?" one asked. He had brown hair and a sturdy build that looked as if he could run all day and never tire. His eyes were kind.

I repeated what Sophie had said, and all at once they were in motion. The blond partner leapt over the fence to check out the other side, and the first officer started back to the front, dialing on his cell phone.

"Where's Lizbeth?" I asked.

Sophie looked at me blankly, and I had to repeat the question before she said, "In the kitchen. In her swing. What if they took her, too!" We ran to the kitchen, but Lizbeth was sound asleep in her swing. Sophie collapsed to the floor by her daughter and began sobbing. "Oh, my boy, my baby! He's going to be so scared. Why do they want him? What are they going to do to him?"

Tawnia and I had no answer, but my sister sat awkwardly next to Sophie and held her.

"I'm going out to the fence," I said. Tawnia nodded. It was a long shot that the kidnapper had left imprints there, but he might have. Or maybe the man had dropped something that contained an imprint.

No such luck. I met the police officer coming back over the fence, his face grim. "Anything there?" I asked. He shook his head.

I waited until he started back to the gate before running my hands over the fence. I was thorough, covering far more of it than the man could have touched. The only objects nearby that had an imprint were the toys that Sawyer had played with in the sand-box—more pleasant tingles than anything else. I went to the set of plastic chairs and tables on the patio and carried the table over to the fence to check out the area on the other side for myself. A house was being constructed there, and all that met my gaze was piles of lumber, small hills of dirt, and rubbish that had been left behind by the workers.

Sawyer was simply gone.

Back in the house, everything was in chaos. Several more police cars had arrived, and officers were with Sophie in her sitting room. Tawnia sat next to her, holding her hand. Outside, a growing crowd of neighbors were talking to police officers. Women held tightly to their babies or to the hands of their toddlers. I didn't need the police to tell me that no one had seen anything.

Except for Sophie.

"It wasn't your husband, was it?" I heard a police officer asking her.

"No! No, of course not. Dennis wouldn't do this. Why aren't you out there finding my son?" Sophie could barely get out the words. Her face was a mess. Mascara ran down her cheeks. Half her hair had broken free of its comb and curled unevenly around her face.

There was nothing I could do to help.

I went to the kitchen where baby Lizbeth still slept soundly.

What did I know?

Nothing really, except if Russo was after Dennis, he could also be after his family. But why give Sophie a car, and probably the money as well, and then take Sawyer? It didn't make sense. There had to be another player.

The baby's eyes came open, and her face crumpled as she readied for a huge scream. Hurriedly, I unhooked her safety belt and slid her out of the seat. I was awkward, but Lizbeth wasn't picky.

"It's okay," I said, kissing her softly. She had a warm and pleasant smell that reminded me of sunshine and made me want to curl up with her and keep her safe. "We'll find your brother and your daddy." But what if we didn't? Lizbeth would never remember either of them or be able to understand the loss her mother would always feel. "I'll do everything I can to get them back to you."

That probably meant going to see Russo again and somehow getting my hands on his personal belongings. Not an easy task. What if he'd been the one who sent my attacker? I hugged Lizbeth tighter, knowing it didn't matter. I'd still have to try. Russo knew far more than he was telling.

"Ah, I wondered if you'd be here."

I lifted my face from the baby to see Shannon, feeling suddenly awkward. "What took you so long?" I countered.

He sighed. "We've got everyone working on it. An Amber Alert is going out in a few minutes. We're sending people to all the main roads, but it's like looking for a needle in a haystack."

"Use a microscope then. We have to find them." Until I spoke, I hadn't realized how close to tears I was.

"We will."

"Alive," I added.

He didn't reply.

I handed him the baby. "I have somewhere to go."

Shannon's arms went instinctively around the baby. "Wait, why are you giving her to me? Where are you going?"

Ignoring him, I walked out of the kitchen, past the police officers in the foyer, and through the front door.

I wasn't exactly planning to walk into Russo's den, though. First I'd try to call him, and that meant another favor from Tracy. She might be at her mother's, but I bet she was keeping tabs on the situation.

Hurrying down the sidewalk, I nearly ran into someone—Ace, the man I'd met in Russo's office. He was still wearing jeans and T-shirt. "What are you doing here?" Even as I said it, I remembered where else I'd seen him. "Wait, I know you. You're a private investigator. I've seen you at the station asking questions." I hadn't seen him recently, but during the first case I worked with Shannon, he'd probably been the only person more annoying to the detective than I was. "Why are you here?"

"I could ask you the same thing."

"Sophie and Dennis are my friends."

"I was hired by Russo to find Dennis."

"So you're the reason Russo's in Portland."

He shook his head, that secret smile still on his face. "Nope. He hired me only yesterday."

"You're Shannon's plant, aren't you?" So that's how he was keeping tabs on Russo. Chalk one up to Shannon—he knew how to use even annoying private eyes.

"Me?" Ace said far too innocently.

"Have you made any progress at all?" I seriously doubted his ability. Then again, he was here not more than thirty minutes since Sawyer had been taken. Did that mean Russo was responsible for the boy's disappearance?

"If I had made progress, what makes you think I'd share it with you?"

I could see he wasn't going to tell me anything useful, so I shoved past him. I'd almost made it to my car when a black Lexus pulled up next to me, the back window rolling down. The car looked suspiciously familiar.

Russo.

Sure enough, he was in the backseat, leaning over so I could see him. "Can we talk?"

I glanced over my shoulder, but Ace had gone inside Sophie's house, and Shannon was nowhere to be seen. None of the police officers or the neighbors were paying attention to me.

Making a quick decision that was based more upon Sophie's tearful face than on logic, I opened the door and slid into the empty seat. Charlie was driving, but he didn't so much as glance my way.

"Okay, talk," I said, as Charlie hit the gas.

"I need to take you somewhere."

This didn't sound good. I thought of asking him about the guy with the knife but decided I really didn't want to know. Besides, he apparently wanted something from me. If he was guilty, he wasn't going to admit it to me now. "Where?"

"To the motel where Dennis was last night. I want to know if you can tell me anything."

"What could I possibly tell you? Besides, I seem to remember you saying something about me and garbage at our last meeting."

He had the good grace to look ashamed. "I had another chat with the private investigator I hired, and he says you're for real. Or at least that the detectives at the police station give you some credit."

"Okay, I'll help. But first you have to answer a few questions." No way was I going to be used to find Dennis only so we could both end up as food for the fishes. I leaned back and folded my arms.

Russo regarded me silently for long seconds—seconds that were taking me farther away from Sophie's and the protection of the police. "Deal," he said. "Shoot."

"Why are you trying to find Dennis? What is he to you?"

He frowned. "It's a long story."

"How far is it to the motel?"

"Have it your way. I'll tell you. Dennis isn't the man you know. His name isn't Dennis."

"That much I've already figured out. I also know he witnessed a murder five years ago. I think he ran away and began a new life."

Russo laughed. "That's not far from the truth. About running away, at least. Dennis is actually Damiano—Damian, in English. Damian Franco. I've been looking for him for five years. He's my cousin."

CHAPTER

10

Dennis's real name was Damian? That was hard to believe. I mean, the name Damian should belong to a tall, good-looking, dark-haired Italian with a prominent nose and an accent, not a regular, ordinary IT guy with brown hair who gardened with his wife and picked out colors to paint his baby daughter's room.

"Dennis is your cousin," I repeated. At least that explained Dennis's mixed emotions at seeing Russo. "If that's true, why was he so afraid of you?"

"Did he tell you he was afraid?"

"I felt it on something he owns." I met his gaze steadily. "He wasn't just afraid but terrified, and that caused him to pack a suitcase and leave his family—probably with the hope that you wouldn't find them. Did you take Sawyer?" That made sense. If this "family" of Dennis's had been searching for him, they'd likely want to find his children, too.

Russo blinked. "What are you talking about?"

"Didn't your private eye tell you? Sawyer is missing. Someone took him from his own backyard less than an hour ago."

Russo's face paled to a shade of gray I would have found amusing if it hadn't set back my theory of his being responsible. He pulled out his cell phone and dialed, barking orders in a language I didn't recognize. I wondered if he spoke that language without an accent as he did English. I didn't understand a word. Maybe if I touched the phone, I would receive an imprint that could tell me what he said—emotions had no language—but Russo was unlikely to allow that liberty.

When he finished, he studied me gravely. "I didn't order the boy taken, but I should have. This means they know Damian—Dennis—is in Portland and have found out about his family."

"They who?"

"On the night Damian disappeared, he and his older brother met with Joben Saito, one of our business rivals. We'd clashed before, and that night was supposed to be the end of our problems. But things didn't go well at the meeting, and Damian's brother was killed."

I didn't ask what kind of business negotiations ended so poorly. Nothing legal, I'd bet, if the result was murder.

"Damian called me after Bartolomeo was killed," Russo continued. "He was scared. Said someone was after him. Saito, presumably. When we got there, Damian and Saito were gone, but the police had a man in custody, and we thought he had to be Damian. When the man went missing, we all believed Saito's men had killed him."

"Why didn't you go to the police?"

Russo laughed. "This isn't the sort of thing you go to the police about. But we've kept an eye on the Saitos ever since because Damian's body never turned up. For all we knew, they still had him. When the Saitos came to Portland, we figured it was to damage our interests in the city, but when I saw Damian at the attorney's, I began to wonder if they were here for him. After all, he had witnessed the murder and could put Saito in jail."

"It's been five years, and Dennis has cut all ties to his family. Obviously, he had no intention of going to the police. Why would the Saitos still be after him?"

Russo's face twisted into something that chilled me. "The particulars are none of your business. But make no mistake—they would love to lay his body on his father's doorstep. Damian is the only living son, and his brother left no male heirs, so Damian is to inherit his father's business."

"He doesn't seem very interested." That Dennis had stayed away from his family after the incident told me far more than Russo likely wanted me to know. He must have wanted to escape, perhaps had been waiting for the right opportunity to disappear.

Russo waved away my concern. "He'll change his mind once he is back with the family. Besides, he has a son himself, now. The boy must be brought up in the business."

"Maybe he doesn't like your kind of business," I muttered under my breath. I knew Dennis, and he wasn't the kind of man Russo was. "What about you?" I said more loudly. "You could run the family."

"I do work hard for the family, but I'm not my uncle's son. Since my mother is his sister, I don't share the same last name. Besides, even if I were his son, I have three daughters. No boys. My second wife is expecting, but the doctor says it's also a girl. My uncle remarried after his first wife's death and has a daughter from that marriage. It may be that my young cousin will someday have a son who could be my uncle's heir, but for now we need Damian and his son."

Did I detect bitterness in the words, or were they a simple statement of facts? Whatever he felt, Russo wasn't showing me, and I was sure he'd take exception if I reached over to touch the heavy ring next to his half-missing finger.

"What if Dennis doesn't want to go back?" I asked.

"He has no choice."

"He might run again."

Russo shook his head. "He wouldn't leave his family behind with us."

"No wonder he chose to run away," I spat. "Stories like this make me glad I have no clue who my birth relatives are."

"Don't judge what you don't know."

I lifted my chin and locked my eyes on his. "I do know, and I don't believe the welfare of a group is more important than the life of an individual. Dennis made his choice, and his family—you—should honor that. If you don't, any love between you is nothing but words."

Russo's glare would have sent a shiver down my spine if I hadn't been so furious. If he thought I was going to help him find Dennis, he was mistaken. I stared out the window again, biting the inside of my lip in an attempt to control my temper.

After a time, Russo surprised me by saying in a relatively calm voice, "Damian and I played together as children. He was a good kid even then. His brother and I teased him for it and played pranks on him, but he never complained and he never cried. He didn't cringe when his father disciplined us or rebel against him. He simply endured. He was eighteen when his mother died, and it was he who comforted his brother and his father. I've always admired Damian, and I've missed him."

What could I say to that? As with Dennis, bits of gray swirled around his feelings and motives. But what shade? Dark gray or light? I wasn't sure it mattered.

We drove in silence a few more blocks and then I asked, "If you really didn't take Sawyer, do you think Saito did?"

"It's possible. Likely. I have my people looking into it now." His eyes went past me. "Looks like we've arrived."

I swiveled to see a small motel that was maybe ten minutes from Jake's grandmother's apartment building. Unlike the area she lived in, the entire block was run down, and the motel in particular badly needed refurbishing. I wondered if Dennis had chosen it on purpose, or if it was where he'd simply ended up.

"Your investigator tracked him here?"

"Actually, the police found the place first. My man has contacts within the department."

I wondered if Russo had any idea that his investigator played both sides, or maybe Shannon was the one in the dark. When I saw him again, I'd be sure to ask.

I sized up my two companions as we headed for a room on the second floor, accessed directly from the parking lot. No way I could take both of them together, or even alone, unless they were completely untrained, but I might be able to get away from them if I needed to. I'd have to watch for the opportunity. Right now they sandwiched me in between them like a delicacy they were reluctant to let out of their sight.

We didn't get as far as the door before a uniformed police officer stepped in our way. "Excuse me. This area is off limits."

I guess he recognized that men wearing clothing as expensive as Russo and Charlie wouldn't be guests at this dive.

"Hey, Peirce, it's me," I said, recognizing the short, red-haired man from my visits to the police station. He'd stood out from the others because of his flaming hair and because he told jokes that had diverted his colleagues' attention from the odd girl in the worn jeans who could read imprints. I'd never forgotten him for that, though I still didn't know the name of his big, dark-skinned, shaved-head companion who emerged from the room at our voices, his hand on his gun.

"I did recognize you, Ms. Rain," Peirce said. "Been a few months."

"I told you to call me Autumn." Peirce Elvey was probably five years younger than me but calling me Ms. made me feel old.

"Right." He gave me a grin that wrinkled the many freckles on his nose. "So, did Detective Martin send you here?"

I avoided answering directly. "I've come to see if I could read anything."

"I think it'd be okay for you to enter. The room was pretty neat when we got here, and they did the fingerprinting already. Pretty much the only thing we found of interest was a shirt someone ripped up and used as a bandage. They took it to see if the blood on it matches our missing man. There's nothing really left to see, but we're going over the room once more to make sure we didn't miss anything."

The significance of Tawnia having described a similar motel room with a bandage on a table was not lost on me. "I'll be careful," I said, feeling a bit guilty for using what little influence I had to get inside. I looked at Russo. "Maybe you guys should wait out here."

I thought Russo would rip my head off at the suggestion, but he swallowed hard and nodded.

"That'd be best," Peirce said. "I can't authorize anyone to enter until Detective Martin arrives. Except Autumn."

"Shannon's coming?"

"Yeah, he's finishing up something else." Peirce's brow furrowed, and I knew he'd heard about Sawyer.

"We'll find him," I said.

Peirce didn't show surprise that I already knew about the boy. I wondered what he would say if he knew Russo had every intention of doing something similar to Sophie, Dennis, and the rest of their family.

I glanced at Russo and saw that some of the anger had left his face. Hidden, most likely. He hadn't expected the police to still be here—or to keep him out. I for one was relieved. Now that I understood his connection with the case, I didn't want to wager on my chances of survival if I actually led Russo to Dennis.

Thoughts of Sophie filled my mind as I entered the motel room. How different this place was from their home next to Tawnia's and probably even more different from where Dennis had grown up. An odd smell lingered in the air—the smell of age, of use, of dirt so embedded it could never be removed. My nose twitched, but I resisted the urge to breathe through my mouth. I'd rather smell the air I breathed. The room was plain, with only the basic amenities. No refrigerator, no microwave, and only a single faded print on the wall.

"You can do the bathroom first," said the dark-skinned officer. "We're completely finished in there." Two other officers, a man with brown hair and a woman with a short black ponytail, were on their knees, looking under the bed.

The bathroom was little more than a closet with a shower and a toilet. The soap hadn't been used, or the miniature bottle of shampoo. One towel was missing, and I assumed the police had taken it. Two wrapped cups on the sink hadn't been touched, so Dennis either hadn't been thirsty, or he hadn't been here long enough to get himself a drink. Since the bed was still made, I was voting on the latter.

There was quite a bit of fingerprinting dust on the sink and on the toilet, and I tried to push back my reluctance as I touched the sink knobs, gliding my fingertips over the area gingerly. Nothing. Next I touched the toilet lid and flush handle, followed by the towel rack, and then back to the sink where I touched the mirror. Imprints. Faint ones from four months earlier. A flash of a woman crying. A woman dressed in a maid uniform. Not related to this investigation.

"Any luck?" Peirce asked.

I shook my head. "No one cared about this room enough to leave any imprints."

"I thought you had something with the mirror."

"Nothing that will help us."

Out in the room, the officers had moved to the table. I didn't see how they could have missed anything because there simply wasn't much to search. I ran my fingers over all the available surfaces, especially those that had the remains of fingerprint dust. Russo and Charlie stared at me from the doorway, filling up the space as though blocking my escape. Trying to ignore them, I trailed my hands along the knobs to the battered entertainment center and the small television. Nothing. I wished I could have touched the bandage, though if the cloth had contained an imprint, it might be too faded to help anyway. More likely, it wouldn't hold anything.

An exclamation from the female officer drew my attention. With a gloved hand, she pulled a small prescription bottle out from under the heating unit. "Sleeping pills," she said, "belonging to Dennis Briggs."

I hurried over. "His wife said he had a prescription for them. Can I see them?"

"Not a good idea. I have to take it in and check for prints."

"You'll probably only find his."

"They might have dropped during a struggle." She frowned at me. "Who are you anyway?"

"She's with me." Shannon was shoving past Russo and his sidekick. "We can wait until you take the prints."

"Here?"

"Here."

The officer didn't question further but went quickly to work.

"I see you've been slumming," Shannon said to me in an under-tone. Annoyance and anger came through his words.

I knew he was talking about Russo. "No more than usual." Giving him a fake smile, I added in a whisper. "You know, you're almost cute when you're mad."

Several seconds of silence passed before he said, "So you think I'm cute."

"I said 'almost.'" I turned away, trying to hide the quirk of my lips that hinted at a real smile. "Why didn't you tell me Russo is related to the man Dennis saw murdered?"

Shannon arched a brow. "Just found out myself a few hours ago. If I'd told you, you'd have probably run right out and confronted Russo again. Oh, wait, you did that anyway."

"No, this time he came for me. And what you might not know is that Dennis is really Damiano Franco."

"Brother of the man he saw murdered?"

"Exactly." Was that an admiring glance? Well, it made no dif-ference to me.

"All the more reason not to trust Russo," Shannon said.

I met his gaze. "I never trust anyone I don't know." *Not anymore.*

The female officer frowned, apparently irritated at not finding what she wanted. Or maybe her ponytail was too tight. She handed the bottle to Shannon, who extended it to me.

I took a breath. Russo was peering inside the room, his eyes almost as intense as Shannon's. I opened my hand, and Shannon placed the bottle on my palm.

An imprint came to life in my mind, one from the night be-fore. Dennis/I sat on the bed, staring at the bottle in his/my hand. Memories of a younger Russo and another similar face with Dennis's laughing smile. The memories weren't violent or even desperate. They were a thirst that couldn't be quenched, a loss that couldn't be filled. An ache without a name. Over all was Dennis's desire for escape.

I knew the other young man was Dennis's older brother, Bartolomeo, and that Dennis still mourned his death. Mourned all alone because he had rejected that life and the comfort his family could have offered, and he couldn't share that past with Sophie. He had sat in this room yesterday holding this bottle and thinking about the brother he'd lost and the cousin he'd left behind. A tear rolled down my cheek. My cheek, but Dennis's emotion.

A noise at the door, Dennis/me turning, terror growing in his/ my gut, but also that tiny bit of ambivalence, a strange longing that reminded me of the tiny rush of warmth in the pen imprint.

Wait. These men he/I didn't recognize. Then again, a lot would have changed in five years. An Asian man grabbing me. He was built like a wrestler, his strong fingers like metal hooks.

"Hey, take it easy. I'll go peacefully."

"What do I care?" the Asian sneered, the scar across his left cheek sagging gruesomely. "The only reason I don't kill you is 'cuz our boss has a few questions." A fist coming up to meet my face. Exploding pain. Blackness.

Struggling for breath, I dropped the bottle onto the bed. Shannon reached out to steady me but stopped short when I began speaking. "He was taken," I said, more to Russo than anyone else. "An Asian man and two others. He thought they'd been sent from his family, but he didn't recognize them. They didn't seem to care when he told them he'd go peacefully. They hit him. That's all I saw. The medication must have fallen from his hand and rolled under the heater."

"Did you say an Asian man?" Russo took few steps into the room, and no one objected. "Is he a big man and did he have a scar on his face?"

"What's the significance of that?" Shannon asked.

"The Saito family is Japanese, and they have an employee who meets that description."

"The Saitos operate strictly in the east. What would they want with Dennis?" Shannon looked between Russo and me.

Russo gave Shannon a glare. "They would kill him as they did his brother five years ago."

"Yeah, I get the family relationship. What I want to know is why they would kill either of them. What did you guys to do them?"

Russo's only answer was a withering glare. I guess whatever secrets the family held, he wasn't going to share them with me and a police detective.

"The man did have a vertical scar on his cheek," I said. "His left cheek."

"Then there's no time." Russo's large fists clenched and un-clenched at his side. "If the Saitos have Dennis, he's as good as dead. And the boy, too. If we have any chance of saving them, we have to act now."

"We don't know where they've gone." Shannon glanced at his phone as it buzzed, but didn't answer.

Russo's eyes narrowed as he contemplated Shannon. "I might," he said finally. "The Saitos have used one of their many compa-nies to rent a warehouse down by the docks. But if you go in with all your force, they will kill Dennis and Sawyer without hesitation. You'll have to go in stealthily, with only a few people. My man Charlie can show you. He's been there."

Now it was Shannon's turn to stare at Russo. "How do I know this isn't just more misdirection?"

"I have nothing more to hide." Russo raised his hands.

"Ha!" I scoffed. "Except what you did to make the Saitos so angry. And the fact that you've come to force Dennis to return to your family."

"His family needs him."

"No, they don't. Not in that way. You could run the business without him. He doesn't want any of it." That wasn't quite true because I knew he wanted some of it, to see his family, to mourn with them over his brother, to remember his mother. That he'd chosen to run instead of staying with them said volumes about what he felt about their business.

Russo was becoming angry again—I could see it in the slight color of his face, the way his expression went blank. "Damian is like a brother to me. He'll see reason."

Like a brother? That made me wonder about the "aunt" Dennis had taken Sophie to meet. Who was the woman? Had at least one of his family members been aware of his survival these past five years? Perhaps even helping him?

"Is your mother still alive?" I asked Russo.

He blinked at the change in conversation. "She was when I left New Jersey. She suffers with a bone disease that keeps her confined to her bed." As when he'd talked about growing up with Dennis, I felt a flash of a real person behind his tough exterior, of sympathy and affection. Whatever else he was, Russo's tender feelings for his mother were genuine.

"I accept your help," Shannon said into the silence that followed. "Your man can ride back with me and tell me what he knows. It'll take me an hour to gather everyone. Do you think we have that long?"

Russo shrugged. "Depends on how long Dennis can last without telling them what they want to know. It may already be too late."

Shannon gave the officers a few directives before we followed Russo from the room. We walked in silence to the stairs.

"'Ha'?" Shannon said to me. "You said 'ha' to an organized crime boss?"

"Whatever works." I breezed past him down the stairs, thinking of asking Peirce to give me a ride home on his way back to the precinct because I wasn't about to go with Russo. I wondered if Russo would drive himself since Charlie was going with Shannon, but outside Russo and Charlie were already talking to another pair of men wearing dress shirts and slacks, their heads close together as they conferred. Too bad my talent wasn't telepathy.

My phone was vibrating like crazy, and I fished it out of my pocket. I didn't recognize the number and there was no name. "Hello?" I said, putting a hand to my ear so I could hear past the sound of the traffic zooming by. Didn't anyone in this area know what a muffler was?

"Is this Autumn Rain?" A woman's voice, panicked beyond recognition—if I knew her at all.

"Who's this?"

"It's Kolonda Lewis. I'm sorry to call you like this, but I'm worried about Jake."

"He seemed fine when I left the shop a few hours ago. He might be there now."

"He's not. Someone there gave me your number. I didn't know who else to call."

"What happened?" Why wouldn't she get to the point?

"Jake called me, all excited about something he'd found out about my properties. Said he was coming over to tell me about it, but he never got here. The phone rang once, and the caller ID said it was him, but no one was on the line when I answered. I've tried his phone since, but it goes to voice mail. I wouldn't worry, but one of my neighbors says they saw some guys pushing someone matching Jake's description into a gray van in front of my house. I don't know what to do."

"What did the men look like? What were they wearing? Did she get a license plate?" The questions tumbled from me, sounding oddly calm and thorough, despite the fact that inside I was screaming. It was as if another part of me had taken over—the same part that was able to read a negative imprint and not go crazy. The part that practiced martial art moves until my healing ribs ached.

"Just a minute. I'll ask." She was gone for long seconds. I could hear talking but not individual words. "Okay, I'm back. She didn't notice what they were wearing, so I guess they fit in. She did say there were two men who jumped out of the van. One was Asian, the other white."

My heart had frozen at the word *Asian*. "Was the Asian big? Did he have a scar on his face?"

More seconds passed as Kolonda asked. "She said he was kind of big for an Asian, but she didn't notice a scar."

Shannon had caught up to me. He was on his phone, too, barking orders, but he stopped talking as he saw my face. "What's wrong?"

"It's Jake," I choked out. "He's in trouble."

11

This can't be happening, I thought. Jake, my Jake, taken by men in a gray van? Kolonda had to be mistaken. But the panic in her voice was real. What frightened me more than anything was the connection with the Asian. Did he work for the Saitos? The only thing that made sense was that Russo might have been wrong about them coming here for Dennis. If they were also in town for business, it might involve real estate, and the last thing Jake had told me was that he was going to look into Kolonda's building problem. Could he have uncovered something the Saitos wanted to remain hidden?

It wasn't the only answer. Whoever was behind the attack on me that morning could be using Jake for revenge.

Unfortunately, I still didn't know who had sent the thug. Russo was slipping downward on the list of my suspects, seeing as how he preferred the direct approach in contacting me, but it was hard to believe the Saitos would have heard of me and considered me a danger. So we were back to Kolonda and her buildings again.

Where was the connection? If there was one, I wasn't seeing it. Maybe Jake was involved in other issues I knew nothing about.

"Get Jon and Tracy ready to move," Shannon was saying into his phone. "And get the backup perimeter in place. Call me when it's done." He stepped closer to me. "What happened?"

"I'll call you right back," I said to Kolonda, hanging up. I took Shannon's phone and punched in her number from the caller ID on my phone and handed it back to him. "Name's Kolonda. She says Jake was taken by some men in a van. One of them was a big Asian." I forced myself to leave him and walked over to where Russo and his men were still talking. Silence fell as I approached. I noticed that the private investigator, Ace, had arrived.

"I need the address of the warehouse," I said to Russo. "Please, tell me where it is."

Russo shook his head. "Charlie will take the police there."

"The detective is setting up a perimeter. The Saitos will know. It'll be too late for Dennis." *And for Jake.*

"You think *you're* going in?" Charlie asked, a grin or a sneer beginning on his face. I couldn't tell which.

"My boyfriend was just taken by a big Asian man."

Russo arched a brow. "Can't be related. What would the Saitos want with him?"

"That's what I want to know."

"Autumn." Shannon came up behind me. "I sent someone over. Don't worry. I'm sure it's a misunderstanding."

The feeling in my gut didn't believe him. I might not be able to trust all my instincts anymore, but I knew something was wrong with Jake. I could feel it.

"If you send a lot of men into the area, they'll know you're there," Russo said to Shannon. "You should go with Charlie and one or two others."

"We're only setting up a perimeter. It'll be far enough away that we'll go in unseen."

Russo barked a laugh. "I've never known the police to go in unseen."

"I have. Your man Charlie will come as far as the perimeter, but he won't be coming with us into the warehouse. I need men who don't have another agenda. I think you'll understand why."

"That is not the deal."

"It is now."

Shannon and Russo continued their conversation, but my attention was on Ace, who had moved away and was heading toward a black BMW with dings on the door, which I recognized as having been in the parking lot of Russo's Chinese restaurant. He walked with purpose, and I bet I knew where he was heading.

When I caught up to him, he flashed me his usual secret grin. "Where are you going?" I asked.

"Need a ride somewhere?"

"To Saito's warehouse."

He laughed. "If I were you, that's the last place I'd want to be."

"That's where you're going. I won't get in the way. I can handle myself, I promise."

"I heard what you did to that thug." He plunged his hands in the pocket of his jeans, his shoulders slouching forward. "But he was a cheap hood. The Saitos are experienced."

"You're the one who told Shannon I went to see Russo."

He shrugged one shoulder. "Dealing with Russo is dangerous. When I saw the flat, I knew it was a trap and thought you might not make it out alive."

"Well, I did. I bet Russo's paying you extra to get Dennis before the police mess it up."

"I thought you told the guys at the precinct that you weren't psychic."

I grimaced. "If you don't take me, I'll tell Shannon what you're planning. Even if you do have a working relationship, I get the feeling he doesn't really like you."

"He holds grudges, that's all."

"Make your choice."

"Fine." He opened the doors with his remote. "Get in."

I swung the door open quickly before he could change his mind. As we drove off, I saw Shannon staring after us. His expression was odd, one I'd never seen before—not angry, curious, annoyed, and not even thoughtful. But rather purposely blank, empty. I shivered.

"So, what's the plan?" I asked Ace.

"I sneak in, grab Dennis, and get out."

"You have a gun?" Dumb question. All private detectives I've ever heard of carried concealed weapons.

"Won't need it. No one will see me."

"Us," I corrected. "Russo must have a lot of faith in you."

"They won't even know we're there."

"What about Shannon? Is Russo afraid he'll mess things up?"

Ace's ever-present grin faltered. "It's not him Russo's worried about."

"Oh, I see. Russo's worried that Dennis might not want to rejoin his loving family and that the police will protect him. So, do you plan to force Dennis to go back to New Jersey with Russo?" Because I was going to do everything to assure that didn't happen.

"He'll want to go." Ace's smile was back.

"I doubt it."

"You'll see. Nothing like a man facing death to want to reunite with his family."

"His family is his wife and two children, not the people he ran away from. You know what they are, don't you? You know what kind of life you'll be consigning him to."

Again the one-shouldered shrug. "I'm just doing my job. The rest is up to Dennis."

"That's a cop-out."

Ace simply smiled.

My cell phone vibrated, and I picked it up. "Hi, Tracy," I said, hoping for news of Jake.

"I only have a minute, but I'm calling to find out where you are. Shannon's in a tizzy because you left with some PI."

"What's a tizzy?"

"Never mind. Just something my mom likes to say. So where are you?"

"In a car. I don't know where. I'm trying to find Jake."

"Jake?"

"You haven't heard?" I gave her a hurried explanation.

"I'm sorry, Autumn. I'm sure Shannon's already done it, but I'll double-check that we've sent our best to see what happened with Jake. I'll even look into whatever information he might have been working on. I know an attorney who works a lot in the real estate scene. I promise I'll do everything I can to find him."

"Thanks, Tracy."

"I'd hate to see anything happen to Jake. He's a good guy. In fact, he might be one of the few men who actually knows how to keep his word."

That was girl-speak for once-again-a-man-I-liked-did-a-stupid-thing. "Who's the jerk?" I asked.

"Ian Gideon called last night and asked me out, but he canceled about an hour ago when I was at my mom's. Said something came up with work. Good thing, I guess, since all this came up and Shannon wants my help, but he's still a jerk."

"Maybe Ian really does have to work. His law firm's pretty big, and I bet they have clients who are important enough to force him to give up a hot Saturday night date."

"Naw, I could hear it in his voice. I know when a man is lying to me. Forget Ian. He's not worth another thought. Look, Autumn, I might be out of touch for a while. Shannon and I are following up on Dennis's kidnapping. But I promise we're not forgetting about Jake."

"Thanks." I hung up and looked at Ace. "The police are on their way to the warehouse. Or will be shortly."

"We'll be in and out before they arrive."

We traveled the rest of the way to the docks in silence. As usual, the Willamette River was bustling with activity. Commercial tugs, boats, and even huge freighters and oceangoing barges floated past. Recreational vehicles also used the river, careful to avoid the shipping lanes. On some days it seemed I was the only one who avoided the river.

Finally, Ace parked the car. "It's not far from here. Come on. Stay with me and act natural."

Easier said than done. I was jumpy and unsettled as we made our way past buildings on the waterfront, and I wondered if it was the proximity of the water where I'd lost Winter, or if it had something to do with Jake. Sometimes I could almost feel Jake's presence, as I did my sister's, yet at the moment I felt nothing. Nothing except the oppressive heat, the humidity sticking my shirt to my skin.

Ace stopped walking suddenly and backed up a step, so whatever he'd seen was hidden from my view. "What?" I mouthed.

He jerked his chin in the direction we'd been headed. "Saitos have a lookout. We'll have to go around."

We went another way, weaving around buildings, old equipment, and a couple of rusted fences. Once we had to talk our way past a security guard, and two more times Ace spotted lookouts he was sure belonged to the Saitos, one on a rooftop and another sitting on a pier whittling. I spotted another smoking and leaning up against a wall. All had at least some Asian blood, though the one on the wharf had only the barest hint. Another trait they shared was the constant roaming of their alert eyes and the radios at their waists. Definitely not indigent men whiling away the hours of the day.

"There," Ace said. We were squatting behind some old shipping crates, and he was looking at a large building that had been newly painted an ugly tan color. A few men were coming and going, but no one was loading any kind of freight that might cover our approach.

"So we go around the back?"

He nodded. Still hunching over, he ran to a group of rusted barrels that might have been sitting there for five decades. I touched them and felt the pleasant sensation of hard work and satisfaction. I wondered if they were worth anything from an antiques standpoint. On our trek I'd passed quite a few things I wanted to research before coming back to make the owners an offer. Thinking of the antiques helped keep my fear to a manageable level. Besides, a woman had to eat.

At the barrels, we waited until no one was in sight before running to the side of the building. I felt relief when no shouts broke the normal dockside sounds.

We went cautiously around the back of the warehouse to a pile of broken wooden crates, dented barrels, and other refuse, including a toilet and used paint cans. Ace climbed this with surprising dexterity, his destination apparently the small window in the second floor.

"What if it's locked?"

"Left it open the last time I was here." Seconds later he disappeared. I waited for him to give me the all clear, but he didn't reappear.

I was on my own. I regarded the place, wondering if this was really the best entrance point. My anxiety over Jake didn't allow me to consider long. I scaled the rickety pile of garbage with more than a little reluctance. Random imprints followed my path. Resentment on a paint can, a burst of happiness from a worn metal box, sleepiness from a steering wheel of some sort, and a lever which held the desire for revenge. Once or twice the strength of the imprints took me by surprise, and I had to fight to maintain my balance. Since my antique rings were still on the sink back at my shop, I didn't even have that meager barrier to protect me. I began holding my hands close to the objects in front of me before using them to climb, avoiding all objects that so much as hinted at holding an imprint. I couldn't tell if the imprints were positive or negative before touching them, and it was better not to take a chance.

By the time I hefted myself onto a large metal container at the top of the garbage heap, my hair was plastered to my skull and my damp shirt clung to my skin. The window, its screen long vanished, was partially open, enough for me to squeeze through.

The window opened up into a narrow room filled with more junk, though of slightly higher caliber than the kind outside. Tables, chairs, cabinets, boxed items. Things someone felt they would use again someday and probably never would. Certainly nothing belonging to the Saitos, who had only recently rented the place, according to Russo.

I slid to the door, slowly opening it. Because the storage room was the last one in the dim hallway, there was really only one way to go. No one was in sight, so I started forward, noticing that only the right side of the hallway had doors—and not many of them. I touched the first knob as I passed, unsure if I could read an imprint from this side even if Jake or Dennis had touched the other side, though the emotional requirement of leaving an imprint would likely be met. Jake might even have purposely tried to leave an imprint, if such a thing was possible.

I was thinking about this so hard that I almost didn't hear the person ascending the stairs at the end of the hall. No choice but to make the unlikely sprint to the storage room or try one of the other two doors. I chose a door, praying no one was inside—and that there was a place to hide.

The room was slightly larger than the storage room and completely devoid of junk. A few couches, a refrigerator, a sink, and a microwave brought back memories of the employee break room at Russo's Chinese restaurant. I had barely slipped into the adjoining bathroom when the door opened.

"You can wait right here," a man said, unmasked violence in his voice. Something heavy fell to the floor. Or was pushed.

"Look, I told you everything." Ace's voice, tight with pain.

"Then I have no need of you." The sound of an impact, followed by the footsteps leaving.

When I peeked out a few minutes later, Ace was out cold but not shot or dead. No blood, except from his nose, which was probably broken. His arms and feet were bound tight. "Ace, wake up." I slapped his face gently. Nothing. Nothing but the knot forming at his temple.

So much for no one knowing he'd been there. I'd have to come back for him later or tell Shannon where he was. I couldn't leave now, not without Jake and the others. I debated whether or not to untie Ace, worrying that doing so might alert someone to my presence. In the end I loosened the knot at his hands so he could take off the rope if he awoke but would appear to be tied if someone came in while he was still unconscious.

When I entered the hallway again, voices were coming from the first door near the stairs. Asian words, probably Japanese. I hurried to the stairs. My heart thundered and I felt cold, though it was even hotter in the warehouse than outside. Though cleared of obvious debris, the place smelled of dust that made my nose itch. My feet made more sound than I wanted on the steps, so as I turned on the first landing, I slowed down. There were no doors at the top or the bottom of the stairs or any place to hide if someone came. I felt exposed.

I reached the bottom of the stairs and peered out. I don't know what I expected, but it wasn't this empty cavern that stretched up for two stories. No wonder there hadn't been doors on the left wall. On the far side of the cavern sat four cars of different colors and a dark van. As I watched, a car pulled out of the huge garage-style opening. I waited for more movement and was rewarded when a short Asian man emerged from a doorway at the back of the warehouse, a cigarette dangling from his lips. He also climbed in a car and drove out of the garage, this time shutting the massive door behind him with a remote. I didn't see any doors besides the one where the man had emerged, but I suspected that the door could lead to a hallway and more rooms, similar to the design upstairs.

Two cars and a van. Where were their drivers? I'd heard at least two people in the room upstairs, but that left one more vehicle driver to account for, and any possible passengers.

No more movement. Taking a breath, I sprinted across the open space to the doorway, stopping briefly to crane my neck around the corner before I entered. No one in sight. But there was no hallway or smaller rooms, just one long room that ran along the entire back of the warehouse. Neat rows of new-looking crates were stacked three high, making them a few inches taller than my height. I was curious to know what was inside the crates but more interested in finding Jake.

I eased along the rows, choosing the space by the far wall instead of the main aisle down the middle. Every so often, I stopped to listen. Nothing. I passed two windows covered with such a thick film of greasy dirt that I couldn't see anything but light through them. On one windowsill, lying next to a large hammer, sat a plastic container filled with nails like those in the lids of the crates.

When I passed several kegs with gunpowder labels, I became even more curious about what the Saitos were involved in—and more nervous about being in the warehouse at all. You meet a lot of people growing up as the only child of hippie parents who have all sorts of questionable friends, including a few in the underground Earth Liberation Front, or ELF. My parents had never advocated violence as a way to encourage responsibility for Mother Earth, but their friends' fanaticism had been both frightening and fascinating to observe. During my brief stint in college, I'd even dated one of the "Elves"—until I realized that all those bombs he was making for fun in his dorm were actually being used around campus and local businesses.

I had learned from him about gunpowder. By itself it wasn't highly explosive, like TNT, but it was powerful enough in large amounts or even small amounts, if it was packed tightly. I'd seen enough of my share of homemade explosives not to want to be around if something happened to set those barrels aflame.

I heard a movement and froze. Was it coming from one of the crates? Impatiently I waited until I heard it again and decided it originated at the far end of the room, either from a crate or behind the last row. I moved furtively, trying not to breathe. The rows ended, and I saw a battered desk littered with wrappers, fast-food bags, partly empty drinks, a roll of duct tape, and another box of nails.

From the corner of my eye, I spied a movement where the last row of crates nearly touched the desk. I crept around the desk and saw a pair of jeans-clad legs lying on the floor. The rest of the body was hidden behind the crate.

"Jake?" I whispered. The legs went utterly still. I rushed the last few steps, rounding the crate.

Dennis was lying in the space between the crate and the wall. His hands were tied with rope that had been wrapped through a large cinder block, which in turn had been affixed to the floor with new concrete, if the open bag next to it was any indication. An old red bucket had obviously been used to mix the stuff. Several pieces of duct tape were plastered over Dennis's mouth, but the part of his face I could see was covered with cuts and bruises.

The terror in his eyes faded as he saw me. "M-um," he said.

I didn't ask him if he was okay. Obviously, he wasn't. "Let me get the tape off." I tried to do it gently, but his pained expression drove me to rip it off quickly.

"Thanks," he muttered.

"Where's Jake and Sawyer? Are they here, too?"

He looked at me blankly for a minute. "What do you mean, Sawyer? Did something happen to him?" His mouth trembled, and the despair in his eyes showed that he was near breaking.

"Is anyone here with you? Anyone? Are they holding anyone else?" My voice was harsh, but I couldn't help that.

"I haven't seen anyone."

"Are you sure?"

"No one is near enough to answer when I call out, and I've heard nothing in this room except those men."

I wilted a bit. Of course Jake wasn't here. I'd been too willing to blame his disappearance on the Saitos when I'd heard about the big Asian man, but his being here in exactly the same place and at the same time as Dennis would be too easy. When it came right down to it, there were a fair number of Asians in Portland. The Asian Kolonda's neighbor saw could have been anyone. Maybe even a man who worked at one of Russo's Chinese restaurants.

"Saito's men are responsible for this, right?" I asked.

Dennis nodded, his eyes watering. "At first I thought they were my family."

"I know."

"What did you mean about Sawyer?"

I debated what to tell him, but in the end he would have to know. Maybe knowing would give him the energy to escape this place with me. "He's missing. Someone took him from your back-yard."

"My family."

"Maybe. We don't know. The police are working on it. But you will only be able to help Sawyer if we get out of here."

"It was Nic. I know it was."

"He certainly seems interested in you enough to do something like that. He's working with a private detective and the police to get you out of here."

Dennis smiled grimly. "That's my cousin, always working both sides."

"There has to be something to get this rope off. You aren't going anywhere with this cinder block."

"Try the desk."

Listening first to make sure no one had entered the room during our conversation, I left Dennis and went to search the desk, hoping to find something I could use: a box cutter, scissors, even a knife. I pulled out drawer after drawer with no luck, until finally I found a pack of box cutter blades. No box cutter, but the blades would have to do.

Carefully, I began sawing on Dennis's rope. It was tough trying to hurry and at the same time not to cut myself, knowing any minute I could be discovered. I tried not to think about Jake and where he might be at that moment.

Dennis had managed to sit up, but by the labored way he breathed, I knew he wasn't going to be able to move fast or far. He cradled his right hand against his chest. I suspected some of his fingers had been broken during his interrogation. His forehead glistened with fever.

I planned our escape as I worked on the rope. Dennis's condition limited our choices. I might have to hide him somewhere in the warehouse until Shannon and Tracy arrived. That way even if the Saitos tried to kill Dennis the minute the police were on site, they would have to find him first.

"Ow." I'd cut my finger.

Dennis's head lolled back against the wall. "You should just go. They'll catch you, too."

"I'm not leaving you. Sophie would kill me. Besides, I almost have it."

Then the gunfire began.

CHAPTER

12

Shouts and more gunfire, coming from the main part of the warehouse. Dennis moaned. "You'd better get out of here."

I dragged the blade through the last strands of the rope. "Shut up." I grabbed his arm. "Come on."

This time we used the aisle on the inside wall. I half dragged, half carried Dennis. He was worse off than I'd thought, and our chances for escape were diminishing by the minute.

Reaching the doorway, I pushed him behind a stack of crates. It wasn't a good hiding place, but better than leaving him where he'd been. "Stay here," I whispered.

"As if I could do anything else."

I eased toward the door on hands and knees, peering through the opening. I couldn't see anything, so I inched forward, keeping low to the cement floor. Figures came into view. Shannon and Tracy, surrounded by four Asian men with guns. Tracy was bleeding from a cut on her face. It looked like I'd found all the drivers and passengers to those cars.

As I watched, another Asian man, larger than the rest, his scarred face familiar to me from Dennis's imprint, came inside dragging the too-still body of what I assumed was the third officer Shannon had brought along. From this distance, I couldn't see if the man was breathing, but red clearly stained his clothes.

It looked like a trap. Whatever measures Shannon had taken, they hadn't worked. None of this was going to end well. The Saitos had killed or wounded an officer, and they would have to get rid of the other two and all the evidence, despite the police investigation that would ensue. I had no doubt they could easily rid themselves of three bodies.

Two more Asian men appeared from upstairs, both dressed in slacks and button-up shirts like their colleagues. One was slender and refined and walked with the air of being in charge. Even the big, scarred man inclined his head with deference as they conversed.

Wait. I knew the thin guy. Not so much his narrow face but the outline of his body, the shape of his high cheeks, the way he held his head. I'd seen him in Dennis's terror-filled phone imprint, bending over a still body, gun in hand. Joben Saito.

Though I'd never met Saito, Dennis's fear froze me in place.

Think, I told myself. *Saito is just another bad guy.*

I had a choice. I could try to get Dennis out one of the back windows while they were occupied and contact the police when we were free. I could call now and risk being overheard as I tried to get someone at the station to take me seriously. Or I could cause a diversion that might free Shannon and Tracy but was more likely to get us all killed.

It wasn't that I liked the most chancy plan, but I didn't have much hope of Shannon and Tracy surviving until their backup arrived. The Saitos must have been ready for their arrival, and if someone had tipped them off, they would also know they had to get rid of Shannon and Tracy quickly.

If I made the wrong decision, I'd have to live with it the rest of my life.

I had to try.

The gunpowder had given me the idea, but I would need something the right size to pack it in. Not too small and not too big either. I didn't want to kill the people I was trying to save.

I hadn't seen anything inside the warehouse that would work, but that pile of junk outside was an ELF bomber's haven—provided I could get the window open.

I moved fast, balancing the need for stealth with the ticking clock. As I made my way toward Dennis, I texted a short message and the general location of the warehouse to the police, wishing I had paid closer attention to the actual address. But if someone believed my text, they would contact the rest of Shannon's team on the perimeter and they would know where to move in.

When I returned to Dennis, he had his eyes closed. "Dennis," I said. "Dennis!"

"Huh?"

"The police are here, but it looks like they sprang a trap. I'm going to make a diversion, see if they can get away. Do you know anything about explosives?"

Dennis thought a moment. His breathing seemed more labored. "I made a few pipe bombs when I younger, but my aunt stopped that. So, no, I don't know much."

"I'll figure something out." Which mostly meant deciding how much gunpowder to use.

I hurried to the far back window that should be buried under the pile of junk Ace and I had climbed earlier. The window opened without too much problem, though junk blocked the opening completely. Frantically, I began pulling handfuls of garbage into the room, pushing aside larger chunks that wouldn't fit inside the window opening. My hands touched odd metal pieces, a pillow, an old flashlight, ancient clothes, a bag of something so smelly, I didn't dare open it.

Occasionally imprints assailed me, but most were long faded. No one had treasured this junk so far down in the pile for a long time, or felt anything traumatic about it. As I brought garbage inside, other trash from above sank into its place. I was beginning to lose hope of finding anything useful when at last I discovered a small can, tin-plated steel by the look of it, and with a tiny opening on the top. It would do. I hoped.

Opening a gunpowder keg with the claw side of the big hammer from the other windowsill, I filled the can with the dark powder. Next, in went the foil burger wrappers from the fast-food bags on the desk. Using a blunt piece of metal I'd found in the junk, I compacted the stuff as well as I could. Did I need more gunpowder? Less? How much was too much?

I remembered something about fuses from my stint in college, but I didn't have potassium or sugar. I did have gunpowder, and my ELF friend had talked about using that for a quick-burning fuse. Well, I needed quick. I straightened out a crumpled napkin, tore off an inch-wide piece on its longest side, and lined it with a bit of black powder. I was supposed to moisten it, I remembered, but I had no time to let it dry. Instead, I took threads from cloth I'd found in the garbage pile, dipped them in the remains of a soft drink, blotting them nearly dry, and rolled them in the gun powder until the string was thickly covered. I rolled this up tight in the piece of napkin, twisting it. Powder seeped out. I didn't think that was supposed to happen.

I felt nauseated as I finished off the can, shoving more foil inside the hole of the lid, followed by a piece of metal I duct-taped over the hole. For good measure I wrapped the whole thing in duct tape.

Too late I realized I didn't have any way to light it.

Tears of frustration pricked my eyes. If Tawnia were here, she'd reach in her purse and pull out a lighter she would probably have there in case she had to make an emergency fire. She paid close attention at our church's disaster preparedness fairs.

There had to be something here. At least one of Saito's men had been smoking, and they might have used a lighter. Could he have left it behind? I rummaged through the drawers but found nothing. All the while, minutes ticked by.

What was I going to do?

There was really only one thing I could do because rubbing two pieces of wooden crates together would take too long, and I'd already wasted too much time. Get Dennis out of here and call the police.

Sticking the small can into my front pants pocket, I hurried back to him. It took a lot of pushing and pulling and prodding to get him to a window not covered by the garbage, but somehow I managed. "You okay?" I hissed after I'd shoved him outside and he'd crumpled onto the ground in a heap.

He lifted his good hand. "Fine."

Feeling for my cell phone, I began to climb out the window, glad I'd charged the battery last night. Or had it been the night before last?

Battery.

I took my foot from the windowsill. I didn't have steel wool, which was the easiest way to start a flame with a battery, but there had been some really thin wire in the garbage that wasn't too rusted. Any friend of an ELF activist could light a fuse with a battery and wire.

I shut the window as it had been before, hoping that if I was caught, they wouldn't think to look for Dennis outside there until he could get to safety. Of course, he hadn't looked like he was going anywhere, much less to somewhere safe.

I sprinted to the other window that I'd left open and began searching through the garbage on the floor for the wire. I found it behind the odorous plastic bag. Wrinkling my nose, I bent the end back and forth until it broke off. Now for the phone battery.

Voices were coming closer, and I ducked behind the crates. I peeked out and saw two men rummaging in a crate near the door. When they left, they held a knife and a length of rope like that which had held Dennis.

Great. I might be too late to do any good.

Holding the wire to the positive and negative ends of the battery, I edged my way to the door. I didn't have to start a fire—just get the wire hot enough so the end of the fuse would catch. The wire was already warm in my hands. I held the end of the fuse up to it. The wire grew hot enough to burn my fingers, and mere seconds passed before the end of the fuse lit. At least that much was working.

A bit too fast. Trying not to panic, I leaned out the door and heaved the can. It didn't go as far as I'd hoped, but it would have to do.

"What's that?" the big Asian growled. His question was followed by a myriad of comments.

"Who's there?"

"Looks like a bomb."

"Everyone get back."

"Let's make the cop go get it."

Nothing happened. Had there been too much water left in the fuse? I supposed that not going off at all was better than blowing the whole place up with everyone in it, though with what I bet the Saitos had planned for us, that was debatable.

"It's nothing," someone said with a laugh. "A dud."

"Get it. And go find who threw it." This I was sure came from Saito himself. I turned to flee. The window was my only hope at this point. Maybe my phone still had enough battery to call for help if I could get clear.

A tremendous boom shook the warehouse. I stumbled and fell.

I wondered if any of them were laughing now.

That's when I noticed the inside wall was on fire, smoke rapidly spreading over the ceiling.

"Stop right there!"

I turned, my hands lifted, nearly sinking to my knees when I saw Shannon.

He lowered the gun he must have reclaimed from his captors. "I thought I saw you roll out that can."

"What about the Saitos?"

"Some are unconscious from the blast, and I took out two who didn't escape outside. Come on. We still have to make it out of here."

"The window," I said.

"I can't leave Tracy and Jon. He's hurt pretty bad."

"Dennis is outside."

"We'll go around and get him. The fire will take time to spread there."

I ran with Shannon to the main room where Tracy was standing over one of Saito's men, lifting several sets of keys from the fallen man's pocket. "I think one of these is to the van. Same brand name on the key chain."

Shannon and I carried the unconscious Jon to the van, whose backseats had all been removed.

"How'd you get here, anyway?" Shannon asked me as we shut the doors. "And inside without being seen? It was as if they knew we were coming."

"Ace brought me. We sneaked in through an upstairs window—oh, no! Ace." That sick feeling was back. I'd started the fire, and it would kill Ace if we didn't help him. "He's still upstairs. They caught him."

We all looked to where the fire was greedily consuming the wall. The metal shell of the warehouse might survive, but the back room and the upstairs would be a complete loss. Ace wouldn't stand a chance.

With a frustrated grunt, Shannon growled at Tracy. "Get them out of here."

"I'll get Ace," I said.

Shannon waved his hand. "I have the gun. Believe me, I'd love to let him rot, but I can't."

I wondered about the grudge Ace had mentioned. What had happened between them, and why would Shannon risk his life for a man he obviously didn't like or respect?

We stared at each other for several precious seconds. I realized I was more worried about him than I wanted to be. "The room at the end of the upstairs hall has a way out the window," I said.

"Thanks." Shannon's gaze shifted to Tracy. "They'll probably be outside waiting for you. If Autumn drives, you'll be free to shoot. Go now. Hurry." Shannon reached out and gave me a little shove.

I obeyed, more out of responsibility than of anything else. I didn't want Tracy and the other officer's life on my hands as well. Sweat poured from my brow, the fire adding to the heat of the day. As I took the keys from Tracy and climbed into the van, two of Saito's men came back inside, guns drawn. The big Asian with a scar ran after Shannon up the stairs. The other came in our direction.

I revved the engine, preparing to barrel though the closed garage door, but Tracy had found an opener. Her face had lost all color, except for the blood from her cut, but she held the gun steady and fired at the oncoming man as I squealed out of the warehouse.

"Where are you going?" Tracy asked as I dragged the wheel heavily to the right, heading around to the back of the warehouse. "They broke our cell phones and took out the batteries, so we'll have to drive to our backup or we'll be no good to Shannon."

"I can't leave Dennis. Here, try my phone."

With one hand, Tracy tried my phone. "Nope. Dead."

Exactly what I'd feared. "Then we'd better be fast."

Dennis wasn't where I'd left him. He'd crawled about thirty yards—unfortunately, in the wrong direction, past the hill of garbage next to the warehouse and toward a huge chainlink fence around the back of the property that he'd never have been able to climb. I slammed on my brakes, jumped from the van, and rushed to his side.

"Help me!" I yelled at Tracy, scanning the window above the garbage heap. No Shannon.

Tracy was already on her way, tucking her gun into her holster. Together, we dragged Dennis to the van and loaded him inside, where he lay back with a sigh of relief.

"Oh, no!" Tracy jumped into the back of the van, past Dennis, where her fellow officer was convulsing, his face turning blue. Checking his pulse, she bent over him and began pumping his chest.

I slammed the double doors shut, knowing I had to drive the man somewhere fast or watch him die. My chest tightened with the knowledge that it might already be too late.

I hadn't taken two steps when the window above the junk pile behind me flew open and Shannon appeared carrying Ace. He set Ace on the garbage, climbed through himself, shouldered Ace again, and clambered down the other side like a crazed man. Smoke streamed from the window.

Seconds later, the big Asian emerged from the smoke, moving through the window with more skill than such a large man deserved. His gun was drawn.

Shannon wasn't going to make it.

I ran to the pile, swooping up a piece of old two-by-four. The Asian jumped the rest of the way to the ground and raised his gun, all his focus on Shannon. I slammed the two-by-four at his head. He staggered but didn't go down. Shannon dumped Ace and reached for his gun. I swung again. No matter his profession, I didn't want to see the Asian gunned down in any future nightmares I might have. The man fell, and this time he stayed down.

"Thanks," Shannon grunted.

"You're welcome. Now we're even. You saved my life at the commune, and now I've saved yours."

"We still have to get out of here."

We hurried to the van. I threw open the back doors, and Shannon dropped Ace inside. Tracy was no longer doing CPR on Jon, and he seemed to be breathing on his own. A little of the tightness around my heart lessened.

"Watch him," Tracy said to Shannon, pulling herself into the driver's seat.

I jumped in, and she peeled out before I had the back doors all the way closed. We weren't half a block away before a much larger explosion shook the van. The windows in surrounding buildings shattered.

Shannon looked at me as if expecting an explanation.

"There was a lot of gunpowder in the warehouse," I said. "Kegs of it. And a lot of crates, but I don't know what was inside those."

"Could be guns or other weapons. Probably shipping them overseas to terrorists."

"Not anymore."

He flashed me a smile. "Nope."

159

Shannon slid closer to the unconscious officer. "Hold on, Jon. You're going to be okay. Just hold on."

I bent over Ace, but besides the bump on his head, he didn't seem damaged. "Wake up!" I shouted at him, my voice only marginally sympathetic. I was still annoyed by how he'd deserted me at the warehouse.

After a few more attempts, Ace's eyes fluttered. "Huh? Oh, it's you. Where are we?"

"Never mind him," Shannon said. "What about Dennis?"

Dennis was unconscious, but he had a pulse. "I don't know. His breathing is bad."

"The only reason he's alive at all is because he didn't tell the Saitos what they wanted to know."

"Yeah, but what was that?"

"Maybe he'll tell us."

We passed a few seconds in silence, and then I said more quietly, "Sawyer wasn't there. Jake, either."

"Ah, so that's why you were there."

"We're lucky she was," Tracy said over her shoulder.

Shannon didn't reply, but he crawled between the two front seats, ready and watching. The gun in his hand reminded me that we weren't safe, not yet.

Tracy took a sharp corner, throwing us into the wall of the van. Dennis opened his eyes at the impact, his left hand fumbling in his pocket. "Need to call Sophie," he muttered. "Make sure she takes care of Sawyer."

"Sh," I said. "I'll talk to her." He obviously didn't remember what I'd said about his son, or his fever was messing with his mind.

He had something in his unbroken hand, but it was too small for a cell phone. "You've got to be kidding," I said. "You have a lighter? All along you had a lighter?"

"Took it from them. But the rollers are too stiff for my left hand. Couldn't get it to stay lit long enough to burn the rope."

I started to try out the lighter myself but dropped it immediately when a terror-filled imprint flared in my mind. I'd experienced enough terror in that warehouse without tapping into Dennis's.

"Did you hear anyone tell them we were coming?" Shannon asked.

Dennis stared at him mutely, and Shannon had to repeat the question. Dennis nodded but before he could speak, Ace said, "It was me. They were going to kill me. I had to give them something."

In one motion, Shannon was at his throat, shaking him. "You miserable little weasel. I should have known."

"Thanks for coming back for me," Ace muttered.

Shannon shoved him away. "I should have let you burn. You almost got yourself and the rest of us killed."

"I'm sorry." Ace lifted his head and met Shannon's eyes. "I'm sorry about everything."

His apology seemed to be for more than his betrayal, but I couldn't ask about it with Shannon glaring at him. Besides, it wasn't my business.

In strangled silence we made it to the police perimeter where we called for an ambulance. Dennis, Jon, and Ace were treated and carted off, and Tracy was ordered to the hospital for stitches on her cheek.

"I can go in later," Tracy said to Shannon. "I want to go with you to get the Saitos."

"Sorry. Hospital first. Peirce will drive you."

"You wouldn't go in." She gave Shannon a dark look, but he was already moving away, barking orders. The wail of fire trucks and police cars made a cacophony in the confusion, and I for one was glad to leave the area. Now that Dennis was safe and Jake nowhere near the Saitos, I had no issue with them. I needed to get to

Kolonda's and figure out what had happened to Jake. She could at least tell me the name of the shady contractor who was giving her problems. That was my only lead at the moment. With my dead cell phone and no wheels, though, how to get there was another issue.

"We'll give you a ride," Tracy offered. "Better yet, come with me to the hospital. We can get my face fixed, check on Jon and Dennis, and then talk to the officers we sent to look into Jake's disappearance."

"Can't you call them now?"

"I already left a message. They'll call me back when they can." She had another cell phone now, co-opted from one of the other officers.

"Okay." Though I knew I'd get more inside information by sticking with her, it still chafed that I was doing nothing immediate to recover Jake. A pit was growing in my stomach. What would I do if I lost him?

CHAPTER

13

An hour later the doctor cleared Tracy to leave the hospital, but she was fuming at the news that Saito and most of his men had escaped Shannon's second raid. The two men taken into custody refused to say a word, except to deny they knew anyone named Saito. Shannon hauled them down to the precinct to see what more he could extract.

"We should have shot them all at the warehouse," Tracy muttered.

"Uh, we were rather busy trying not to get shot ourselves," I reminded her. "Not all of us succeeded."

She grimaced. "Poor Jon. Let's check on him and Dennis and get out of here. If those officers haven't called about Jake by then, we'll go to Kolonda's and investigate ourselves."

Jon was in the ICU and not yet conscious, though his condition was stable. Tracy teared up at the news of her colleague. "He'll be okay," she said. "He's a strong man, always a fighter."

I hadn't known Jon at all, but I felt Tracy's concern. "I hope he will."

Outside Dennis's door stood a uniformed police officer, who let us in after verifying Tracy's clearance. He frowned at my bare feet, but like all of the hospital personnel, he didn't say anything—probably because I was with Tracy. Even without a uniform and her gun concealed, her every movement screamed detective.

Dennis was conscious and stable, though suffering from a bruised kidney and numerous broken bones. The medications he'd received made it hard for him to focus, but he gripped my hand and said, "Thanks for everything. I'd still be there if you hadn't shown up."

"So you owe me one." I felt uncomfortable with his thanks since the real reason I'd gone was to find Jake.

"About my son," he began.

I'd been giving that some thought, too, and Russo was once again my primary suspect. If I was right, Sawyer was safe for the moment—at least physically. The only thing that bugged me was Russo's reaction when he'd heard the child was missing. Was he really that good an actor? Probably, but I saw no reason for him to go to such effort to act so convincingly when I had no proof and he could always deny everything to the police.

"You said at the warehouse you thought your cousin had him," I said.

Dennis gave a short nod. "Has to be him. They want an heir, and if I'm not available, Sawyer will do. But I won't let them have my little boy or allow him to be sucked into that life. I've been loyal to my family, even though I know they'll never believe that. I've always known they'd see me dead if they found me and I refused to return to them. But I'll tell the police everything I know before I'll go with them or let them have Sawyer. It's been years since I left, but I still know enough about their operation to make it worth the police hiding us. Not until Sawyer's safely home, though. I want protection, a new identity. For all of us."

"I'm sure that can be arranged." I leaned on the edge of his bed, exhaustion creeping through my body. I needed protein or sleep—or both. "You're sure Saito didn't have Sawyer?"

"Saito would have used him against me."

"What did Saito want from you?"

"Information."

"About your family's business? After five years?"

"Like I said, I still know plenty Saito or the cops could use, but that's not why he's after me."

"Why, then?"

Dennis's eyes dropped as he said quietly, "He wanted to know what happened to his son."

"His son?"

"Yes."

Dennis didn't say more, and I looked at Tracy for help.

"Our information says that Saito's oldest son went missing about six years ago," Tracy said. "His body was never found. Because he was suspected of arms dealing and drug trafficking, he was on the police radar, but he simply vanished. Probably living it up in Europe."

"No, he's dead," Dennis said. "Saito knew that already. He wanted justice—and he wanted to know where his son is buried."

"And how would you know all that?" I asked.

Dennis's jaw worked, and his eyes went from me to Tracy and back again, as though deciding if he should speak. His nostrils flared as he took a breath. "Because I killed him." Dennis choked on the last word, and tears gathered in his eyes. "Well, Bart killed him, but I was there. I could have stopped him. It was my fault every bit as much as it was Bart's. I helped him hide the body. Saito and his son were cutting into family profits, so we took out the son.

He was a terrible man, but it wasn't our job to decide his fate. He left behind two small sons. I couldn't live with myself after that. His death haunted me. I decided that if I could ever find a way out, I'd take it."

"Saito suspects you?"

"Bart told him we did it. Right before Saito killed him."

"That meeting five years ago wasn't for negotiation then?"

Dennis stared at the wall, his voice empty. "We were supposed to lure Saito there and get rid of him once and for all. I didn't want to go, but I couldn't let Bart go by himself. He was so cocky because it was just us and Saito, and he'd already killed Saito's son. But Saito was too fast. He shot Bart and then asked me where his son's body was. He would have killed me, too, if it hadn't been for the police sirens." His voice grew higher and more agitated. "Saito was distracted, and I knocked his gun out of his hand and ran. He came after me. I tripped and fell, and I thought it was all over, but I guess he decided not to kill me before he knew for sure where we'd put his son. The police arrived, and he took off. I ran away, too— and kept running."

"Your aunt helped you, didn't she?"

Dennis's eyes snapped back to mine. "How did you know?"

"From some things Nic Russo said about her, and Sophie told me you went to see an aunt once. I didn't think you would have been able to hide so well without help."

"She gave me money. Connected me with someone who could arrange a new identity. She hates the life as much as I did. She stayed all those years only because of me and Nic. Well, and fear of what my father—her brother—would do to her."

"Does Russo know?"

He shook his head. "Definitely not."

I remembered the affection Russo had displayed for his mother, and I wondered if she could intervene in Dennis's situation now, perhaps mediate between him and her brother. Not likely if she was still trapped in the life she detested.

"They'll try to kill me now," Dennis said. "If they think I'll say anything. Nic is loyal to my father. His own father disappeared when he was only a baby. He was always more my father's son than I was."

"Your father won't just let you go?"

Dennis shook his head. "It's all or nothing with the Franco family, but I can't live that life."

"Unless it's for Sawyer."

The pain in his face told me that was true. He wouldn't abandon his son, and I knew Sophie wouldn't either. They'd lost the chance to live their own lives.

"He'll be coming to see me soon," Dennis said.

Tracy and I shared a determined glance. "Don't stop fighting yet," Tracy told him. "Russo doesn't know you're alive. We're keeping that under wraps for now."

Dennis nodded, but we all knew that if Russo had Sawyer, it wouldn't really matter. He would own Dennis, heart and soul.

We left Dennis's room more depressed than when we entered. Tracy drew out her phone and began texting. "I have to let Shannon know what we're up against." She sighed. "He sure doesn't seem the murdering type, does he?"

"Dennis? That's because he's not. You heard him—his brother dragged him into it. What choice did he have?"

"Good point. Hopefully the prosecution will see it that way."

"If we don't get him away from Russo, it won't matter. The Franco family will have a team of top attorneys ready to defend him. He'll never be allowed to testify, so it will be his attorneys' denial against your testimony."

"And yours."

"Not if it's to send Dennis to jail. I'm trying to save him, not throw him back into the bosom of his viperous family when he's done everything he can to leave that life. The police need to find Sawyer so Russo has nothing to hold over Dennis. Then Dennis can pass along information—perhaps not even related to his family—that'll be enough to cut a deal with the prosecution."

Tracy nodded. "Could be the prosecution wouldn't go after him anyway. Pretty hard to prove a murder with no body. No way his lawyers would allow him to give us that information."

We were heading toward the elevator that led to the lobby, and though I was itching to find out about Jake, I forced myself to say, "We're not going to check on Ace before we leave?"

Tracy snorted. "I don't care about Ace. Besides, he's too ornery to die."

"What happened between him and Shannon, anyway?"

"You heard about that?"

"No. It's the way they act. They work together, but they don't seem to like each other at all."

"It's about a woman." She rolled her eyes. "It's always about a woman."

"They fought over a woman? I find that hard to believe."

"Me, too. Happened before I was out of school. She was a police officer, and she and Shannon dated for a while, but she quit to go into private detective work with Ace. He'd left the force a few years earlier and kept teasing her about joining him until finally she did. She was killed during one of their investigations."

No wonder Shannon hated Ace. "Was she still seeing Shannon at the time?"

"On and off, I think. She liked Ace too. Believe it or not, he can be very charming."

Creepy was more the word I'd use, with his odd, ever-present smile, but where women and men were concerned, sometimes it was impossible to understand attraction.

Despite my curiosity about Shannon's love life, which was none of my business and therefore more interesting, I was only half listening by this time because a familiar chord of recognition was growing in my chest. I looked up to see Tawnia coming from the elevator. With her was Sophie, carrying baby Lizbeth.

"Autumn!" Tawnia was moving fast for a pregnant woman.

"Thank you so much!" Sophie threw herself at me, barely avoiding squishing Lizbeth between us. "I spoke to Dennis on the phone. He wasn't making much sense, but he said you found him."

"It's true," Tracy said. "Without Autumn, things might have ended very differently."

"Are you okay?" Tawnia looked pointedly at the bandage on Tracy's face. Now that I paid attention, Tracy appeared rather gruesome with dried blood staining her shirt.

"I'm fine. Just a few stitches," Tracy said.

Tawnia rounded on me almost accusingly, her eyes taking in my garbage-ruined shirt. I was glad I'd washed my hands, face, and even my feet in the hospital bathroom. "They said there was an explosion."

"Yeah, uh, I had to make a distraction." I could see my sister wanted to lecture me on putting myself in danger, but I was saved by Sophie's next words.

"About my boy. Is there any word?"

Tracy shook her head. "Not yet, but we do have leads. Someone saw a black sedan leaving the area. We're fairly confident that whoever took him didn't intend to hurt him."

"Dennis thinks it was his cousin," I added.

"Cousin?" Sophie looked confused. "I don't understand. Everyone keeps asking me about Dennis's family, but he doesn't have family, except that old aunt who died."

I gave her a sympathetic smile. "Dennis will explain." It wasn't going to be easy for him, telling his wife about his past life, and especially his part in a murder.

"Give your ID to the officer at the door," Tracy told her. "You're cleared to go in." She looked at Tawnia. "Unfortunately, you aren't unless an officer is in the room."

Tawnia waved the words away. "I'll be okay. I can hold Lizbeth in the hall." She looked at me. "Are you really all right?"

I wanted to tell her about Jake getting mixed up in Kolonda's apartment problems, but there wasn't time. If I got started now, I'd be in no condition to search for Jake. "We'll talk later," I said to her. "Tracy and I have some wrapping up to do."

"Wait." Tawnia opened her purse and withdrew a tiny picture of the two of us, the one we'd taken together last year after she'd cut her hair so we could see how alike we looked. Except unlike the larger copy I kept in my apartment, this one she'd drawn herself, line after intricate line, using watercolor pencils to fill in the tiny bit of color. Removing the protective plastic sleeve, she placed it in my hand. Love flooded me as I took the drawing, so sweet and warm that it felt like honey on my tongue. Not so much a vision of a certain place and time, though I could clearly see Tawnia's hands working over the page, but a constant, delicious feeling.

"Does it work?" she asked.

"Yeah." I was perking up already.

She gave me a smug grin. "I thought of how much you mean to me every second I worked on it. I finished it this afternoon. It's small so you can always carry it with you."

I hugged my sister. "Thanks."

I put the drawing back in the plastic and in my pocket, but before we could leave, Sophie's hand reached out to Tracy's arm. "Please find my little boy. He's going to be so scared."

"Or he might be wrapping everyone around his little finger." I gave her an encouraging smile. Sawyer was one of the most fearless kids I knew, and what I was saying could well be true.

"Thanks," Sophie whispered, but she was crying again as she started down the hall.

"I'll take care of her." Pressing something else into my hand, my twin started after her.

"Take care of little Oak, too," I called.

Tawnia looked over her shoulder and grinned. "I'm not naming my baby Oak."

"Not even a middle name?"

Not answering, she hurried after Sophie.

I looked at what she'd given me. It was a pink-wrapped Bellybar, like those she'd practically survived on during her first months of pregnancy and still carried in her purse for emergencies. Plenty of protein and sugar to keep me going. I wanted to yell after her and ask if she also carried a lighter.

Tracy read the wording and arched a brow. "Is there something you're not telling me?"

"Yeah, right." I ripped open the wrapper and took a bite as we stepped into the elevator. "Try calling those officers again."

This time someone answered. Tracy frowned in concentration as she listened to the officers. "Well, go back to the scene," she said. "Do another sweep. There has to be something."

She listened for a minute more before rolling her eyes. "The university medical facility? No, you don't have time to check out a robbery there. This has priority. They took what? Yuck. People are really sick these days. Look, ask dispatch to send someone else, or it'll have to wait. Let me know if you turn up anything. Do a wider perimeter just in case." She shook her head as she hung up.

"What?" I said.

"Someone broke in and took a donated cadaver at the university." Tracy made a face. "Probably a fraternity prank."

"I meant with Jake."

"The officers have talked to all the neighbors and went to see Tony Blancher the contractor—who apparently is such a disagreeable man that they'd love to throw him in jail if they had any excuse at all—but they've found no new clues as to who grabbed Jake or why. The neighbor stands by her claim, though. They're sure she's a reliable witness."

"So what now?" I'd planned to go over to Kolonda's myself, but it was unlikely I could find something in the street that the police and Kolonda hadn't, and Jake wouldn't have left imprints on the ground through his shoes.

"Now we take a little drive to see that attorney I told you about who works in the real estate scene. Maybe she has something for us." There was a light in her eyes as she spoke, and I knew her decision to act relieved the tension she felt at not being involved in interrogating Saito's men.

"I hope so," I said. "Though you do remember it's your day off, right?"

"I have nothing better to do, anyway, since Ian Gideon broke our date."

"His loss."

"Darn right it is. The jerk."

I smiled at her choice of words. I'd never heard Tracy cuss, not even when she was really upset. I admired that.

When we reached the lobby of the hospital, the sight of Nicholas Russo pulled me up short. I hesitated only an instant before launching myself at him. His appearance reminded me that the Saitos weren't the only ones with an Asian connection. Kolonda's neighbor wouldn't be able to distinguish Saito's men from Russo's restaurant employees.

Russo's bodyguard, Charlie, pushed me away, his hand going to his waist where I knew he kept his gun.

"Don't even think about it," Tracy warned Charlie. Her iron grip prevented me from going at Russo again.

"Where is he?" I hissed. "Where'd you take Jake!"

Russo blinked at me. "I don't know what you're talking about."

I could almost believe him, he was so sincere, but I knew he made a business out of lying.

"I swear, if you hurt him in any way, I'll hunt you down and make you pay!" Big words, but that was how I felt.

Russo didn't look in the least disturbed, which made me angrier. "I don't know anything about your boyfriend. I'm here because of Damian."

"How did you—" But I knew how he'd heard. Ace had been hurt, but he'd been conscious. He must have asked for a phone the minute he arrived at the hospital.

"The fact that you know who Jake is tells me you could be responsible." Tracy's voice was icy enough to strike terror into any normal perp. "As for Dennis, you stay away from him. The officer at the door has strict orders not to let you see him."

Russo frowned, his face darkening. "Why? I'm his cousin. I'm *family*. Family is everything. Damian knows that, or will remember it soon enough."

"You stay away from him," I echoed. "I didn't save him to turn him over to you."

"He'll want to see me. I may be the only chance he has to see his son alive again."

"Is that a confession?" Tracy snapped.

Russo blinked slowly. "A fact. Nothing more. I know how to get things done. I found Damian, didn't I?"

"Thanks to your private detective's big mouth, we almost got killed." I stepped closer to him, but again Tracy held me back.

"I realize that." To my surprise, Russo's broad face became conciliatory. "Apparently, I am in your debt for saving my cousin's life.

Think what you like about me, but I do care about my cousin."
A smirk touched one corner of his mouth, and I was sure he was
mocking me.

"If you owe me, then tell me where Jake is." It couldn't hurt to
ask.

Russo's eyes held mine, the warm blue of the sky, and I could
almost believe he felt compassion. "I'll see what I can find out."
With that he stepped past me, leaving me feeling frustrated and
revengeful. And longing for Jake.

"Come on, Autumn. I'll call and let the officer know not to let
Russo see Dennis. It'll be okay."

She was wrong. I was betting Russo had Sawyer and that meant
Dennis and Sophie would have no choice but to do anything they
could to get their son back. Tears stung my eyes, but I wouldn't let
them fall. I had to concentrate on Jake.

Peirce had left his squad car for Tracy, so a short time later
we stood at the door to a two-story house in an upscale part of
Portland. The door was opened by a fifty-something woman with
dark hair swept on top of her head, revealing her long, graceful
neck. Her body in its flowing, wide-legged yellow pantsuit was trim
and firm. She looked great for any age, and I wondered if it was due
to good genes or a large paycheck.

"Claire, this is Autumn Rain, who's working with me on our
missing person case. Autumn, this is my friend Claire Philpot."

"Nice to meet you," we said, shaking hands. Her eyes traveled
down to my bare feet, which she regarded a bit too long for my
comfort. That seemed odd, because she wasn't wearing shoes either, only thin socks, and by the few pairs near the door, I was
sure her house was a no-shoe house anyway. I'd washed my feet
thoroughly at the hospital, so they were cleaner than Tracy's shoes.

"Come inside," she said, regaining her composure.

Sure enough, Tracy removed her shoes at the door, revealing a tiny hole in her sock near the joint of her left big toe.

The large entryway felt cool and lovely compared to the warm evening air outside and the heat I'd been feeling since the fire.

"I'm glad you came," Claire said as she led the way to a plush sitting room. She had light brown eyes that might have been plain, except for the perfect accenting of her makeup. "I think you'll be interested in what I uncovered. Please, sit down. You both look a little the worse for wear. When you called, I asked my housekeeper to prepare a tray. I take it neither of you has had dinner?"

Tracy and I exchanged a look. I didn't think my dirty clothes would leave a stain on Claire's leather sofa, and the blood on Tracy's blouse was long dried, but we did indeed look bedraggled. I hadn't eaten since lunch at the store, and Tracy probably hadn't since she left her mother's party. In fact, until that moment I hadn't realized how late it was—eight-thirty. Only five and half hours since I'd left my shop, though I felt I'd lived a lifetime in that warehouse. Worse, it would be dark soon, and I was no closer to finding Jake.

"Thank you," Tracy said gracefully. Despite her ruined clothes, she looked at home against the expensive decor, and it flitted through my mind again what a mistake Ian was making. No doubt he'd ask her out again, but he'd get nowhere with her now. He'd have to derive his comfort from whatever he'd felt was more important than courting Tracy.

The housekeeper brought a tray loaded with fruit, vegetables, and different kinds of finger sandwiches. I greedily ate the ones made with wheat bread, while Tracy started in on the white. I wanted to ask if the fruit was organically grown, but I knew it would be rude, and at this point, I was happy to take what I could get. When asked what we preferred to drink, I went for herbal iced tea, while Tracy asked for a soft drink.

"So," I said, the second I could make myself stop cramming in food. Though Tracy was only nibbling, I made up for both of us. I told myself I had to keep myself strong for Jake.

"A friend of mine heard from a friend of hers, whose husband is a city councilman, that the city council has discussed rezoning the area your missing man was interested in."

"Let me guess," Tracy said. "They're changing it to a commercial zone."

"Exactly—if it's all approved, of course. Apparently, at least one investor has already submitted a plan for a huge, block-long shopping center, with several key stores and restaurants committed. It's really an excellent place for commercial development, as the newer residential developments surrounding the area currently have a long way to travel for necessities. Not only will this clean up some of the more rundown buildings and generate a nice tax income for the city, but it will add convenience to a lot of people's lives."

"What if the current owners don't want to sell?" I asked.

Claire smiled. "If the plan is approved, they'll be offered enough that they'll be begging to sell."

"When would that approval go through?"

"I'd say by the end of the year, first of next. But deals like this don't happen overnight. It has to have been in the works at least a year. Behind closed doors, of course."

"So whoever owns the property at the time the announcement is finally made will make a hefty sum selling to developers, right?" I took another sandwich, my mind working hard.

"Unless they want to develop the property themselves. Build a store or whatever."

My sandwich hesitated in midair. "Have there been a lot of property sales in that area?"

Claire's smile grew wider. She looked at Tracy. "I see why you're working with her. She gets right to it."

I wasn't sure if that was as much a compliment on my

intelligence as it was a snide dig on my scraggly appearance. I decided not to take offense. I didn't care what this rich, beautiful woman thought as long as she helped me find Jake.

"You don't know the half of it." Tracy grinned. "Seems she helps solve all my cases these days. They ought to hire her."

Not that I would accept, though I was thinking about charging a fee for my consulting services. It would go a long way to paying the mortgage on my store. "Well?" I prompted.

Claire returned her attention to me. "The county has recorded many more sales than usual in the past few months, far more than can be attributed to the recovering economy. I'd say someone is certain the rezoning will take place. Some of the former property owners might be upset when they learn they could have sold for drastically more only a year later, but there'll be nothing they can do about it."

"Who's buying the land?"

"Several different contractors and developers, but at least six I know are dummy corporations. It'll take time to trace them back to the real owners, though. We won't get any more information today."

"It's enough." Tracy speared a piece of cantaloupe with her fork.

"Could be Russo," I said. "He's into construction and restaurants, and he wouldn't think twice about cheating Kolonda and others out of a nice profit."

"It could be anyone," Tracy countered.

"I don't know who this Russo is," Claire said, "but I have to disagree with you, Tracy. Not everyone would kidnap a man to assure they get a property for a lower price."

I should have felt satisfaction at Claire's observance, but what I felt was hunger and impatience. After all the imprints of the past few days, I needed more protein . . . and to find Jake.

Tracy stood. "Thank you for your help, Claire. I owe you one."

"Let me know if you'd like me to look into this further." Claire arose fluidly and moved toward the door. "I'll give you my discounted rate." A clear message that while she'd been happy to check into things for the police, her charity only went so far.

"I'll put someone at the precinct on it. I'll let you know if we need anything more."

I grabbed a last handful of grapes and shoved them into the front pocket that hadn't held my makeshift gunpowder bomb. Unfortunately, my action didn't go completely unobserved.

"Would you like more sandwiches to take with you?" Claire asked, a touch of cool amusement in her tone.

"No," I said. "But thank you. It's been a long day."

Her eyes traveled down to my feet and back again. "You are an interesting person, Autumn Rain," she said. "Something tells me there is more to you than meets the eye. My late husband always told me I had a feeling for these things."

I could sense no hint of her former derision, and since I had experienced no imprints that warned me against her, I took her words at face value. I found myself wishing I could give her something in return. Except I didn't know if she needed anything or that I could give it to her if she did. "Thank you for your help," I said, extending my hand to shake hers. She wasn't wearing a ring, so it was an easy thing to do. "Let me know if you ever need any antiques or herbs. I own Autumn's Antiques here in town. I'll give you a good deal."

She smiled. "I'll let you know."

Back in the squad car, Tracy said, "She was impressed by you. I'm surprised because she mostly hates everyone. Or mistrusts them. She's had to work hard to get where she is. After she married, she gave up being an attorney to raise their two children and only came back into the game a few years ago, right before her husband died of a heart attack. He was an attorney, too. There was some question from his employer about his having misused funds. She always maintained his innocence, but I guess she'll never know what really happened."

No wonder Claire radiated that standoffish air. An event like that changed a person. I took the grapes from my pocket, offering them to Tracy, who took a few. "I want to talk to Kolonda's neighbor, and I want to tell Kolonda what we found out so she won't sell."

Tracy grimaced. "Whoever is buying up those properties isn't exactly going to be happy about us ruining their plans."

"Which is exactly why I'm going to call the newspaper after we talk to Kolonda. The less this character has to gain, the less reason he has to keep Jake."

"Depending on who we're talking about, it might mean he'll take out his frustration on Jake."

I hadn't thought of that. "Okay, so we'll find Jake first and then call the papers."

Tracy's phone buzzed with an incoming text. She looked at the screen and smiled. "Yes! They found something. They didn't say what, but it's got to be important." She typed out a response.

We drove in silence to Kolonda's. It wasn't far, but darkness was falling fast, and I willed Tracy to hurry. Kolonda's house, if somewhat smaller than Claire Philpot's, was every bit as elegant, at least on the outside. A far cry from Jake's apartment, or even his grandmother's place. Worlds apart.

The officers at the scene came toward us as we parked, triumphant smiles on their faces. Tracy jumped from the car. "What is it?"

One man held up a plastic bag containing a black cell phone. "Definitely his. Found it in those bushes." The officer pointed to the tasteful landscaping in front of Kolonda's house. "But the witness says he was standing over there when they grabbed him. That's a good twenty feet away."

"He could have thrown it." Tracy reached for the plastic bag.

"If it's his, we should be able to find out who else he talked to before he went missing," the officer said. "Backtrack his path."

"Great job, guys. I'll take it from here." Tracy turned to find me grinning.

I recognized Jake's cell phone, of course. A little black one that didn't require a monthly web charge. Neither of us wanted to be bothered with e-mail on our phones or felt the need to surf the Internet when we were away from home or our stores. "If he threw it, that means he was calling when he was taken."

"Maybe he meant for you to find it."

I'd been hoping the same thing, and I was grateful he'd been able to think clearly, given the circumstances. That was Jake. He did what had to be done and usually managed to add in a little flair while he was at it. I was happy whoever took him hadn't been worried about the phone enough to go after it.

I reached for the bag.

"Not here. In the car," Tracy said, glancing at the other officers, who were returning to their car. "We don't want to appear to be tampering with evidence."

I hurried back to the car and opened my door.

14

Tracy handed me the plastic bag without touching the phone. They would likely look for prints, but it wouldn't be too odd if mine were on it—I was Jake's girlfriend. I wondered, however, why he'd called Kolonda first with his discovery instead of me. It felt weird that he had done so. Then again, when Sawyer had gone missing, I hadn't called him but had plunged straight into my investigation. I hadn't asked him to go with me to see Russo, either. What did that say about our relationship? People changed and grew as they dated, as they explored being a couple to see if they were a good fit for the ultimate commitment, and I realized that as much as I cared about Jake, I really didn't know where we were heading.

I pushed the troubling thoughts aside. I hadn't called Jake because I was simply doing my job, a job I'd been called to do because of my special talent. I hadn't asked for this ability in the first place, but I was starting to believe it was my purpose in life.

To right wrongs, to help people, to discover truths—even if they weren't what anyone expected.

What we'd discovered about Dennis certainly hadn't been in any of Sophie's wildest dreams.

Stop delaying, I told myself.

I reached into the bag. I wasn't sure if I was more afraid of not finding an imprint about the kidnapping or discovering Jake's recent feelings about me. About Kolonda. No one should have such a narrow peek into anyone's life, especially not the person they loved. Moments of joy or anger or frustration are fleeting and can't adequately show the sum of a person's true feelings. While they may hint at the truth, imprints weren't a fair way to judge an entire relationship, for good or bad. Dennis's imprint on Sophie's bracelet proved that much.

I slid my hand under the phone. The plastic casing was warm, as though even in the bushes it had caught the rays of the setting sun. The instant I touched the phone an imprint came through. Something new, recent. Excitement at seeing Kolonda. Fear that he/I wouldn't measure up. Confusion at his/my feelings for her.

I wasn't surprised, but I was hurt. *It doesn't mean anything,* I told myself. Anyone would feel the same about an old flame—especially one as beautiful and needy as Kolonda.

The imprint continued as strong arms grabbed Jake/me from behind. He/I threw a punch at the Asian, following up with a satisfying kick to the man's knee. Whipping around to slam my hand, still clutching the phone, into the other attacker—a nondescript white man with brown hair. Pain burst in the back of my head. I fell to one knee, and hands began dragging me to the gray van. Fear pounded in my heart. Why were they doing this? What did they want? Who were they?

The door of the van opened, and Jake/I caught a glimpse of another man's face before a blindfold cut off his vision. Recognition flooded me. I knew that man. Me, Autumn, not Jake. The brief view wouldn't likely be enough for Jake even to recall the man if he were to see him later in a lineup, but I had talked with this guy at length, studied him, and it was more than enough. The last bit of the imprint was Jake's hand thrusting out as he blindly tossed the phone, and the thought: *Find me, Autumn*.

The abduction had taken mere seconds, but it was enough to tell me what I needed to know. Other images were coming from the phone now. Older, rapid imprints, none easily identified. Vague, as though at different times he'd felt strong emotion while using the phone—frustration directed at his sister, Randa, warmth at the thought of me, excitement at finding a new herb for the shop— everything blended until I could barely pick them apart. I let the phone drop back into the bag and turned to face Tracy.

"What is it? You don't look so hot."

"I know why Ian canceled your date."

Her head moved back and forth slowly. "It can't be."

"He was in the van. Jake saw him. He didn't recognize him, but I did. I didn't recognize the Asian at all. Not Saito's man."

"If Ian's involved, that means Russo could be, too. Either Russo's the developer building that shopping center Claire talked about and Ian's cleaning up for him, or Ian knows the plan and is working a side scheme all on his own."

"His law firm's income isn't enough for him?"

"The more money some people get, the more they crave." Tracy's voice was bitter. "At least we know who has Jake."

"Where would he keep him?"

"I don't know. I say we pay Mr. Gideon a visit."

"You sure you're up to it?"

"Oh, yeah." Eagerness glittered in her eyes. "But let's stop at Walmart and grab another blouse. It's probably the only place open now. We're going to make a nice little social call to Mr. Creepo Gideon."

I didn't see Tracy as the kind to shop at Walmart, but my estimation of her shot up. This scorned woman was going in for the kill.

A tapping at my window drew our attention, and we turned to see Kolonda standing outside the police car. I hit the button to roll down the window, but nothing happened until Tracy turned the key in the ignition.

"Uh, I wanted to know if you'd found any leads," Kolonda said before the glass had descended halfway.

I was loath to tell this woman anything—this woman who might be close to reclaiming Jake's heart. I glanced at Tracy, who said, "We do have a lead to a man we think might be working for another man, though we have no proof of them taking Jake at the moment."

I looked back at Kolonda. "That reminds me. Didn't you say you kept the pen of that contractor who tried to get you to sign over your buildings? Did you ever find it?"

Kolonda blinked her surprise. "What does that have to do with anything?"

"If you have it, we might be able to identify the man responsible for taking Jake."

"I already know who owns the pen."

"I mean the man who hired him. Please, do you have it?" I felt some satisfaction that Jake hadn't explained about my ability. I'd as much given him permission at his grandmother's apartment, but he hadn't talked about my weirdness after all. I felt a rush of gratitude to him for protecting me from the ridicule so often directed my way by those who claimed to be educated—never mind that science hypothesized the possibility of my ability's existence.

Or had he been ashamed?

No, not Jake. He wore dreads, after all, and had gone all over town with me in my bare feet. I found myself smiling and feeling more determination to find him.

I'm coming, Jake.

"Well, if it will help. I think I have it inside. Do you want to wait?"

"Sure. But hurry. We need to find Jake as soon as we can."

To her credit, Kolonda sprinted up the walk and into her house. Three minutes ticked by before she returned, holding the pen carefully between two fingers. "I already touched it a few times, so I don't know if you'll find fingerprints."

I didn't care a hoot about those kind of prints, but I let her drop it into the plastic bag Tracy handed me. Apparently the police department bought them in bulk. "Thanks."

"I feel so responsible," Kolonda said. "He was only helping me, and if that contractor did something to him . . ." She stopped. "I know you two are together, but Jake's special to me. He always has been." Tears started in her eyes.

"We'll find him," I said. "Meanwhile, don't sell out to anyone, no matter what they say."

Her eyes widened. "You think they'd let Jake go if I sold them my buildings? I'll do it. I'd do anything to help him."

I was sure Kolonda's two buildings weren't the sole reason they'd taken Jake. This deal was far larger, involving an entire block and millions of dollars. If anything, Jake's snooping was likely the reason for his capture, not Kolonda's refusal to sell out. Whoever was ultimately behind this wanted to keep all reference of the rezoning from the newspapers until he finished buying properties.

"We don't think anyone will contact you," Tracy said. "But if they do, call me." She handed Kolonda a card.

"I will. Thanks."

Kolonda backed away, her sadness evident. For the first time, I noticed her eyes were red and swollen as though she'd been crying.

Crying wouldn't find Jake. I gritted my teeth and stared straight ahead.

"Beautiful woman." Tracy eased the car into motion. "A relative of Jake's?"

"Old girlfriend."

"Doesn't sound like she wants it to be over."

"Tell me something I don't know." The question to answer was how Jake felt about Kolonda.

"Are you going to read the pen?"

"Of course." As I touched my finger to the fat metal casing, a wave of greed flooded me, sticky and sweet. I was staring into Kolonda's beautiful face, anger surging through me. No, not me, but the man whose imprint I was seeing. *Stupid broad. Just give it up. I told you I ain't takin' responsibility. Get used to it.* My/his eyes took in a caved roof and the mess of insulation and debris spread throughout the room. "Look, I'll get back to you," he/I said aloud. "But you might be better off selling out to me. I'll come by your office later at the university and bring you a contract."

"I don't want to sell. I want you to fix this like you should have in the first place."

"Sorry. Ain't my responsibility."

He/I turned to go, a skyline of one tall building standing among shorter ones filling my sight.

The imprint ended, and another sluggishly followed. I was looking into Ian's face, greed pouring through me. I shook his hand. Nothing more.

I sighed and released the pen. "Confirmation about Ian's involvement in the real estate deals. He and the contractor signed a contract that involved a lot of money. But that imprint's old. About

a year. I bet they've managed to buy or mess up quite a bit of properties since then."

Tracy snorted. "On the construction side, all they'd have to do
is always be the lowest bid and then do a shoddy job. That'd be
enough to encourage people to sell out later."

"Until Jake got involved."

"We still don't know if Ian's acting on his own or for Russo."
Tracy turned a corner that I recognized was close to Walmart.

"I'm hoping it was Russo." In fact, an idea was forming in my
head of how to find proof that he was involved and using that proof
to help Dennis and his family. It was a long shot, but carefully
planned, it might work.

"Really?" Tracy arched a brow. "Because I'd think he'd be the
kind who would simply threaten people or make them disappear
completely instead of wasting time doing shoddy construction
work."

She had a point. I'd better hope Ian was working alone.

• • •

We arrived at Ian Gideon's at ten twenty-one, thanks to
Walmart's self-checkout and someone at the precinct who found
Gideon's home address in record time. Tracy and I both wore new
tops, so we looked better than we had, but I longed to change my
jeans, which, if I sniffed with too much concentration, smelled
faintly of rotten potatoes and gunpowder.

Ian lived in an apartment building, and I doubted he'd have
been able to take Jake there without alerting someone, much less
keep him quiet. Of course, his first stop could have been the river,
but I didn't think Ian, even working with Russo, would be so casual
about murder. Then again, I didn't know the man very well. The
only imprint I'd read from him had been on his ring when we'd

shaken hands at the law firm—obviously a misleading imprint that had little to do with his true character.

"I'll distract him," Tracy said as we approached the glass doors to the building, "while you touch things. He must have left imprints somewhere."

"Got it." I was beginning to wish we'd stopped for a hamburger. My longing for food always cranked up a notch when stress was involved. Which, come to think of it, was pretty much all the time these days. The imprints I'd experienced in the past two days had made it worse, pushing me to voracity. "Wait. What if that employee of his told him about my ability?"

"You mean that imbecile who called us when you showed up at the law firm, Ben or whatever? Ha. He didn't believe a word you said, and I doubt he'd want to get on his boss's nephew's questionably crazy list for you."

"I hope you're right."

"I am. What you should be hoping is that he's home."

"Might be better if he's not. Either way, I'm going inside."

Tracy stared at me, but I didn't back down. I was determined to find clues that would lead me to Jake, one way or another. Deciding it wasn't worth a debate, she pushed the buzzer to an intercom on the sixth floor.

"Who is it?" someone asked after a long minute of silence.

I couldn't tell who it was, but Tracy had talked to Ian more than I had.

"Hi, Ian. It's Tracy. I was in the area and thought I'd stop by to say hi. I was hoping you'd be off work by now."

"Uh . . . Sure. Great! Come on up." Despite the hesitation, he did seem happy to hear from her. Must mean that Jake wasn't there, which I had already suspected but felt disappointed about anyway.

On the way up in the elevator, Tracy called the precinct. "Any news on Sawyer Briggs? That's too bad. Tell Detective Martin where

I am if he asks. Meanwhile, I want any information we can find on any properties Ian Gideon owns. Please send that and the list of Russo properties to this cell. Thanks."

Ian was waiting for us in the hallway when we emerged from the elevator, a bottle of wine in his thin fingers. Surprise registered on his narrow face when he saw me.

"I would have called," Tracy said, her voice slipping into flirtation mode, "but it really was on the spur of the moment. Autumn and I were in the neighborhood."

Ian took her hand, holding onto it as he spoke. "I'm actually here just to grab a bite of dinner. I have an appointment in about an hour back at the office—something I'm taking to court on Monday—but I couldn't stand being at work another minute. The funny thing is, I was about to call you. See if you had time for a chat. It's much better that you're here." He grinned and held up the bottle of wine. "Have time for a drink?"

"Sure." Tracy smiled, which seemed to make Ian lose his train of thought.

"Uh, come on. My apartment is over here." He led the way through the well-lighted hallway to a door he'd apparently left open.

His place was obviously a bachelor pad. No flowers or women's magazines on the coffee table, no assortment of photographs or anything I generally associated with women, such as throws or knickknacks. Chrome seemed the overriding theme in the apartment, everything modern and expensive, from the white, silver-tipped draperies and gray leather couch that looked brand-new to the chrome-and-glass coffee table and silver floor lamps. Occasional splashes of blue appeared in pictures on the wall and in throw rugs over the wood floor. Unlike some bachelor pads I'd seen, I guessed that the decorator had been paid far too much for far too little. Poor Ian. He needed a woman's touch—preferably from a woman with taste—and by the slight flaring of Tracy's nostrils at a particularly horrendous blue accent pillow, I knew she thought the same thing.

"Please, have a seat." Ian indicated the gray couch, onto which I settled with a little sigh. It was far more comfortable than it looked, and my estimation of the room's designer went up infinitesimally. Not enough to make up for those draperies, though.

Ian sat in a chair close to Tracy's side of the couch, twisting the cork from the bottle. I didn't see where he'd gotten the glasses, but there were three of them so they had to be close by.

"None for me," I said, as he poured. "Though I'd love a cup of herbal tea, if you have any without caffeine."

"Yeah, in the kitchen. I think." He hesitated before adding, "I'll make you some."

I stood. "Don't bother. You two talk. I'll help myself—if that's okay."

"Sure. It should be in the cupboard above the sink, I hope. I don't drink it much." He shrugged apologetically.

Before I'd gone three feet, he'd already forgotten I was there. His eyes were riveted on Tracy, whom I knew well enough to detect the tenseness in her shoulders and the forced way she laughed. He was attracted to her, which I found sad under the circumstances because, after what we'd learned, Tracy was more likely to pull her gun on him than to accept another date. If I didn't find a clue to Jake's whereabouts soon, I might go ahead and help myself to her gun.

"What happened to your face?" I heard Ian saying. I didn't listen for her response.

As I moved through the wide arch where I could see the kitchen, I touched one of the silver lamps, but there were no imprints. A two-foot silver statue, which looked antique but was an obvious rip-off to someone with an experienced eye, contained an imprint of a woman hoping Ian wouldn't question the price tag she'd given him for the object, which she had bought new and sold to him after adding the antiquing. The profit she'd made was enough to make even an honest person think, however briefly, about changing professions.

Laughter drifted in from the living room as I searched in the cupboard above Ian's stainless steel refrigerator using a chair from the chrome-and-glass table. He had herbal tea all right, but even if I overlooked the thick film of dust on the carton, one glance at the ingredients told me it was awful. Ginger, of course, one of the last teas I'd ever choose, and unlike Jake's new tea, this one had black-berry leaf in it. I didn't like blackberry leaf, no matter how much sweetener I added, though if used in a smaller amount, I supposed it would be almost undetectable. Even if I didn't know Ian was holding Jake, I'd dislike him solely on the grounds of this brew. No one should inflict such tea on guests.

A little more searching revealed a saucepan that would work to boil the water. Not that I intended to drink the tea and so could have used the microwave, which I ordinarily shunned, but boiling water the old-fashioned way would give me more time to search the kitchen. As the water heated, I trailed my hands over everything in sight—stainless steel appliances, the book on the counter, the dishes and pans, the stack of mail. There were imprints, but they were vague and fading. Nothing about Jake. I pushed on, opening another drawer. This one was full of junk.

Ah, I thought. People often had these kinds of drawers—I had two myself—and I kept a lot of stuff I used often or couldn't bear to throw away.

"You finding everything?"

I blinked at Ian, my hand poised over his drawer. "Spoons," I said. "I need a spoon to mix in the sugar." He couldn't know that I never used regular sugar, could he?

His eyes narrowed. "Not in there."

"Obviously." I withdrew my hand and shut it with my hip. He jerked slightly as it slammed a little too hard. "Sorry," I muttered.

"In there."

I retrieved a spoon from the drawer he'd indicated, glad that it held no imprints. Fortunately, no one ever cared much about spoons. I hoped he'd leave, but he pushed a shiny silver container of sugar toward me, leaned against the counter, and folded his arms.

Great. How was I going to get into that drawer with him staring at me? I thought I'd seen keys in there, which were bound to hold imprints. I had the feeling his car wouldn't be the ordinary kind. Probably something worth more than I made in ten years and that garnered a lot of attention from attractive professional women.

"So," I said, pouring the water into the mug I'd found previously and adding a tea bag. "How was it you landed a big client like Nicholas Russo? Weird, isn't it, that Dennis turned out to be Russo's cousin?"

"Cousin?" But there was no real surprise in his voice or his lean face. Ian had known, perhaps all along, despite what he'd told the police earlier about his ignorance of a connection between Russo and Dennis. However, a lot had transpired today, and exactly when he had gained this knowledge was still open for debate.

"Didn't you hear? Apparently, Dennis disappeared after witnessing his brother's murder, and his family thought he was dead. They want him back, of course."

"What family wouldn't? I'm sure he's happy to be in contact with them again."

"Not really." I left my gaze on Ian as I stirred my herb tea, but if I expected him to shift uncomfortably or visibly reveal his guilt, I was out of luck. "If you're as good a lawyer as I think you are," I added, "you probably know why."

"Our firm has no awareness of any underhanded dealings, if

192

that's what you're implying." The arrogance in his confident tone made me want to scream.

I reached over and opened the junk drawer again. "You don't have any paper in here, do you? I'm wondering if you can give me Russo's phone number. There's something I need to discuss with him."

"Give me your cell number, and I'll send it to you."

"Uh, my cell phone isn't charged and I'll need to call him before I'll get a chance to plug it in." I spied keys in the drawer, and my hands tingled in anticipation.

"Here's the number." Ian shoved a card from his wallet at me, but I dropped my hand anyway, letting them close around the keys.

"What a cool key," I gushed. "What kind of car do you drive?" Not that the key was anything but ordinary.

Irritation crossed Ian's face. "A Lexus convertible. Nothing special." He took them from my hands, and I let them go because all I felt on it was pride and a little bit of lust, both more than a few weeks old. I didn't want to experience those kinds of emotions, especially not his.

"Oh, do you have a garage here?" Inside the drawer I spied a key card like the ones hotels use for their rooms. This one had GARAGE written at the top in large block letters.

"No, that's from work."

Sure enough, down at the bottom of the key card in tiny letters were the words Simeon, Gideon & Associates. I reached for it.

He stopped me by shutting the drawer. "We should go back to Tracy. She'll be wondering where we are. Too bad I have to leave in a bit. I really wish I had more time."

"I'm sure Tracy does, too. I know she was looking forward to seeing you." How could I get him to fess up? Maybe if I followed him to wherever he was going, he'd lead me to Jake, though with my luck, he really would be heading to his office for work.

"Come on." He handed me the steaming mug and placed his hand on the small of my back. Though separated from him by a layer of fabric, my flesh crawled.

I saw it then, what I'd been missing all along. Peeking out from the thick metal leg of a kitchen chair near the far wall was a tiny plastic soldier in a blue uniform.

I moved quickly away from Ian, crossing the tiled floor and scooping up the toy, easily identifying it as an antique. And not just any antique but one whose rifle was no longer connected to one of the soldier's hands—one of the two figurines I'd given Sawyer. A toy he often carried in his pocket.

I stared at the soldier and then at Ian, a chill shuddering through me. I'd come here expecting to find a trace of Jake, but apparently Ian had other things to hide.

CHAPTER

15

W hat's this?" I asked—or tried to. Because an imprint was coming fast. Strong hands grasping, Sawyer's fear. A cry for his mother. A white man, one neither Sawyer nor I recognized. Struggling until something was pushed against his/my mouth and the world went dark.

This imprint was followed by older, more pleasant ones. Satisfaction of playing with the toy, memories of the day I'd given it to him. "You sure you want that one?" I asked him in the imprint. "It's broken. See?" But he liked the broken one because it was "funner to shoot," though he would never really shoot anyone. It was all pretend. He also liked the lady with the funny eyes who didn't wear shoes.

When I could finally focus on Ian again, I found him staring at the toy in my hand. "One of my nephews must have left it," he said.

"It's antique. Not many children have them or play with them if they do." Was that a worry line on his forehead? My heartbeat increased.

"What's taking you guys so long?" Tracy asked, entering the kitchen. "Are you drying tea leaves or something?" Her false smile ended when she saw my face, and her hand moved closer to the weapon I knew she had hidden in a holster at her back. "What is it, Autumn?"

Anger boiled inside me. "This is Sawyer's." I held up the soldier. The imprints were replaying, and I was barely able to talk. Hurriedly, I slipped it into the pocket of my jeans next to my useless cell phone.

"You mean Dennis's son?" Ian snorted. "I don't think so. He's never been here. Could have come from my cleaning lady's child, for all I know."

Ignoring him, Tracy looked at me. "You sure?"

"He left an imprint."

"Where's the boy?" Tracy demanded of Ian, her face hardening. "Where did you take him?"

"I don't know what you're talking about. What would I want with Dennis's son?"

"Did you do it for Russo?" I sneered. "That's how he's going to force Dennis to return to his so-called family, you know. By threatening to take his son."

"I'm not involved in any such plan. I'd never do anything to hurt a child."

I took a step toward him. "I suppose you don't know where Jake is, either. Or know anything about a van and an Asian man jumping him on the street."

That brought a reaction, but not the one I'd intended. In a single motion, he dived toward the table, grabbed the mug of tea where I'd set it, and flung the contents at Tracy. She drew her weapon just as smoothly, though the pain of the hot tea must have stung. But Ian was already hurtling toward her, producing his own pistol. One of the guns went off as his collision with Tracy toppled them both, the bullet going wide and ricocheting off the fridge. Tracy's gun skidded over the floor, the noise loud in the sudden silence.

Tracy lay on the tile, unmoving, though I could see her chest rising and falling. Ian pointed his gun at her, his movements less certain now, as though he wasn't comfortable with firearms. Neither was I.

Concentrating, I kicked at his hand, sending his gun flying. Now we were even. Well, as even as I could get with a man who was so much taller and probably a lot stronger, despite his leanness. Ian recovered and came after me. He didn't move with the skill of the well-trained, but he'd had at least some boxing experience somewhere along the line. I was more agile than he expected, easily avoiding those first punches and countering them with my own. His reach was longer, which cut down my effectiveness because I had to throw and get out of reach before he clobbered me. Fortunately, my legs were longer than his arms, and he didn't seem to know how to use his own legs to hit me, so that evened the score a bit further.

The air in the kitchen grew stifling and heavy as I worried about Tracy. Had the bullet hit her when it ricocheted, or had she banged her head on the tile when Ian attacked? More than anything I wanted to see if she was okay.

Ian sent a punch that took me off guard, slamming into my torso below my right breast—fortunately not the side of my healing ribs, though from the impact he might have broken a few new ones.

He grinned, his thin face wolflike. "You should have listened when I tried to warn you off this morning."

"You sent that thug after me at the gas station near Russo's restaurant?" I circled him warily, planning my next attack. Foot to his knee and then to his groin, followed by two jabs and an all-out punch to his head. It might work if I could place the first kick exactly right. Too bad I didn't have my keys. Last I remembered seeing them was at Sophie's when Sawyer was taken.

Ian shrugged. "I talked to Tracy on her way to her parents' house. She told me you were going to see Russo. I was simply protecting my client."

"Your client or yourself? How many properties are you going to be able to sell to the shopping center developers?"

"What do you know about that?"

"Enough to go to the newspapers. What I want to know is how Russo really became your client. No way that was coincidence."

He laughed. "No. It was brilliance. I discovered Dennis's past during the background search I conduct on all new employees. I'm a master at backgrounds, you see." Ian's voice was so casual we could have been sitting in his office with a desk between us instead of circling the kitchen looking for an opportunity to strike. "Wouldn't you like to know who your father was—your real father, that is? And your grandparents? I could find them all."

"Like you found Dennis's family? How much did they pay you?" I grimaced in disgust.

"I find it much better to seek a long-term relationship with a legitimate client than to collect a prize. A bit of lucrative business thrown my way is nothing to them, and it means everything in the eyes of my firm's partners—particularly my aunt."

"So instead of getting a payment to betray Dennis, you got his family's business."

He grinned. "And a raise. I was hoping for partnership, but my aunt keeps putting me off."

"How could you sell Dennis out that way?" Ian was backing toward the block of kitchen knives, so I rushed him, landing a successful roundhouse on his thigh and compelling him back toward the table.

"He was involved in the murder of Joben Saito's son. He could have been the trigger man, for all I know."

That reverberated close to the truth Dennis had confessed to me at the hospital. If Ian was that good, maybe he could trace my birth mother's family and discover who my biological father was. The need to know always burned inside me, though mostly as a tiny flame that grew smaller when I was with my sister, her presence having a satiating effect on my curiosity.

"Whatever you're into," I said to Ian, "it's over now. You injured, maybe even killed, a police officer. It'll go easier on you if you stop this insanity and call an ambulance."

Ian hesitated, appearing to think about what I'd said. He shook his head, like Tawnia's new dog throwing off water when we swam in the ocean. "You're right. I've gone too far."

I could see the danger of that line of thought. "You still have your aunt's law firm. I'm sure they'll back you, won't they? They'll help you fix things."

"Yeah, right." His face twisted in an ugly grimace. "Even if things went back to the way they were, when my aunt finally does kick the bucket, her share of the firm will go to that snot-nosed baby cousin of mine, who isn't even out of law school. My career means nothing to her. I realized that a long time ago."

It occurred to me that Ian was in a situation similar to the one Russo had been in with Dennis, except Dennis had disappeared, effectively turning over the reins to his cousin. Did Russo really plan to return Dennis to the family, or were his plans far darker?

"You could start your own law firm," I said. "If you tell them where Sawyer is, they'll go easy on you. And Jake. Is he still with the Asian?"

"You should have listened to my warning. Both you and your hoodlum boyfriend should have stayed out of it."

That did it. Jake had dreads, but he wasn't a hoodlum. He was a hard worker, he attended church every Sunday, and he was kind to everyone. Most important, he was my friend.

I faked a roundhouse, and Ian turned to block, exposing his knee. It was all I could wish for. Knee, groin, face. Only my last, knock-out punch was off, though Ian tripped and hit his head on the table.

"Where is Jake!" I yelled.

I hadn't noticed that he'd fallen next to Tracy's gun. Grabbing it, he let off a volley of shots as I dived toward his gun that lay to the right of the table. Another shot slammed into the wall above my head. Lucky for me he had terrible aim.

My luck didn't hold. In the next instant, hot, slicing pain skidded over my right calf, seeming never to stop. White flashes of agony obscured my vision. I forced myself to roll over and face him. I had hold of his gun now, but before I could do anything with it, Ian shot again. The empty click sounded almost as loud as the bullets had in the silent kitchen. He threw the gun down and disappeared through the door.

He hadn't needed to flee. Already I was immobilized by the imprints in his gun. Fear, exultation, and greed filled my head. "I'll let you go," he/I was saying to Jake, who lay on brown carpet, tied and bloodied, as though he'd fought to get free. "Once everything is taken care of, you won't remember a thing. I can't have you going public with this. I have too much to lose." In Ian's mind I saw just how much—yes, he'd been working for Russo, but he had far more properties for himself on the side. He would be set for several lifetimes.

More than a motive for kidnapping.

"I'll go public," Jake growled.

Ian/I laughed. "After the doctor's visit, you'll be lucky if you remember your own name." He/I motioned, and the Asian man I recognized from the imprint on Jake's phone tied a cloth over Jake's mouth. The last imprint was of a window and a tall building standing out among its neighbors.

I shook my hand free of the gun.

I'd seen that building before, though at a slightly different angle. But where? I struggled to remember. Then I had it: the pen Kolonda had kept from her visit with the contractor. She'd been showing him the caved-in ceiling at one of her buildings, so that meant Jake had to be somewhere nearby.

Gathering my strength, I crawled to Tracy's side, my wound sending shards of agony up my leg. The pain seemed everywhere, though it was worst in my calf. I knew I should look at it, but I had to take care of Tracy first. She was breathing but unconscious. I could see no blood. I reached for her phone, at the last minute grabbing it with the end of my shirt. I couldn't risk any more imprints for the moment. I needed my wits about me.

I pushed the number with the tip of a fingernail that was slightly longer than the others. "What is it?" growled a voice.

"Shannon, it's Autumn."

"Why are you using Tracy's phone?"

"Because she's unconscious. We need an ambulance at Ian Gideon's apartment right away. They know the address at the precinct. It's on this phone, but I don't know how to—"

"Is she okay?" His clipped tone told me I was running off at the mouth again. Not my fault I was losing it.

"I don't know. But Ian has Jake, and he knows where Sawyer is. Maybe Ian grabbed Sawyer for Russo." That didn't feel exactly right, though. Not because Russo had seemed genuinely upset about Sawyer's disappearance but because I'd started to wonder why Russo would take Sawyer before the search for Dennis was concluded. Dennis had been easy enough to trace, and the fear of what Russo might do to their son should keep both Dennis and Sophie in line without his actually taking the boy. He could always kidnap the child later if Dennis tried to talk to the police or go into hiding again, a thing Russo seemed positive he wouldn't do. Russo didn't strike me as someone who put himself to useless tasks.

"I'm on my way," Shannon's voice cut through my tumult of thoughts. "The ambulance will be there first. You stay put."

"No."

"Why not?"

"I need to find Jake."

"Autumn, stay there. I'll help you find him." His voice held a note of pleading that at any other time would have had me mocking him.

"There isn't time." Ian had been serious about hurting me, which means he'd made the leap from kidnapper to potential murderer. The bullet gouges in the wall near where I'd been sitting were proof enough of that.

"At least tell me where you're going."

"I think Ian owns a place near Kolonda's buildings. Maybe. Kolonda's the woman you talked to earlier. Jake was going to see her when he was taken. Hurry, Shannon. I don't know if Tracy's okay." With that I hung up because I was sounding desperate, and there was a part of me that wanted to wait for him. Not, however, the part that loved Jake.

Tracy's eyelids fluttered, and I bent closer to her. "Tracy? Can you hear me?" She moaned, which I took as a good sign. "Help is coming. Shannon's coming." She seemed to relax at that, but I still had to fight my guilt as I took her keys, climbed to my feet, and hobbled toward the kitchen door. I glanced once at Ian's abandoned gun, but I really didn't know how to use it, and the imprints might immobilize me at a crucial time. I would have to use other means to save Jake.

If I could find him in time.

CHAPTER

16

The ugly draperies finally found a good use when combined with the scissors in Ian's junk drawer. The silver-tipped material actually looked good wrapped tightly around my right leg like some hippie statement my adoptive parents would have understood and applauded. Not only did the wrapping stop the blood but it hid most of what had dripped. The gunshot was a surface wound that didn't look as bad as it felt, so there would be no worries about having to dig out the bullet later. Once I got moving and focused, I could almost ignore the pain.

I left the door to Ian's apartment open. I could already hear the mournful wail of the ambulance as I left the building and hurried to Tracy's squad car. I wondered how long I'd have before the police started looking for the vehicle. Hopefully, it'd be long enough.

In the car, I took Jake's black cell phone from the plastic bag, careful to secure the plastic between my skin and the phone so I wouldn't relive the imprints, and dialed Kolonda's number. She answered on the second ring.

I started the engine. "I need the address to your buildings." I knew the general area, of course, since learning of the impending shopping complexes, but as Kolonda gave me the address and tried to explain exactly where they were located, I felt a sinking disappointment. I was hopelessly directionally impaired and finding them could take time I simply didn't have.

Wait. The squad car had a GPS. I'd start toward the right area of town and program in the address at the next stoplight.

"Is this about Jake?" Kolonda asked before I could hang up.

"I think maybe he's being held in a building near there. I'm not sure where."

"What can I do?"

"Pray."

"I meant it when I said I'd give up my properties for Jake."

"This is bigger than just your buildings."

"I should never have given him up." There, it was out.

"Maybe," I said, "but you did." I hung up because there was nothing more to say, and the last thing I needed to do was to get in a car accident while telling Kolonda to stay away from Jake.

The GPS on the squad car turned out to be something you could use only if you had a degree in electronics or had gone through officer training—neither of which I could claim. After three tries at three different lights, I gave up and took to watching the buildings. I was sure I could find the general area and hopefully pinpoint it from there.

I prayed and hoped Kolonda had taken my advice to do the same.

Up and down the streets I drove, tears stinging my eyes. I was nearly ready to turn on the squad car lights and demand help from the nearest pedestrian when I saw the building. Ignoring the honking from the guy in a van behind me, I pulled abruptly over. Checking the pen's imprint once more verified that this was the right street. Now I wished I'd brought Ian's gun, because I wanted to recheck the angle of that imprint, but instead I closed my eyes and tried to remember. This had to be the place, though the building seemed farther to the left than in the imprint from the pen. My job would be to find the building that had the right angle.

There weren't any parking places along the packed street, so I left the squad car double-parked and hotfooted it up the sidewalk. Now that it had rested, my wounded leg rebelled at the effort. There weren't many people out and about at this time of night, despite the jam of parked cars, and the furtive looks of a few youths sitting on apartment steps made me wonder if I was safe. I couldn't worry about that now. Holding my head up, I hurried down the street with a confidence I was far from feeling.

When I found the right angle at last, my heart plunged. It could be one of two buildings, and they were both larger than the rest on the street, possibly containing dozens of apartments. Signs advertising availability told me which apartments were vacant, and I knew Jake would likely be held in one of those, but the sheer number of vacancies was overwhelming. How was I going to find him? I didn't even know for sure if he was there. Searching would eat up valuable time. It was all I could do not to collapse onto the sidewalk and start weeping. *Oh, Jake. I'm sorry.*

Then I thought of Tawnia.

Stepping into the shadows of the stairs leading up to the first apartment building, I dialed my twin's number.

"Jake?" Tawnia asked eagerly.

"No, it's Autumn."

"I heard about what happened to Jake. Is there any news? I've been trying to call you. Why aren't you answering your phone?"

"Battery's dead. Listen. I need you to draw a picture. I need a number."

"That's another reason why I've been calling. I keep drawing a picture. A tall building next to several shorter ones."

"Good. I need the other side of that street. A number. A number on the outside of a tall building or an apartment number."

"Autumn, I can't." Tawnia sounded scared.

"You have to. He has Jake and Sawyer."

"Who?"

"Ian Gideon."

"The hot attorney who was gaga over Tracy? You've got to be kidding." But she knew I wasn't. There was silence for a long moment and then, "I'm sorry, Autumn. I'm trying, but nothing is coming. No number, no building, nothing except a parking garage. A small one. I've never seen it before."

A parking garage? Why did that seem familiar? There weren't any parking garages here in this older section of town, not if I could judge by the numerous cars squeezed against the curbs.

"Autumn, are you okay?"

"I can't lose Jake. I can't." I'd lost too many people. I'd rather see him with Kolonda than gone from my life so permanently.

"I can't lose *you*."

We were a sorry pair, my sister and I, our early losses making us needy and fearful. But she had Bret and soon would have the baby, and her adoptive parents were still alive, if not deeply involved in her life. So even at the risk of her losing me, I had to continue.

Why was a parking garage familiar? Wait. Tonight I'd seen a key card for a parking garage—a garage at Simeon, Gideon & Associates. It was the only garage I could think of that might be related. Jake might have been here earlier, but he could have been moved to the garage—I didn't doubt Tawnia's gift any more than I doubted my own. Well, that wasn't exactly right because I certainly did doubt my own, but I knew both were real and mostly reliable.

"Thanks, Tawnia."

"Where are you going?" My sister's voice was panicked.

"To Simeon and Gideon. Will you get hold of Shannon and tell him to meet me there?"

"No need," a voice said from behind me. "I'm here." I whirled and saw Shannon standing to my left, out of breath. On the other side of the street his unmarked Mustang sat in what must have been the only parking spot available in the entire area, the door standing wide open. His tousled hair reflected light from the few streets lights that the resident hoodlums had not yet gotten around to breaking or that had been recently replaced. He made a solid figure in the darkness, something to turn to, and with his beautiful aqua eyes, he looked a bit like an avenging angel.

"How's Tracy?" I asked, letting my hand rest on his arm.

"I don't know. I came right here to see what trouble you were getting into. They'll let me know when they have something to say."

That he'd come to find me instead of going to Tracy said something, but I wasn't sure I wanted to know what.

Shannon looked pointedly at my hand where I gripped his arm. "I take it you're glad to see me?"

He was trying to lighten the atmosphere, but I wasn't biting. "I can't work the GPS, and you're the one with the gun." I started for his car.

Shannon came after me—fast but without appearing to hurry. "So why are we going to Simeon and Gideon?"

"I think that's where Jake is."

"And Sawyer?"

"Maybe."

I was grateful I wouldn't have to find my way in the dark to the law office alone. I was also grateful for his company, though I'd never admit as much to him. At least I was doing a good job at not limping because he didn't bother to run around and open my door.

The street still held a bit of warmth, though the sun was down, and it felt good against my bare feet. There was a growing coldness in my wounded leg that I didn't like one bit.

Shannon was already inside the car when I saw Kolonda—not coming from one of her buildings farther down the street but emerging from the building I'd almost entered. She had to have left right when I'd called her in order to beat me to the area, though I really had no idea how long I'd driven around before finding the place.

"Well?" Shannon asked, leaning over to look at me.

I motioned for him to zip it. Giving me a scowl, he did.

With Kolonda was a broad, swarthy man I'd never seen before. He wore work clothes, his white T-shirt badly stained, and his fore-head ending in sparse hair that was long enough to be pulled into a ridiculous ponytail. He stood at Kolonda's height, short for a man, and he walked with his hand on her elbow, which seemed odd to me because it was obvious they ran in different circles. His sloppy dress, the scraggly goatee, and even the solid way he walked told me they had nothing in common. This man probably hadn't made it through high school, and Kolonda valued education above all else. If she wasn't his tutor, they could have nothing to talk about.

Unless it had to do with her rental buildings. Or Jake.

As I watched, the man put her into a battered blue truck and went around to the driver's side. I hoped she'd open the door and make a run for it, but apparently she hadn't finished whatever busi-ness she wanted to conduct with the man.

I let myself sink to the seat inside Shannon's car, trying to ig-nore the fiery ache in my leg.

"You know her?" Shannon asked as he pulled into the street after them.

"That's Kolonda Lewis."

"I see."

"I'm not sure who that guy is, but something's not right. He's definitely not her type. He might be the contractor who was trying to buy her buildings. What's she doing down here so late, anyway?"

"We'd better follow them."

"No. We have to get to Jake." He was my responsibility. Kolonda wasn't. I felt guilty because I knew Jake would want me to care about her, but I simply wasn't that good.

Shannon dialed a number on his phone. "Any news?" He sighed. "Okay, good. Hey, you interviewed the contractor today when Jake Ryan went missing. What's he look like?" He listened a moment. "That's what I thought. Thanks."

I stared at him, but he didn't enlighten me until I said, "Well?"

"Tracy regained consciousness, but she has a concussion. She keeps slipping in and out. The doctors are doing tests now."

I wasn't sure if that was good or bad news. "And the contractor?"

"Name's Tony Blancher, and the guy with Kolonda matches his description. Not the type to leave a good impression."

"I hope she isn't doing something stupid."

"Like what?"

"I don't know." There had been desperation in her voice the last two times we'd talked. If I'd been in her place, I don't know that I could have sat at home waiting. Then again, I wasn't a teacher from a privileged family. I was a woman accustomed to making do with little, taking calculated risks for those I cared about and landing on my feet. Moreover, I had a talent that helped me at least as often as it caused chaos.

The truck in front of us turned abruptly, but Shannon didn't follow. I fought down another twinge of guilt. Jake first—and the little boy whose toy soldier was searing a hole in the pocket of my jeans.

Moments later, Shannon turned on the siren and the lights embedded into the dash.

"You hot?" Shannon asked.

His eyes went briefly to my lips and then back to the road. I ran my fingers above my top lip and felt drops of moisture there. "I'm fine," I said, but I'd felt hot since the explosion and hotter since my run-in with Ian. *Stupid leg, anyway.*

We were across town in half the time, Shannon silencing the siren several blocks from the law office.

"He might not be there," I warned. "Tawnia didn't draw him. But something's happening here, and it must be connected."

"You telling me we're here because of Tawnia's drawing?" The dubious tone in his voice irritated me. Tawnia and I had proven ourselves over and over again. What would it take to satisfy this man? I didn't remind him that I was the reason both he and Dennis were still alive.

"Not here," I told him, as he pulled up in front of the building. "There's underground parking somewhere. Not sure where." I wished I'd been able to touch the garage card key in Ian's drawer because then I might have something else to tell Shannon. Of course, it could just as well have held nothing.

He stared at me. "How do we get in? We'll need either an opener or a code."

"A card. We'll have to think of something."

"There has to be a way from the inside," Shannon said. "There's probably a night watchman, considering how large the company is, and I bet a few of the attorneys are burning the midnight oil. Come on." He strode toward the building, and I had to hurry to catch up. My leg was stiff and numb. I hoped that was a good sign.

The double glass doors were locked, but after a bit of banging, a scrawny watchman appeared with a mustard smear on his chin. He had a Taser but no gun that I could see. The tag on his chest read

Robison, but whether it was a first or a last name was left to the imagination. When Shannon flashed his badge through the glass, the man opened the door a few inches. "I can't let you in unless I contact one of the partners," he said. "We have a lot of sensitive files here."

I wondered if there was a file on me. If Ian had already begun to research my background, he might have found my birth mother's family and possibly my father's. But, no, there hadn't been time for that. I'd only met him yesterday, so unless he'd completed a background check on all of Dennis and Sophie's acquaintances, he wouldn't have any information on me or my sister.

"We don't want the files," Shannon said, his voice barely restrained. "Look, uh, Mr. Robison, we need to get into your parking garage."

The guard took out his phone. "I'm sure it'll be fine. I'll just call Mr. Gideon."

Shannon pushed open the door and snatched the phone from the guard. "Sorry. Can't let you do that."

"How do I know you're really even the police?"

"You'll have to trust me."

The guard groaned. "You're going to get me fired. I have kids. I need this job." He curled in on himself as though giving up, but I recognized a fake-out move that Edward often used in our tae kwon do class, one I'd always considered a bit underhanded. Anger flared to life. I kicked at his knee with my left foot, following it with a hard right punch and elbow jab that helped him find the floor. He moaned more loudly.

"Was that absolutely necessary?" Shannon said.

"You're welcome." The man had no grace when it came to my saving his hide. I had no illusions that my attack had been successful only because I'd taken the guard by surprise, but I was beginning to feel more confident with my moves.

Shannon lifted the guard to his feet. "Do you have security monitors?"

"A few."

"Any in the parking garage?"

"Two."

"Show me."

We followed the guard past the reception desk and into the same hallway that housed Dennis's small office. The area was lit with a minimum of fluorescent lighting, but it was bright compared to outside. The building was warmer, too, which I hadn't expected. They must turn the air-conditioning off at night. My right leg hurt worse since I'd placed so much weight on it during my encounter with the guard, and Shannon eyed me suspiciously. "You okay?"

"Peachy." Better than Jake was, I suspected.

The security room was about half the size of Dennis's office. A long desk spanning one wall held four monitors and what looked like a half-eaten gourmet sandwich from one of Portland's better delis. One monitor showed the lower lobby, and a second displayed the upper lobby where the partner attorneys had their offices. Two more cameras were in the parking garage, one at the elevator connecting the garage to the building, the other at the entrance and exit where an automatic door kept out the riffraff.

"Not much help," Shannon muttered as he cuffed Robison to a chair.

"Wait." I pointed to the far monitor. A battered blue truck came squealing up to the garage doors, and the driver leaned out his window to swipe a card. I caught a glimpse of another face beside him before the door opened and the truck left the camera's view.

Shannon looked at the guard. "That truck come here often?"

"Never seen it before." Under his breath he added, "Lots of stuff I've never seen before."

"What do you mean?" I asked.

The guard's eyes narrowed. They were brown and small and reminded me of a ferret I'd had as a child. "Forget it. I ain't telling you." Guess he was the type to carry a grudge.

"Oh?" Shannon's eyes glinted. "You want to tell me?" He removed his gun from his holster, and though he didn't wave it around, Robison became instantly more talkative.

"Just a lot of coming and going tonight, that's all. Nothing I can really pinpoint. Look, please don't hurt me. I have kids!"

"No, you don't," I said. There were no pictures of him with a family, though there were several family pictures that must belong to other security men. He wasn't wearing a ring, either.

"Okay, but I do have a sister and a nephew!"

"Relax. We're not going to hurt you." Shannon holstered his gun.

"Then you really are from the police, right?"

Sound from a speaker interrupted whatever reply Shannon might have made. A light above the monitor showing the garage elevator gleamed red, telling us where the sound came from.

"What are you doing here?" Unmistakably Ian's voice, though the camera angle and picture quality were poor.

"I brought that black chick," the contractor told him. "She's willing to sign."

"You shouldn't have come here, Tony."

"I need the paperwork." Tony ducked his head subserviently, but the firm way he stood told me he wasn't as submissive as he pretended.

"We'll do it tomorrow."

"She wants to see him tonight, or she won't sign."

Ian grabbed the front of Tony's shirt and shoved him out of the camera's view, but the brief sight of them together like that, with Ian towering over the short contractor seared into my mind. Tony grunted as he met up with the cement wall out of our view. "You told her we had him?" Ian growled.

"How else you think she was willing to sign? They won't say nothing. Neither of them. Not if they know what's good for them."

"You idiot. There's more you don't know. There was a complication at my apartment. I'll have to get rid of him now. Maybe both of them."

"Nah. I'm sure it's nothing your aunt can't get you out of. I seen her work. You guys defend murderers, and they always get off scot-free."

Silence for a few seconds before Ian came back into view as he stepped away from the other man. "Maybe you're right. If we get them out of here, there'll be no proof, and tomorrow they wake up in the desert miles from here, unable to remember their own names for the next year, if they ever remember them. Go get the girl and your truck. Hurry, I'm meeting with someone across town in twenty minutes."

"Another client?" Tony rubbed a big hand over his receding hairline.

"Sure. Big payoff. You get these guys out of here and to that doctor before the police arrive, and I'll see you get a share."

"I'll meet you by the storage rooms." The contractor hurried off, but Ian's gaze went to the camera, his lips pursing. Cursing and muttering about another mess to clean up, he jumped, taking a swipe at the camera. All at once we saw nothing except a short expanse of cement wall.

"Guess he'll be coming up here," Shannon said, "to clear the evidence. If not now, then after he hands them off."

Robison shook his head. "This is all recorded by computer. With the right codes he can delete the footage from anywhere. Look, this is all happening on my watch—I'd like to do something to help. I know the layout of the storage area in the garage."

Nodding, Shannon undid the handcuffs. "I'll send for backup, but they might not arrive in time. We need to get to those storage rooms now."

"Sure. This way." Robison hurried from the room, glancing back once to see if we were following. He was kind of cute in an unrefined sort of way, though definitely not my type.

"Will it do any good telling you to stay here?" Shannon said to me, punching a number on his phone as we jogged down the hall and out to the foyer where the elevator and stairs were located.

I didn't dignify his question with an answer. I was too busy trying not to hobble. Too busy worrying about what drugs Ian Gideon might have already given to Jake. Did Ian have another gun? Did the contractor? And who was Ian meeting with? He didn't seem to be planning on taking Jake, so did it have something to do with Sawyer? The thought of that little boy being a pawn in whatever scheme Ian had dredged up was almost worse than handing him over to Russo. Yet if Ian hadn't taken Saywer for Russo, what did he want him for? He wouldn't be stupid enough to hold the boy for ransom from Russo, would he?

With no answer in sight, I quit worrying about it. I wish I'd asked Tawnia to send her drawing to Jake's phone so I could see if it held any clues to help us find him. That had to be my priority for the moment. And Kolonda. Guess we'd have to save her, too.

We used the stairs so as not to alert anyone in the garage to our presence, but the foresight was unnecessary because no one was around when we emerged. I hadn't picked up any imprints from the elevator or the wall where I touched it, either, but I'd expected as much.

Hold on, Jake. I knew he was close the minute I stepped from the stairwell. I could feel him. I blinked back tears.

"Something wrong?" Shannon asked me.

I shook my head. "He's here."

"We know that. We heard Gideon say as much, remember?"

His response was more gentle than the words implied, and for that I was grateful. He was right. Maybe I wasn't as attuned to Jake as I wanted to believe, yet I felt him more strongly as we approached the storage area. It was something I couldn't explain, only to Tawnia, who understood exactly how it felt.

Shannon had his gun out again, and we began to creep along. "Must be in that back corner," he whispered.

"Yeah." Robison was hanging back now, and I didn't blame him for wanting to be out of the line of fire. So far he hadn't been much help. The garage was relatively small and the storage area simple to find. The blue truck parked in front and the slightly open door were other giveaways.

"Stay back," Shannon ordered before running to the cover of the truck. I obeyed, or mostly obeyed, ducking behind a cement pillar opposite the truck and peering around it. Robison didn't follow me, for which I was glad.

Shannon approached the door to the last storage room, holding his gun ready. In a burst of motion, he kicked the door open with his foot, slamming it open. "Police! Come out with your hands where I can see them!"

Muffled cursing, and then Tony, the burly contractor, came into view with his hands in the air. Ian came next, but he had Kolonda in front of him. I couldn't tell if he had a gun.

Kolonda's eyes locked on me, though how she'd spotted me peering from behind the pillar, I didn't know. "Jake's in there," she called. "He's hurt!"

"Let go of the girl!" Shannon demanded. "There's no way out. We have the place covered." A lie, though Ian couldn't know that, and it would be true soon enough when Shannon's backup arrived.

"Fine!" Ian shoved Kolonda at Shannon, who stopped her momentum with his free arm. Ian didn't have a gun, but I wondered what would have happened if he'd found another one. "Look,

I don't know how that man in there got in my garage," Ian added. "But I had nothing to do with it."

Tony shot him a dirty look. "Me either!"

I would have laughed if I hadn't been so worried about Jake. I rushed forward, unable to hide my limp at that speed. It didn't matter. I'd found Jake, and Shannon could order me to the hospital now, if he wanted. The storage room was lit by a single bulb—not much foresight, or perhaps a bit of penny-pinching. I saw pieces of furniture, a few fake plants, filing cabinets, and framed pictures. Lying in the middle of the floor was Jake. He was bound hand and foot, and a gag had been tied over his mouth. His face was bruised and swollen. He wasn't moving.

"Jake!" I threw myself down beside him and felt his neck for a pulse. It was there, and surprisingly strong. In the next minute, Kolonda was kneeling next to me, untying his feet while I worked on his hands. His eyes fluttered. "I'm here, Jake," I said, ignoring the tears sliding down my cheeks. "Are you okay?"

One eye finally opened, the other apparently too swollen to do more than flutter. "Hi, Autumn. I knew you'd find me, but did you have to bring him?"

I looked up and saw Shannon standing over us, his gun still on Ian and the contractor, whom he'd brought back inside the room.

I knew I was grinning like an idiot. "Sometimes you don't pick your company." My eyes happened to fall on Kolonda as I said this, and Jake's eyes followed.

"Kolonda," he murmured. "What are you doing here?" From his tone I could tell he wasn't exactly unhappy to see her.

"Looking for you. Oh, Jake, this is all my fault!" She moved closer, her hand going to his cheek, her eyes dripping tears. She didn't get a red nose and face when she cried but looked rather fresh, as though she'd simply spritzed her face. It wasn't fair.

Shannon took out his cuffs. "Would you mind putting these on our attorney friend?" he said to me. "We can use some of this rope for the other guy."

"Glad to." I stood, catching the cuffs as he tossed them.

Anger filled me. Murderous anger that burned white hot. *Stay calm*, he/I told himself/myself. *A simple change of plans, that's all. Focus.* He/I needed to get free, knock off the attorney before he could squeal on the boss or let on that they were meeting tonight, and then get out of here. A picture of Saito flitted through his/my mind at the idea of "boss."

The imprint was only a few minutes old and whoever it belonged to was planning murder. My eyes flew to the door as Robison appeared, gun in hand. "Watch out!" I screamed.

Too late.

CHAPTER
17

Shannon jumped to the side as a shot rang into the stillness, followed immediately by a second shot from the same direction. I couldn't see what happened, though, as I was hit by another imprint, an older one of a man who'd been arrested in a domestic violence situation. More fury. Blinding rage. Struggling. The imprint hadn't yet faded when another surged to life, this time from a gangbanger who moments earlier had shot his second-in-command. I heard a sob that I vaguely recognized as my own.

Another imprint began. A woman who—

The handcuffs were yanked from my grasp, and I nearly collapsed with relief. Shannon hadn't thought about the criminals this metal had touched or how it might affect me. I thought it might be he who finally rescued me from the imprints, but it was Jake kneeling in front of me, still holding the cuffs. Kolonda was behind him, pulling him down, away. They were okay.

Shannon picked himself off the cement next to me, apparently unharmed, so that left Ian and the contractor as possible targets.

No, not the contractor. Tony was huddled by the far wall, his arms thrown over his head but very much alive.

That left only one person. My eyes swung to a lump on the floor that minutes ago had been a proud, defiant Ian.

"See what you can do for him. I'll get the guard." Shannon hurtled out the door after Robison.

Kolonda had succeeded in getting Jake to lie down, so I walked alone to Ian, kneeling beside him. "You going to help me here?" I asked Tony as I rolled him over.

"What do you want me to do?" The contractor's eyes were dilated with fear.

"Give me your shirt." Ian had been shot in the stomach, and the way he was losing blood, I didn't give him much time unless I could stop the bleeding.

"My shirt?"

"Now!"

The short man reluctantly wriggling out of his shirt might have been amusing on another day, but now his slowness annoyed me. If Ian died, we wouldn't know what deal he'd been working with Saito, and though a few things were clicking into place for me now—namely how Saito had found Dennis—there was a lot that still needed answering. Like where he'd stashed Sawyer.

I balled up the shirt and pressed it against the wound. Ian wasn't moving. "Ian," I said, speaking close to his ear. "Where's Sawyer? Where did you take Dennis's son?"

No answer. I glanced over at Jake, who was seated now, appearing mostly propped up by Kolonda. "You didn't see Sawyer, did you?"

Jake shook his head. "Sophie's son? No, and our slick attorney there didn't say anything about him."

"Sawyer?" asked Kolonda. "I thought this was about my properties."

Pretty, spoiled, little princess still thought this was all about her. I stifled my annoyance by glaring at the bare-chested contractor. "What about you? Do you know anything about a missing boy?"

"I wasn't a part of anything like that—I swear. Just a few real estate deals." Tony slunk to the door as he talked.

"Don't do it," I said. "Running from the scene of a crime . . ."

He darted out the door, and I sighed. Unlike the mysterious ferret-faced guard, the police should be able to locate the contractor easily, and no doubt additional charges would be added to the list he'd already incurred.

Ian was still bleeding, and I was running out of clean cloth to press against the wound. "Can't you help me here?" I asked Kolonda. "He's going to bleed to death if we don't stop this."

That got her up and searching for something to bind the wound, which at least distanced her from Jake. He looked bad, a sure sign he hadn't made it easy on his kidnappers, but it didn't look like anything time couldn't heal. He scooted over to me, his leg fitting comfortably against my good one.

"Such a waste." He stared down at Ian's inert form.

"He's been doing real estate deals not only for Russo but for himself. Millions of dollars at stake. I suspect most of the deals aren't legitimate." In fact, I was betting on that. If there was enough proof that Russo was involved with deals that weren't on the up and up, I might be able to force him to look the other way while Dennis and Sophie disappeared again. It'd be a tough sell, though. One I couldn't even try if Russo actually had Sawyer.

"I was planning to go public. No wonder he freaked."

At least Jake understood. He was watching Kolonda now, an odd look on his face. My heart did a funny lurch. Was I losing him? Jake had been my closest friend and constant supporter in the year since Winter had died in the bridge collapse. I'd known for most of that time that I loved him. Yet I also knew that tragedy sometimes brought people together who wouldn't ordinarily find each other. What that might mean, I couldn't say.

My muscles screamed with the pressure I had to keep on Ian's wound to staunch the flow of blood, and my leg was so far beyond numb that I was almost surprised to see it still attached.

Jake was watching me now. "You're hurt."

"A scratch." I remembered Shannon had once said something like that to me. I tried to grin but failed.

"Will this do?" Kolonda returned with a yellowed, embroidered tablecloth that probably cost more than I paid for food in a month.

"Perfect." I wedged it over the shirt and continued my pressure, which at least saved me from being drenched with blood and exposed to who-knew-what. Ian still hadn't regained consciousness. Lucky for him.

I was glad when Shannon reappeared in the doorway, though it wasn't Robison he shoved into the room in front of him. The half-dressed contractor fell to his knees and wouldn't meet my gaze.

"Well?" I asked, hoping he'd passed Robison off to other officers outside.

Shannon shook his head. "Got away. Planned escape."

"He works for Saito."

"Really?"

"Who works for Saito? What's going on?" Jake interrupted, a hurt in his voice that had nothing to do with his physical aches. Guess I wasn't the only one who had jealousy issues.

I explained about the fake guard and the imprint he'd left on the cuffs, but I didn't get far into the tale because people began arriving. First the police, who made short work of the contractor, and then the paramedics, who rushed Ian off to the hospital, and more paramedics who tended to Jake.

"Look at her, too," Shannon said, motioning to me. "Something's wrong with her leg."

I sighed and submitted to a paramedic, who unwrapped my leg and told me I should go to the hospital. I didn't want to go because I was thinking about Sawyer and feeling I was missing something. "Just wrap it again for now," I told him in a low voice so Shannon wouldn't hear. "Something to hold me for a bit."

As he finished wrapping my leg, I felt Jake's phone vibrating in my pocket. I took a piece of the paramedic's gauze and fished it out. My sister, of course. "Hello?"

"Autumn. Thank heaven you're safe! I've been calling and calling, and you haven't picked up."

"It's been a little busy."

"I was so scared," she whispered. "I drew a picture of you and Jake. You were holding something in your hands, and you were frozen. There was a man with a gun. I just about jumped in the car to try to find you."

"It's okay," I said. "We're okay. We found Jake." She couldn't have helped even if she had come, and I hoped she knew her baby meant far more to me than any danger she might possibly save me from.

"Sawyer wasn't there?"

"I'm sorry."

"I'm the one who's sorry. I got you into this."

"Don't be. It's what I do."

I was glad she didn't ask me to make this the last time because despite all the terrors of the day and all the aches in my sore body, I hadn't felt more alive since my last case. Maybe Winter had been right when he said some people couldn't help what they were called to do. Sometimes you had to step up and take the role you were meant to fill.

"How's little Riverreed?" I asked.

Tawnia laughed, making me feel less exhausted. "Riverreed. I'll think about it."

"Really?"

"No."

"I didn't think so. Look, I have to go."

"Call me if you need me."

"I will." I hung up to find Shannon watching me.

"What's wrong with your leg?" he asked. "Maybe you'd better go to the hospital."

"I hurt it earlier. But it's wrapped, and the paramedic gave me a painkiller, so I'm fine for now."

His silence told me he doubted my word, and he would be right. I felt weak and fragile both from my wound and from those horrifying imprints on the cuffs—and jealous at the way Kolonda was still fawning over my boyfriend. I needed a good imprint or a ton of protein to shake this feeling.

Jake was already pushing away from his paramedics and limping toward me. "Here, take this." He shoved something into my hand.

"What is it?"

"Power bar. I bummed it off one of the paramedics." He gave me a wink and settled next to me.

A rush of feeling made me weepy. "Thanks."

He leaned his head against mine and said nothing. The understanding that he was finally and truly safe flooded me. It so easily could have gone another way. I closed my eyes momentarily and drank in the sensation.

Before long, I became all too aware of Kolonda and Shannon watching us. Was it my imagination that Shannon was fiddling with his watch? Maybe putting it on? Why would he be doing that? Actually, I could use that watch right now because as content as I was to have Jake safe, my legs felt boneless, and a single protein bar might not go far toward changing that. Then I remembered Tawnia's drawing. Smiling, I put a hand in my pocket, working a finger underneath the protective sleeve. Love seeped slowly through my body, soothing the worst of the imprinted memories.

Shannon's gaze followed the movements of my hand but lifted away almost immediately. I was glad he didn't ask.

The paramedic who'd dressed my wound still hovered nearby, looking as though he was going to say something—probably something about having to report a gunshot wound—but I waved him to silence. "I'll go to the hospital soon. Detective Martin will see that I do, I'm sure. Thanks for your help." I stared at Shannon, daring him to contradict me, but he didn't say a word. I must have convinced him. Of course, he didn't know that I'd been shot, and I wasn't going to enlighten him or Jake about that—not until after I figured out what had happened to Sawyer. Besides, with the imprints from my sister's drawing, the power bar, and Jake's presence, my leg and I were both feeling better.

"Ian must have been working both sides," I said, thinking it through aloud. "It's the only thing that makes sense if the Saitos were going to all that trouble to watch him."

Shannon nodded. "So Ian finds out about Dennis's past and contacts not only his family but the Saitos as well."

"Why not? He gives the Francos back their prodigal son and gets Russo's business. Then he gives Saito a chance at revenge. Double the profit. Bet he has business deals with Saito as well. He was going to meet with Saito tonight."

"You know this from the imprint on the cuff?"

I shivered. "From one of them." It was a low blow, but Shannon had it coming. He should have looked out for me. You did that for your partner, even a temporary one.

His eyes held sorrow. "You couldn't drop the cuffs?"

"No." I'd been completely drawn in. Whether because I was

tired or because the imprints had been so strong, I really didn't know. It was frightening even to think about.

"I'm really sorry."

"It's over." I shrugged. It wasn't really. The images couldn't be erased from my mind so easily. Better not to experience them in the first place. "Look, despite whatever deal Ian made with Saito, he obviously didn't trust Ian, so he planted the guard."

"Who decided to kill him when we showed up."

"Yeah. Protect the boss at all costs. Pretty lousy way to do business, if you ask me."

"Or a good one. Ian probably would have sold out Saito."

I wasn't too sure, but we'd probably never know. Jake and Kolonda were paying close attention to the conversation, but the dazed look on Kolonda's face made me wonder if she was in shock. Apparently, the paramedics thought so, too, because one was checking her pulse. Two others were back to looking at Jake.

"That Joben Saito tried to kill Ian means Ian must have something big on him," Shannon said. "Something he wanted to make sure Ian didn't implicate him in."

"Proof of murder?" I suggested. "Saito killed Dennis's brother. Ian must have known that."

"It all happened so long ago that I doubt there's much proof remaining. Except Dennis, whose word is questionable after his involvement in the murder of Saito's son."

Goose bumps crawled over my scalp. "Kidnapping, then."

Shannon shook his head, his face growing hard. "Ian Gideon wouldn't do that. Not to a child. If he planned to give Sawyer to Saito, he had to know they would kill him."

The idea of Sawyer being given to the Saitos was every bit as repulsive to me, but unless there was another player, which seemed unlikely, Ian had taken Sawyer for either Saito or Russo. If it'd been Russo, we'd have probably heard something by now—either from

Ace or some other source Shannon had employed to investigate Russo, or maybe from Dennis himself, if his cousin had hinted at taking Sawyer to prevent him from talking to the police. So that left Saito.

"Fact: Ian was going to meet with Saito tonight," I said. "Fact: Sawyer was in his apartment." I took the soldier from the pocket of my jeans, hearing Jake draw in a swift breath of air as he recognized the toy. I dropped it into Shannon's hand before the imprint of the abduction could play all the way out.

Our eyes met with complete understanding. "We have to find Sawyer before Saito does," Shannon said.

18

How are we going to find Sawyer?" Jake asked, lifting an ice pack from his eye.

Shannon opened his mouth, probably to order us all to our homes or the hospital, but I beat him to it. "I need to go back to Ian's apartment. There has to be something I'm missing. Maybe I can find a clue there."

"I'll have the other officers meet us," Shannon said. "They'll have to go over everything again now that we have this new information. Don't touch anything until it's cleared, okay?"

"I'll try to restrain myself."

Jake made a strangled sound of amusement.

"Jake, shouldn't you go to the hospital?" Kolonda looked drawn and unfocused.

"I'm okay. I need to help find the boy."

Her eyes begged him, saying she needed him, pleading for him to go with her, to take her somewhere safe. Jake wouldn't be a man if he didn't notice, if his protective urges didn't kick in.

I wondered if he would fall to Kolonda's silent pleas.

"Maybe an officer could . . ." I trailed off, looking at Jake and then back to Kolonda. Shannon's eyes riveted on mine, plainly understanding. If he didn't find someone to take Kolonda, Jake would feel obligated. Not that Shannon really cared, but I knew exactly how I felt about it.

"Good idea," Jake said, and I felt myself relax.

Shannon nodded. "Come with me. I'll get you squared away." With a last baleful look at Jake, Kolonda obeyed.

As they moved off, Jake slid a cool, clammy hand into mine. Kolonda was right—he should have gone to the hospital. But he wouldn't leave me now, not like last time, when he'd gone into a burning building and saved lives, never knowing that because he wasn't with me, I would almost die. He'd have to get over the guilt someday, like I had the nightmares. I didn't hold any of it against him. Shannon had come in time.

Shannon glanced back at me, as if aware of my thoughts. His eyes were hooded, almost navy in the dim light. I had no idea what he was thinking. Not like Jake, who was easy to read, though he hadn't always been.

Jake rubbed his fingers over mine. "Thanks for coming for me."

Again that weepy feeling, which I pushed away. "You'd do the same for me. Come on. Let's try to find Sawyer."

Ian must have stashed the boy somewhere and was planning to hand him off tonight. I had to believe that, because if Saito already had Sawyer, the game was over, and two people I cared about would mourn that little boy for the rest of their lives.

No, I had to believe Saito didn't have him. Yet.

Still, they might know where Ian was keeping him, so he was in danger even with Ian out of the picture. They could have had him followed or traced or whatever other methods criminals used.

"You do have someone ready to question Ian the minute he

wakes, don't you?" I asked Shannon, as we caught up with him near the elevators.

"*If* he wakes. We don't know that he'll make it. It doesn't look good."

I fought down a snarl. It wasn't Shannon's fault. Robison—if that was really his name—had ended up being something entirely different from what we'd thought.

What was I missing? There had to be something. Where would Ian have taken Sawyer?

In Shannon's police car, I made Jake sit in the front with Shannon so I could be alone with my thoughts. Jake didn't look happy about the seating arrangement, but I knew he was glad I wasn't near Shannon.

Men.

A glimpse of my face in Shannon's rearview mirror clearly showed the new bruises from my attack that morning, but on the whole, I looked a lot better than Jake did. He caught my gaze and winked at me with his good eye. Unlike certain detectives I knew, he didn't hold a grudge.

We were halfway to Ian's apartment when I remembered. "His housekeeper," I said, leaning over the seat. "Ian has a cleaning lady. He said the soldier I found there probably belonged to her son. What if there really is a cleaning lady with a child? Who better to take care of Sawyer?"

"Definitely a possibility." Shannon glanced at me in his rearview mirror.

"If Gideon's building is anything like most places around here," Jake said, "other residents might employ the same housekeeper. Often they'll give a discount for people in the same building."

Shannon took the next corner a little too sharply, and when I grunted with the shards of pain moving down my leg, he flashed me an apologetic look. "I'll have the officers question the neighbors when they get there. Question them again, I guess, since they already did that earlier when they found Tracy. Can't risk missing anything."

He began rattling orders into the phone, and after a few moments his voice became irritated, a tone I'd previously thought he reserved for me. "No, I didn't send anyone to the university. Way too late now, anyway. If they call again, tell them we'll send someone tomorrow." He disconnected without saying good-bye.

Minutes later we altered course when an officer called to give Shannon the address of a Mrs. Greta Duval, Ian's housekeeper. It was after midnight by this time, probably closer to one, if my internal clock was working right, but we couldn't worry about that now. If she wasn't involved, she should be happy to help out. At any rate, as a mother with a young child, she should be home at this hour.

We were almost at the address when another call came in. "Are you sure?" Shannon barked. "I'm on my way. Wait until I get there."

"What is it?" I demanded.

"They've located Joben Saito. I've had everyone watching for his people since the explosion at his warehouse today. He and a couple of goons are in a limo heading to the river north of the Hawthorne Bridge reconstruction."

My breath caught in my throat. I should have known. The collapse of the bridge had brought my greatest sorrow and my greatest joy: Winter's death and the knowledge that I had a twin. The bridge was being rebuilt by none other than my engineer brother-in-law, and it would be stronger than it had been before, but I had a problem with all bridges lately. I couldn't cross them without remembering how it felt being trapped in my car as it plunged into the cold, dark expanse of the Willamette.

I swallowed hard and found I could breathe again. "You think he knows where Sawyer is?"

"He seems to be in an awful hurry."

"Let's go, then. Just in case."

Jake said nothing throughout our exchange, but I knew he was in agreement. I also knew he would protect me with his life, and I was hoping that didn't get him killed. We were both running on adrenaline now. I bet that, like me, he couldn't rest if he tried.

We pulled up a block from the river, where Shannon led us on foot to a place by the bank. Three other officers waited near a stone wall that bordered the area. They welcomed Shannon with relief, though they frowned at Jake and me when we appeared—all but the red-haired Peirce Elvey, who gave me a grin. Nice to see a friendly face.

"Saito's in the car," said Peirce's partner. His black skin and shaved head blended perfectly with the night. "That big Asian and that other guy are dumping something into the river. Looks heavy."

I squinted at the men with the trunk, trying to distinguish features that the clouds overhead obscured from our view. The Asian was recognizable by his bulk, but the other man could have been anyone.

"You sure Saito's in the car?" Shannon asked.

"Yep. They stopped off at a construction site on the way. We have someone checking it out now and doing a trace on who owns it, but so far there's no sign of why they were there."

I looked at Shannon. "You think they kept the meeting with Ian?"

"Maybe they took whatever he planned to give them." His voice was carefully controlled.

"Whatever's in that trunk, it's going in the river," Jake choked out. "It's deep here. You'll need divers to get it back."

"What if Sawyer's in—" I couldn't finish the sentence, though it was the only reason I could think of that Saito himself would be present. He would finally exact revenge for the part Dennis had played in Saito's son's death. Everyone stared at the two men struggling under the weight. Either the trunk was loaded with a lot of something, or it was made of lead.

Clouds drifted away from the moon, shedding more light on the bank, and the men with the trunk began to hurry.

"It's that guard," Shannon said, at the same moment I recognized the man we knew as Robison. "Elvey, you're with me," Shannon continued. "We're going for the big Asian and his friend. You others take the car." His eyes fell on me and Jake. "You two stay here. Better yet, call for backup. Push redial." He started to hand me his phone but on second thought gave it to Jake. I didn't know whether to feel offended or grateful that he didn't want me picking up imprints from his phone.

The shooting started about thirty seconds after they left us, ten seconds after Jake finished talking to the precinct. "We have to see what's happening," I hissed as Jake pulled me closer to the wall.

He nodded, and we both slowly peeked out, our eyes going first to the men with the trunk. They had dropped it and were using it for a shield as they fired at Shannon and Pierce. Peirce shot cover from a rotting structure on the bank while Shannon sprinted over the ground and leapt over the trunk onto Robison. The two rolled down the bank, struggling. The Asian continued to exchange fire with Peirce.

Thirty yards away, car doors opened, and men fired on the other two officers. One officer fell, but he rolled and began firing again in the next second. The car's engine revved, and with the doors still open, it barreled not away from the scene, but toward where Peirce was holding off the big Asian. Peirce dived to one side as the car crashed into the ruins. The unlikely move gave Peirce and his fellow officers an advantage because now they surrounded the car.

Except no one was paying attention to the big Asian with the trunk.

"Jake!" I gripped his sleeve. "He's going to dump it!"

The man, driven by whatever loyalty held him to his master, was tugging the trunk with low grunts, his muscles rippling through his long-sleeved shirt.

Closer to the river, I saw Shannon taking a step toward the Asian, only to be tackled again by Robison.

Jake and I shared a glance. He nodded slowly. I took a breath.

We ran—or hobbled, rather—along the wall several yards before vaulting over it, angling to the river's edge. Our path took us beyond where Peirce and the others were battling it out with the car, and I could only hope Saito and his men were too busy to notice two more shadows.

I pushed myself harder, feeling the weeds and refuse along the bank digging into the tough soles of my bare feet. I was faster than Jake, even with my hurt leg, which wasn't saying much. It seemed to take forever to get to the water.

My attention was solely on the trunk as I moved. I had a vision of being shot and not feeling it. Of dying so quickly that I wouldn't have time to understand that I would never save Sawyer.

I reached the water, but with a final grunt that echoed out over the water, the Asian lifted the trunk and heaved it in.

CHAPTER
19

I dived in after the trunk. What else could I do? Before the water covered my head, I had a faint glimpse of Shannon's shocked face, his fist pulled back to deliver a powerful blow to the fake guard, and Jake slamming into the Asian. Then I was under. For a moment I panicked, feeling the icy, liquid death closing over my body. Unseen hands seemed to push me down, down, down.

Winter had been in the water a week before they found him. My father. He wouldn't have been on the bridge at all if he hadn't gone antiques hunting with me.

The trunk. I could barely see the shape in the dark water— probably it was more instinct than actually seeing. I reached out, grasping the edges, preparing myself for a shocking imprint.

I felt . . . nothing.

Just the weight of the box, which, though considerably less in the water, was more than I could lift. I pulled, and my body shot downwards, under the trunk. I pushed again, flapping my legs wildly, but I couldn't tell if I was going up or down. Was the trunk filling with water? What made it so heavy?

I pushed harder. Something brushed my leg, and I imagined a hand before I remembered the fish in the river. My lungs felt like bursting, though I knew I hadn't been in the water long enough to need air.

Yet.

Down. Or up. I couldn't tell. There was no sun to guide me.

The need in my lungs grew. I tried pushing in the direction of what I thought was the bank. If only I could find some purchase for my feet.

There, I felt something. I kicked out, but whatever I'd felt only bruised my foot and continued down the river. Was I drifting, too? What was happening with Jake? With Shannon? The need to know burned as brightly as the need to breathe.

I was going to have to leave the trunk or drown with it. The knowledge came with a deep sorrow. What would I tell Sophie and Dennis?

I felt my hands slipping but not of my own accord. My sight blurred.

No. I would survive. I wouldn't let the river take me as it had Winter.

I pushed outward, one last time and then angled for what I hoped was up. Within seconds I heard shouting, which I joined the second my head split the water. "Down here! It's right here!" Too late, I wondered if it would be the Asian and Robison who greeted me.

But it was Jake who stood anxiously over the water, calling my name. Behind him, I saw Shannon checking the Asian's pulse. Jake waded into the water and grabbed me.

"The trunk!" I reminded him.

We went after it together, joined by Shannon. Between the

three of us, we got the trunk up the bank. Only then did I see Peirce and the dark-skinned officer standing near the car with a stoic Saito. Beyond the big Asian, Robison lay unconscious, one foot in the river.

"Open it," I said to Shannon. I was shaking now, as much from fear of what we would find as from the cold water.

Shannon took out his gun. For a moment, I thought he'd shoot off the lock but wasn't surprised when he used the butt to break the lock. No danger of ricochet. I was on the opposite side of the trunk, so as he peeked in, the lid obstructed my view. He dropped the lid immediately.

"What is it?" Jake asked.

Shannon shook his head and didn't answer.

Not good. Worse than not good if he wasn't even feeling for a pulse. Tears leaked from my eyes as I slumped to the ground. My short hair was plastered to my head, reminding me of that other time when I had waited on the bank by the Willamette, worrying about Winter.

What was I going to tell Sophie?

Near the car, Saito was still impassive, an uncaring monster responsible for a child's death. I hoped he rotted in prison forever.

Shannon was talking into a borrowed phone, directing more officers to the location. He had a large gash on his forehead and occasionally dabbed at it with impatience. Jake stood staring at the trunk, his face frozen. I knew exactly how he felt. I wanted to yell at Shannon for continuing to do his job, for not caring enough, but I could see the tightness in his face, could feel the anger radiating from him. He cared.

Someone had better make real sure Saito stayed far away from Shannon.

And from me.

"I want to know who's responsible," I said. "There's got to be something I can read. Give me something."

"We know who's responsible," Shannon said.

Jake shook himself back into the conversation. "Could have been the attorney. Maybe that was the deal. To do it himself."

Shannon considered a moment, looking first at me and then at Jake. The antagonism I usually felt between them had vanished. Whatever had happened with the Asian while I was in the water had changed something. I might never know what, and at the moment I didn't care.

"It could be bad," Shannon said. "The imprint."

Jake flinched, but he took one look at my determined face and said, "She'll handle it."

I wasn't so sure, but I was going to try. I owed Sawyer and his parents that much. I nodded.

Shannon motioned us back. "I'll see what there is but don't get close. Trust me when I say it's not pretty. There's not much left."

"It doesn't have to be much." In a murder situation, pretty much anything could hold an imprint. Strong emotion did that to objects. On our first case together, I'd been able to identify a little girl's kidnapper from touching her bicycle. We hadn't found her in time, but we had managed to lock the man away.

When Shannon opened the trunk, I couldn't help looking and then had to turn away, gagging. I saw a blue-checkered shirt that resembled the one I'd heard Sawyer had been wearing when he went missing, but the rest wasn't recognizable as anything human, not anymore. I was glad for the dark and my distance.

Shannon gave me a hard look as he shut the trunk again. Before he could show me what he'd taken, more officers arrived. Leaving the trunk to them, Shannon motioned us further down the bank where he produced something between two fingers. An antique soldier mounted on a horse. Sawyer's most favorite of the soldiers I'd given him. Back at Ian's he'd probably let the housekeeper's son play with the other soldier, reserving this one for himself. When they'd gone, the other child had left his borrowed toy behind.

I hesitated, glancing behind me at the men kneeling around the trunk. At least one was a medical professional, or they would have to call one. There would be an autopsy. What kind of world did we live in that a young child was a pawn in a deadly game of revenge? I pushed my sodden bangs from my eyes and reached for the soldier.

The tall, blond man set a change of clothes on the table. I recognized the man as Ian and that the imprint took place in the kitchen at his apartment. At the same time I knew Sawyer had never seen him before. Sawyer/I stared up at him with dislike—a complete dislike that had no solid reasoning. This man had sent away the bad guy who grabbed him in the sandbox and promised to take him home, yet Sawyer/I didn't trust him. He wore a fake smile, and his voice was greasy.

"Put these on," the man said.

"No." I loved my shirt. It was like the soft one Daddy wore when we went camping.

"Do it," the man said. "Those clothes are dirty. You can't go to your parents wearing dirty clothes."

Did he mean it? Going back to Mommy and Daddy and Lizzy?

The woman began taking off my shirt like Mommy always did. She was Edgar's mommy and she was nice. "I'll give the child a bath when I get home," she said. "What time are they coming for him?"

"Seven or eight."

The man put my shirt in a bag. I tried not to cry. I didn't want to be a baby in front of Edgar. I liked Edgar. He was playing with my other soldier by the table.

The thin man handed the woman a folder. "Here are the adoption papers. Make sure they get them when they come." The man was staring at my horsey soldier. I grabbed it tight in both hands. *Mine!* He came at me like a snake. No, not my toy!

I blinked as the imprint cut off. Another took its place, an older, more pleasant one from a week ago, but I shoved the soldier into my pocket to make it stop.

Jake and Shannon were staring at me anxiously. "It's not him. What's in that box isn't him." I felt like screaming it. "Ian took his clothes earlier at his house and sent him away with a woman. He gave her adoption papers to pass on to someone else who was coming to get him."

Shannon blinked. "I know what I saw in that trunk."

"You either trust me or you don't."

"Wait here." He jogged to the knot of officers around the trunk.

"It's not him." I leaned into Jake, a hysterical giggle bubbling up inside me.

His arm went around me. "Then what's in that trunk?"

"I don't know. Wait." I pushed away from him. "Ian said they were coming at seven or eight. I think the imprint was before dinner, but I don't know if he meant tonight or tomorrow morning. What if we don't get there in time?"

"I'll get Shannon."

Not without me he wouldn't. We both hurried toward the trunk, our wet jeans making odd flapping sounds.

"Definitely not a recent demise," a man was saying. "This person has already been embalmed. In fact, I think we may have found the missing cadaver that was stolen from the university this morning. Or part of it. That man was seventy-five and died of cancer. This blood didn't come from him. In fact, it might not even be actual blood. Doesn't seem to be coagulating properly, and the smell is different. There's no doubt they wanted the trunk to sink, though. The bottom is lined with six inches of metal."

Shannon turned to face us, a grim smile on his face. "Let's go for a drive."

I wish he'd taken my word for it, but we hadn't lost that much time.

Someone put a blanket around me, and I looked up to see Peirce's smiling face. "Thanks." I wanted to tell him I was glad he hadn't been hurt, but words didn't seem adequate.

He grinned, his freckled face looking much younger than he really was. "You looked a little cold."

In Shannon's unmarked squad car, he slapped a large rectangular bandage on his forehead before triggering his lights and siren. I was glad there wasn't any talk of leaving us behind. If I was going to continue consulting on cases, he would have to get used to taking me with him. Besides, from the images I'd seen in Sawyer's imprint on the toy soldier, I didn't feel the housekeeper posed a physical danger.

From the backseat, I leaned forward to ask, "How could Ian Gideon draw the line at murdering a child but not at separating him permanently from his parents? It doesn't make sense."

"Warped minds," Shannon said. "I've stopped trying to figure them out."

It still bothered me. Ian was willing to hurt Jake, perhaps kill him. He hadn't seemed fazed at taking down an officer, shooting me, or bilking people out of millions. Yet I believed he really liked Tracy, and he hadn't given Sawyer to the Saitos. Why? A shade of gray I couldn't understand.

"He must have paid someone to break into the university," Jake said. "Wouldn't be hard to find a student who needed money."

"A lot of trouble to fool Saito about the boy's death." Shannon glanced back at me. "My bet is that it boils down to money, not Ian's conscience or any bit of good in him. White child, healthy, male. Even though he's three, he probably got a good price from someone who wasn't eligible for a regular adoption. Someone who wanted a child fast. Plus, if things went wrong, he wouldn't go to jail for murder."

"What if Sawyer's not there?"

Shannon didn't have an answer, but I felt the car speed up.

"We'll plaster the news with his face," Jake said. "Tell everyone he was illegally adopted. Someone will have seen him."

"Unless it's a foreign adoption." Shannon's voice was low. "There's also a dark side to child trafficking that doesn't include anything resembling a real adoption. The fact is, the first twenty-four hours are the best time to find him alive. We're running out of options. We'd better hope he's there."

I slumped back in my seat, folding my arms across my stomach, and prayed.

As when we'd been heading to the law firm's garage, Shannon turned off the siren a few blocks from our destination. "We don't know how involved she is. Better to surprise her."

The residential area was much like the one Tawnia and Bret lived in, or it had been a decade ago. The houses were not quite as new, but most were in good repair and the yards well-groomed. There were a few For Sale signs, and some of those houses were vacant and the lawns dying or overgrown, but for the most part it was a nice middle-class neighborhood. Not one you would suspect of being involved in child trafficking.

When Shannon pulled up in front of the house, all the lights were off. He examined the sleeping neighborhood a moment, before simultaneously drawing his gun and opening his door.

"Wait," I said. "Put the gun away. Let's just go ask her."

"She could be dangerous."

"She has a little boy. Sawyer likes her. She's working for a re-spected attorney who told her everything is on the up and up. She might sense something's not quite right, but she doesn't know for sure."

Emotions ran over Shannon's face, but I couldn't tell what they were—frustration, irritation, admiration? Could have been all three, and more. "Okay, but any sign of danger and you two get out of the way."

"Yes, sir." I looked at Jake, who grinned. He eased out of the car, and I noticed his stiffness because I felt the same way. After today was over, I was going to eat three steaks and sleep for a week.

Shannon motioned to the squad car that had pulled up behind us. Peirce and the dark-skinned officer slid smoothly from their seats, weapons drawn. I hadn't noticed them following us, but I'd been a little preoccupied. "Go around back. Make sure no one leaves." They nodded and hurried off.

At the door, Shannon rang the bell and waited. There was room for only two of us on the porch, and Jake indicated that I should stand next to Shannon. Seeing a woman might be less intimidating than a mulatto man with dreadlocks who looked as though he'd barely survived a gang beating.

We were about to ring again, when the sound of dragging footsteps made us stiffen to attention. The porch light flicked on, and I could see motion behind the peephole. "Who are you?" said a woman's voice that I recognized from Sawyer's imprint.

"Mrs. Duval?" I said before Shannon could speak. "We're here for the child Mr. Gideon placed with you."

"You aren't supposed to be here until morning."

"Please let us in."

A long-suffering sigh we could hear even through the closed door. Then the lock clicked, and the door opened. Greta Duval, wearing lounge pants and a T-shirt, was younger than in Sawyer's imprint, but then to him every adult must seem old. She had beautiful, sleek black hair that hung straight around her face, as though somewhere in her genealogy she might have had Middle Eastern ancestors. The rest of her was pure American, from the smattering of freckles to her ordinary brown eyes.

She studied Shannon and me, faltering as people always did at my bare feet. Could she tell that we were soaked? "You must be the new parents. Too anxious to wait, I bet. Well, he's been anxious to see you, too, ever since Mr. Gideon told him you'd be coming for him. He's a nice boy, and I'm happy he's getting a second chance at having a family." She paused, taking a manila folder off the battered upright piano behind her. "Here. You can look at the papers while I get him. He'll probably be asleep. I'm not sure I can wake him."

"No need." Shannon said, "I'll carry him."

"Just stay here. I don't want to wake my son." Mrs. Duval had seen Jake behind us and her eyes narrowed. "You are here because Mr. Gideon sent you, aren't you?"

"Yes, of course," I said.

She turned to go, but Shannon passed me the folder and put a hand on her arm. "I need to go with you."

Mrs. Duval clutched at the neck of her T-shirt. "Who are you really?"

Shannon eased his badge from his wet slacks and held it up for her to see. "I'm Detective Martin with the Portland police. We're investigating the kidnapping of three-year-old Sawyer Briggs. We believe he's here, and I can't allow you to leave this room without me. We don't believe you had any part in the kidnapping, but we don't know that for sure, and we can't risk that you might do anything to the boy."

Mrs. Duval was shaking her head, her skin suddenly too white against the black hair. "I wouldn't hurt him! And I didn't know he was kidnapped. Mr. Gideon told me his parents had been killed in a car accident. That's all I know."

Anger spurred me to words because Mrs. Duval had handled the folder of adoption papers with enough anxiety and guilt that she had left an imprint. Not enough to evoke a vivid scene in my mind, but the emotions were clear. "You felt something was wrong," I said quietly. "You should have called the police to make sure."

She brought her hands to her face and wept. "Okay, I guess I did think it odd that Mr. Gideon asked me to help him, and he was acting strange. But I really wanted to believe him."

"Is there anyone else in the house besides you and the two boys?"

"No. No one. My husband works the night shift. I'll show you where the boys are."

Shannon went with Mrs. Duval. I handed the folder to Jake, relieved to get rid of it. He rubbed my hand sympathetically. The minutes seemed like hours until at last Shannon reappeared with his gun holstered and Sawyer in his arms.

Sawyer moved restlessly and opened his eyes, blinking several times before he was awake enough to recognize me. "Autumn!" He held out his hands for me, arching away from Shannon. I took him in my arms and hugged him tightly. He started crying. "I want my mommy. Can you take me to Mommy?"

"That's why I'm here, buddy. We've all been looking for you. Everyone's waiting. You're safe now. I promise."

He clung to me weakly and sobbed soft tears of relief that I echoed.

Behind Shannon, Mrs. Duval had her fist to her mouth. She was also crying. "I'm so sorry. If I'd known, I would have talked to him about what happened, but I didn't want to make him remember his parents if they really were dead."

I turned and made my way from the house, with Jake close behind. Shannon followed, calling the other officers so they could watch Mrs. Duval. Jake opened the back door of the car for me, and I slid inside.

"It's okay," I murmured to Sawyer. "It's okay." I wrapped him in another blanket Shannon took from his trunk and held him close as we drove away.

20

Turned out Jake and I went to the hospital after all because that's where Sophie was with Dennis and Lizbeth, who was sleeping in her arms. When we opened the door to the room, she gave a small cry and came running. A startled Shannon found himself holding Lizbeth, while Sophie snatched a newly sleeping Sawyer from my arms.

"Oh, thank you! Thank you!" She showered his face with kisses and cried until she woke both him and Dennis. Sawyer wrapped his arms around his mother's neck as though he'd never let go. Harsh sobs came from the bed.

Jake and I left Shannon to explain and went with a nurse someone had sicced on us—probably Shannon in one of the numerous telephone calls he'd made on the drive to the hospital.

"It's over," Jake said, letting out a deep sigh.

"Not for Dennis and Sophie. They'll still have to go back with Russo." I looked around. "I expected to see him here, or one of his men."

"If you're talking about that big black-haired man with the bodyguard," the nurse said, ushering us into a room, "he was here all day, mostly on the phone, but he left an hour ago. Something about his wife being in labor."

Russo had told me his wife was expecting another girl, and of course nature would choose now to send the baby. "He'll never make it to New Jersey in time."

"I don't think he was going to try. Apparently they're doing a video feed." She rolled her eyes. "What's the world coming to? I mean, I know he cares about his cousin, but if my husband wasn't around when I had a baby, he'd be sleeping on the couch for a year."

Not my place to enlighten her about Dennis's importance in the Franco family. Nic Russo's wife could have a dozen baby girls, and all of them together wouldn't be more important to the Francos than Dennis or his son. Not while Dennis's father was still in charge.

"What about the guy who was shot earlier—Ian Gideon," I asked. "Was he brought here? Is he going to be okay?" As much as I disliked the guy, my plan to keep Russo away from Dennis and Sophie hinged on finding proof that he was involved in something shady. Getting Ian to cut a deal might be the only way to get Russo to back off. My plan fell down a bit when I thought about how little Ian cared for the rest of the human race, but I was desperate.

The nurse's expression changed. "Look, I'm not supposed to hand out information to anyone except immediate family, but they said if it wasn't for you, he would have died in that parking garage. I'm sorry. It's not looking good. We've called his family so they can say good-bye. That's all I can tell you."

Jake and I exchanged a look. Robison had been aiming to kill and obviously knew his job well. That he would serve time for the murder, or that Ian had done so much wrong, didn't make the bleak finality of death any easier. Or help Dennis and Sophie.

The nurse bent to her ministrations, her loquaciousness apparently at an end. I received a shot of painkiller in my leg and only a few stitches, which belied my worst fears, and a lecture from a doctor who looked like he was still in high school about the importance of immediately reporting a gunshot wound. I promised to make note of that for the future.

Jake was grinning at the scolding I received—right up until they gave him a boot for the simple fracture in his lower right leg, a removable cast for his left arm, and staples in his scalp. They also told him he'd fractured his left orbit, the bone holding his eye, but the doctor had high hopes of that not needing surgery. We were to watch for drooping of the eye or sudden changes in vision.

When the nurse went to get Jake's pain medication, I would have teased him, except that he looked so miserable—and I was feeling the strong impressions that bound me to my twin. Standing, I shrugged off the blanket I still wore around my shoulders and went to the door to peer down the hall.

Thinking of my sister, I remembered her miniature drawing, and I wedged my hand in my pocket, fishing for it. Like the rest of me, the drawing was soaked, despite the plastic cover, and I felt a keen sense of loss.

Jake's eyes caught mine over the ruined mess. "She'll make you another one. She'll understand." He was right. Though special, the drawing wasn't irreplaceable. I nodded my thanks, though there wasn't really a need. Jake and I understood each other.

"I'll be back in a minute," I told him. Because instead of Tawnia, Russo had appeared at the far intersection of the hallway, and I knew where he was heading. Though an officer was still posted outside Dennis's door, Russo was determined, and he might find his way in.

I was every bit as determined. Maybe I could reason with him. I thought I might have glimpsed a bit of humanity behind his tough exterior. Had I been fooling myself? I pushed myself faster, rounding the corner where they had disappeared.

One door down from Dennis's room, bald Charlie spotted me and said something to Russo, who stopped and turned. "Ah, Miss Rain. I should put you on the payroll. I hear you saved another member of my family."

"You'd better hold off on that," I said. "I had a good talk with Ian Gideon, and when he wasn't shooting at me, he was telling me what a scam you've been running. It'll all be public now. Your family name is going to be at the top of the headlines. There'll be an investigation."

Russo's congenial expression vanished. "Is that a threat?"

"Just letting you know what's going to happen."

"All my businesses in Portland are legitimate."

"Not according to Ian Gideon." I was bluffing. Could he tell? Behind Russo, Shannon came from Dennis's room and headed our way.

Russo chuckled. "My attorney would never be so stupid as to testify against me. He knows that."

"What if he's dead?" Shannon said.

Russo watched Shannon come around to stand beside me. "Is that another threat? And here I was about to thank you for helping Miss Rain find my cousin's son."

"What I mean," Shannon continued as if Russo hadn't spoken, "is that Ian Gideon is going to die, thanks to your old friend, Mr. Saito. At the moment he's on life support, and his family is deciding whether or not to donate his organs that survived the attack. Given the nature of the case, the police will be taking possession of all his records. I'm sure we'll find what we need in them to send you away for a very long time."

"As I told Miss Rain, all my dealings here are completely—" Russo broke off, his thick brows knitting. "Ah, I understand. I guess Mr. Gideon's records could show anything. What do you want from me?"

I stared at them both blankly before I finally caught on. Shannon would never plant false information, but Russo couldn't know that.

"Leave Dennis alone." I stepped toward Russo. "Just let him go. If you've already told his father that you found him, say he died from injuries. Anything. You said you cared for him once, and I believe you meant it. Your own mother helped him get away. If you take him back to New Jersey, you'll ruin a lot of people's lives. Dennis isn't cut out for that life. You know that as well as I do. And Sawyer—" The thought of his growing up involved with Russo's questionable businesses made me furious enough to leap over tall buildings to save him. "You don't need Sawyer. You run the business anyway, and you can have your own son someday. Or a grandson. You have what? Four daughters now? One of them is bound to have a son. Or you could get over the archaic notion about sons and one of your daughters could be your heir."

Russo held up his hand with the missing finger, a hint of a smile on his lips. "I don't have four daughters."

"But the nurse told me—didn't the baby come?"

"Oh, the baby came. I saw the whole thing from my hotel. Imagine that." He was still smiling, but there was an oddness to his expression that worried me.

"Did something happen?" If the child hadn't made it, or if something had happened to Russo's wife, for all their problems, he wouldn't be in any kind of a mood to make a deal for Dennis's freedom.

"The ultrasound said it was a girl, but it turns out they don't know everything."

"It's a boy?" I exchanged an incredulous look with Shannon.

Russo nodded. "A son. Strong and healthy." He paused, as if allowing that to sink in.

Would this change anything? Perhaps that would depend on how much power Dennis's father retained in the organization.

"And now what?" I asked.

"I find myself in a dilemma." Russo's face became impassive. "All these years my cousin has been missing, and even before that, I worked to build our business. I am my uncle's right hand. He's older now, and his health is failing. I control almost everything for him."

"Let me guess," Shannon said. "He'll want you to turn it over to Dennis."

"He's obsessed with finding his son. His only living son. To carry on the Franco name, you understand, though Russo has become almost as widely known. My uncle's obsession is why I gave Ian Gideon any business at all. He said he had a lead to my cousin's whereabouts, but that it would take time to locate him. Oh, the real estate deals Gideon offered me were good enough on their own, but the chance of finding my cousin was much more important. Had I known Ian was hiding Dennis at his firm all along—" Russo's voice was expressionless, but a glint of admiration shone in his eyes. "Well, I would have rectified the situation."

"But you knew when you came here that Dennis was alive."

"I came to make sure after Ian finally told me. I didn't think Dennis would run."

"The question is," Shannon said, "what are you going to do now? If your dealings are legit, I can promise you'll have no worries on that score."

Russo appeared to consider. "My uncle doesn't know about Dennis or his family. There have been many disappointments, and I stopped telling him each time I found a lead. There was also the chance that when I did find him, Dennis wouldn't come back with me, and I'd have to take certain steps to protect the family." Something in the way he said it made me wonder if eliminating Dennis had been his agenda all along. Or maybe he hadn't known what he would do when the time came. Maybe he still didn't know.

"Pretending you never found Dennis would work best for everyone," I suggested.

"Except for my uncle." Still no expression.

I lifted my chin. "I don't care about your uncle. He isn't worth Dennis's life. Or Sawyer's."

Russo stared at me for a long moment. "Okay," he said finally. "But on one condition." He took my hand, his thumb gently rubbing the skin between my thumb and forefinger. The sensation wasn't unpleasant, but I didn't like the control he radiated.

"And what would that be?" I asked. The tenseness in Shannon's face echoed my own uncertainty. I doubted either of us would like what he was going to say.

"I believe in your strange . . . ability." Russo's thumb pressed more firmly, his touch becoming decidedly unpleasant. "I know you won't voluntarily come to work for me, and I know the detective here"—his eyes flicked to Shannon—"wouldn't take any of my usual methods of encouragement lightly, given his attachment to you. So what I want is a promise that you'll help me out on something in the future. Not now, but maybe next year, or ten years from now. Whenever I need it."

"Help you? You mean you want me to read something?"

"Yes."

I studied him for the space of several heartbeats. I could feel Shannon watching me, but I didn't meet his eyes. This was my offer. My decision.

"Don't do it," Shannon growled. "I'm beginning to think he

doesn't want Dennis back in the fold after all. He said as much himself. He'll let him go to protect his name and his son's future."

I wasn't so sure. I believed Russo was torn between loyalty to his uncle and his own self-interest. The habits of a lifetime were hard to break. "You have to promise never to contact Dennis again."

Russo shook his head. "Now that I've found him, I plan to check in on my cousin every now and then. My mother would want that. But I do promise not to interfere with his life."

That was what I wanted to hear. It confirmed my idea that there was more between them than ugliness. A sense of family. More shades of gray, perhaps, but when it came right down to it, once the threat of prosecution was gone, I couldn't force Russo to keep his promise. Only his sense of honor, his sense of connection with Dennis could do that. Russo himself might never know what his intentions had been toward Dennis. I knew I didn't.

"Okay," I said. "But I have a condition, too. Whatever I tell you can't lead to physically hurting someone."

"That's for me to decide." Russo's face darkened, and his grip became painful.

I didn't flinch. "No. It's my talent, and that means I'll have to know enough about the situation in advance to be sure I'm not doing something I'll regret."

Russo considered me as though he had never seen me before. Gradually, his grip lightened, and his expression cleared. "You have a deal." He dropped my hand. I wanted to rub it, but I wouldn't give him the satisfaction.

"What about your men?" My eyes drifted to Charlie, who was close enough to hear everything without crowding Russo.

"My men are loyal, at least those with me. They'll do what I tell them." Russo inclined his head. "Now, I think my cousin and his family will want to hear about my new son . . . . and my plans."

Shannon waved to the officer, guarding the door. "Let them in," he called. The officer nodded.

I watched Russo and his bodyguard leave, wondering if it would all work out and what I would do if it didn't.

Russo paused and turned at the door. "One more thing," he said, raising his voice so it would carry. "I've done some research on you, Miss Rain, and you might be interested to know that I've found your maternal grandmother. When you're ready to learn about your biological family, contact me. Keep in mind, there'll be a price."

He left me wondering where someone had hidden all the air.

"You okay?" Shannon laid a hand on my back. "He's trying to lock you into working for him. You know that, right? The records were sealed. He can't know anything."

Shannon was still a bit of an idealist, for all his experience. I had no doubt Russo could uncover the information he promised, but I had seen to what lengths he would go, and I'd feel a whole lot better finding another way to trace my ancestry.

The feeling of my sister was even stronger now, overriding my desire to run after Russo and choke the information from him. I started down the hall toward where I'd left Jake.

Shannon's hand on my arm stopped me. "I wish you hadn't promised Russo."

"Because my talent should only be used for police work?" My tone was sharper than I'd intended. "Why, Detective, at least he believes in me. Only a few months ago you were ready to put me in jail rather than believe. Nothing has really changed. You still don't trust my judgment."

He blinked. "We're talking about Russo here. You know what kind of a person he is."

"You're right. I do know. He's one of the bad guys. But he loves his cousin and his mother."

"You're impossible."

"That makes two of us." I was standing closer to him now—too close. Close enough to be acutely aware that he needed a nice long shower as much as did. I could see the hair growth on his face, the lines of worry, the dusty smudges under his eyes that signaled lack of sleep. My desire to argue died within me. Seconds stretched out between us.

Without looking away, Shannon thumbed over his shoulder. "I should check on Tracy."

"How is she?" I'd forgotten all about her. Some friend I was.

"They said she regained consciousness earlier. She has some nasty internal bruising in her head, but she's going to be fine."

"Good."

I waited for him to leave, but he didn't. His eyes remained fixed on mine, as though he wanted to say more. I might even have wanted him to say it.

"There you are." Tawnia's voice. I turned to see her rounding the corner. Jake was with her, hobbling awkwardly in his new boot. Despite his disheveled appearance and the swollen black eye, he was grinning and looked as good to me as ever. His smile faltered when he took notice of my proximity to Shannon.

In the next instant, Tawnia was hugging me. Tears stung my eyes, and I clung to her for a long while. "I've come to take you home with me," she said. "And Lizbeth, too, if Sophie will let me." To Shannon, she added, "Thanks for calling me."

For once I was glad of his interference. "Where's Bret?" I asked.

Tawnia pushed me out to arm's length. "What makes you think he's here? I did very well for the first thirty-two years of my life without him, thank you very much."

"You're expecting, it's the middle of the night, and I know Bret."

"Fine. He's parking the car." We both laughed.

Jake rolled his eyes. "Women."

Shannon nodded and slapped Jake on the back. Another first for them. If I didn't know better, I'd say they were becoming friends. I wasn't sure I liked the idea.

"What happened by the river?" I asked. "Between you two, I mean."

Jake shrugged. "Shannon saved my life. That big guy was going to stomp me."

"We saved each other." Shannon held out a hand to Jake. "Thanks for your help tonight."

Jake shook his hand. "You're welcome. If it's all the same to you, though, I think I'll go back to tending my herbs."

"Good idea. Maybe Autumn should do the same with her antiques."

I smirked. "Not a chance. But we're going to have to talk about a consultation fee. I'm spending way too much time at *your* job."

"On that, I agree."

I doubted he was talking about the money, but I was too tired to care. "If Tracy's awake, tell her I'll come see her tomorrow."

Once again his eyes held mine. Not fair for him to have those beautiful eyes. "I'll do that. Good night." He turned and left.

Tawnia headed toward Dennis's room to talk to Sophie. The guard muttered something about Grand Central Station at rush hour but told her he'd ask permission.

"So," Jake said, pulling me down the hall, away from Tawnia and the watchful guard. "Are we okay?" He glanced in the direction Shannon had taken and back at me.

I stopped walking. "I don't know. Are we? I got the sense that you and Kolonda were . . . I don't know."

He shook his head. "I loved her once enough to want to marry her, and if things were different, maybe I could feel that way again, but I'm another person now. And I'm in love with someone else. With you."

The odd feeling I'd experienced with Shannon began to dissipate, but Jake wasn't finished. "Except it seems I'm not the only one who feels that way."

I tensed. "What do you mean?"

"I mean Shannon. I thought he'd get over his infatuation with you. Or that it wouldn't matter, but I think somehow it does matter. Or is starting to."

That could only mean he sensed a change in me, and I wasn't sure he was wrong. I'd both hated and resented Shannon for much of the time I'd known him, and he'd annoyed me to no end. But I respected and trusted him, too. I enjoyed our verbal sparring, and, worse, I was beginning to suspect that I looked forward to seeing him.

Jake put an arm around me, and I leaned into him with the ease of habit. "Look," he said, "there's a lot of history between us, a lot that doesn't have to do with us, really, but with Winter and our shops. All of that sometimes confuses things. Don't get me wrong—our history is something to build on—but in the end I want us to be together because we would both rather be with each other than with anyone else. Not because we feel like we should or because it's easier. Or because we don't want to let the other down." He fell silent as a nurse passed by.

When she was gone, his hand went to my shoulder and he turned me to face him. "After everything that happened today, I want you to have no doubts about how I feel. I love you, and I want to be with you." He planted a kiss on my lips. Not a demanding, world-stopping kiss, but one that left no doubts.

Jake was already my best friend, and I loved him more than anyone except my sister. He made my heart race when he kissed me, and we'd laughed together far more times than I could count, something I cherished. I'd dreamed of being with Jake forever, but I needed to be sure. I cared too much about him to do anything that might mislead him.

"Jake, I—"

He put a finger over my lips. "Later. I know."

I'm glad he did because I wasn't sure what I'd been going to say. But I didn't ever want to lose him.

Tawnia was coming toward us, a cranky, red-faced Lizbeth held awkwardly to her swollen stomach. "Change of plans, folks. I'm going to help you find Bret so he can get you home. I'll be staying here to see if I can get Sophie through the rest of this night. She's pretty wrapped up with Sawyer at the moment, but she doesn't want to let either of the children go too far—not that I blame her. I promised I'd hold onto Lizbeth every second and bring her right back after I get you two on your way. In the morning, maybe I can convince Sophie to go home with me for a few hours."

"I could stay and help." I wouldn't really know what to do with a baby, especially for hours at a time, but I could walk the halls with her if I had to. Or play with Sawyer when he awoke. Good practice for when my niece or nephew finally made an appearance.

Tawnia rolled her eyes. "Are you kidding? You aren't touching this baby. Not only are you still wet, but you look like you should be checking into the hospital, not leaving it. You both do. You're even shivering! Come on. Let's go find Bret and get you home and into your beds."

We let her usher us toward the elevator. Jake, who'd been quiet during our exchange, an amused grin on his face, snapped his fingers. "Hey, Tawnia, I have an idea for you. After everything that's happened today, what about naming your baby Miracle?"

Tawnia rolled her eyes. "You experience miracles. It's not a name."

"Actually," I said, "I was thinking more along the lines of Destiny."

"Destiny," Tawnia repeated as the elevator door dinged open. "I still don't know what makes you think it's a girl."

Jake caught my gaze for a solemn moment before offering his hand. Smiling, I let his warmth fill me as the elevator doors closed.

About the Author

Rachel Ann Nunes (pronounced noon-esh) learned to read when she was four, beginning a lifelong fascination with the written word. She began writing in the seventh grade and is now the author of over thirty published books, including the popular *Ariana* series and the award-winning picture book *Daughter of a King*.

Rachel and her husband, TJ, have six children. She loves camping with her family, traveling, meeting new people, and, of course, writing. She writes Monday through Friday in her home office, often with a child on her lap, taking frequent breaks to build Lego towers, practice reading, or go swimming with the kids.

Rachel loves hearing from her readers. You can write to her at Rachel@RachelAnnNunes.com. To enjoy her monthly newsletter or to sign up to hear about new releases, visit her website, www.RachelAnnNunes.com.